D1355607

abond Twenty-One Vagabond Twenty-O

Moon Country

Peter Arnott

Vagabond Voices
Glasgow

© Peter Arnott 2015

Published on 29 May 2015 by
Vagabond Voices Publishing Ltd.
Glasgow
Scotland

ISBN: 978-1-908251-47-3

The author's rights to be identified as author of this book under the
Copyright, Designs and Patents Act 1988 have been asserted.

Printed and bound in Poland

Cover design by Mark Mechan

Typeset by Park Productions

The publisher acknowledges subsidy towards
this publication from Creative Scotland

ALBA | CHRUTHACHAIL

For further information on Vagabond Voices, see the website:
www.vagabondvoices.co.uk

For My Family

Moon Country

0.0

The world is everything that is the case.

0.0.1

All the stories told about it turn out to be true.

0.0.2

For example, if this was London or Mumbai or somewhere, then the likes of Tommy Hunter might have got himself lost. But Oor Wee Toon is just not big enough for the likes of Tommy Hunter to be here and nobody notice.

0.0.2.1

If Tommy was still here, is what I'm saying, there would have been signs.

0.0.2.1.1

The animals would have scattered, sensing something, like fire on the prairie. The skies would have darkened. Graves would have opened. Cattle stampeded. Comets would have crossed the sky and dinged off the face of the moon.

0.0.2.2

But there's been nothing.

0.0.3

It's surprising how bleak that makes me feel.

0.1

It's not that Tommy Hunter ever *wanted* trouble. It's just that sooner or later he always *was*.

0.1.1.1

Seismic. Off the Richter scale. In Sensurrround sound. Like a geological feature.

0.1.1.1

You couldn't help but see him, no matter how hard you tried not to look. Like a zit on the face of the earth. Something you could see from space.

0.1.1.2

Like that bubble of lava that's sat underneath Yellowstone Park. Sooner or later that's gonnae erupt and cover us all with six feet of irradiated, molten pus, its plume of chthonic shite blocking out the sun, bringing all of our stories to a close.

0.1.1.2.1

Not a minute before time, if you ask me.

0.1.2

All there is left of Tommy Hunter, then, is the stories about him. And all of the stories about Tommy Hunter turn out to be true. Even when they contradict each other.

0.1.2.1

Like the last time he turned up. All kinds of things got said about that.

0.1.2.2

Where did all that money come from to start with? Envelopes of the stuff he carried about with him in a carpet bag. A fortune he flung about the place with the largesse of some medieval monarch purging his soul of temporal entrapment: doing good, of course, but also prefiguring, in his penitent disbursement of the stuff of life, our final dissolution and the contingency of all things.

0.1.2.3

There were lots of stories about that, and they were all true. Or they might as well have been.

0.2

There are those who say, for example, that Tommy struck it rich randomly, sitting like a statue of homelessness in London somewhere — Camberwell Green or somewhere.

0.2.1

When a man he's never seen before, and who has never seen him before, a long, black man in a long black coat and a black felt hat just walks up to him and drops a carpet bag full of money on the bench beside him.

0.2.1.2

For no reason at all.

0.2.1.2.1

Tommy doesn't look up to see his face. Just listens to the clack clack clack of expensive footfalls die away. The messenger doesn't break stride and is not to be identified.

0.2.1.2.1.1

The messenger's purpose is not to be interrogated. His purpose is only to be fulfilled.

0.2.1.2.

For it was written that heaven would deliver unto Tommy Hunter that which made Tommy Hunter a force for right and truth and justice in the land.

0.2.2

Were he to have existed in order to have made this spontaneous donation, the Angel of the Wedge would have been strategically spot on. Even forces for right and truth and justice don't get far in this most fallen of possible worlds without the financial wherewithal. Not if they're Tommy Hunter they don't. Not if you're a guy who can't walk into a post office to buy a stamp without the alarms going off. Similarly, it would have been no good sending Tommy a cheque or a BACS payment, because if you're someone whose name on a computer will set off a worldwide electronic aneurysm then you can't open a bank account or write off for a MasterCard or shit like that. You can't be part of the world, not this world, not a world where everything is known about everybody, not a world where if you buy a kumquat in Tesco then some cunt in the CIA will know that you're a target for exotic fruit marketing.

0.2.2.1

Guys like Tommy can't exist in a world like that.

0.2.3

Others have suggested a socio-historic sequence of events to account for Tommy's stash, which is every bit as credible as the angel thing.

0.2.3.1

So, it might just as well have been that on a dusty day in April a red-bearded tramp in an old tweed coat, no shirt, Jesus sneakers, no socks and a set of cut-off jeans walked into a venerable solicitors' office in West Nile Street, the wind blowing rags of chip paper in his wake. Mrs Golightly, faithful receptionist, will have looked up over the purple rims of her bifocals into the face of Satan himself, Old Nick quietly demanding, in a voice like Clint Eastwood but with an accent that could have welded ships, to meet with Mr Hugo Moncrieff, a senior partner lost to gout and corruption some half a dozen years before. On being informed of that Georgian gentleman's predecease, the apparition will have chuckled softly to itself, and said its own name, "Ah'm Tommy Hunter," with the inconsequence of an asteroid detonating off the coast of Mexico, this self-nomination sending an eel of fear wriggling through Mrs Golightly's sexagenarian vitals, and setting her fingers to fumbling blindly across the intercom, thereby summoning a random gaggle of junior partners, secretaries and personal assistants to cluster nervously behind the modishly curvilinear reception desk, staring helplessly at this ill-smelling irruption from the Gehenna of the penal system, only one of them finally recognising him, kindly old Mr Meyer, brought into the firm to handle the Newton Mearns trade back in 1974. Old Meyer's nut-brown face will have cracked in welcome saying, "Come on in, Tommy, son," extending a Semitic and arthritic paw to gather in the lost sheep.

0.2.3.1.1

And as they sat together in the dark plush of the meeting room, the Ragged Man and the Old Jew, sentimentally conjoined by some trope of wandering, perhaps, they will have talked about the old days — about Frank and Eleanor, Joseph and Janice, maybe even about old Jack Webster — while a minion will have got sent with a banker's draft for thirty-seven thousand pounds across the road to the Royal Bank of Scotland.

0.2.3.2

Course, he maybe just dug it up, his share of the ancient loot, resurrecting a worm-eaten bin bag from a hole by a loch, Rob Roy's castle reflected in the muddy tarn, fourth tree down from the stone shaped like a pirate's skull.

0.2.3.3

Or mebbe he just saved up his wages up from the jile. He was in there for long enough and he never smoked as far as I can remember. That's most likely the truth of it, and the truth has no obligation to be interesting.

0.2.3.4

But call me whatever the fuck, I favour it was this way.

0.2.3.4.1

I see Tommy Hunter haunting the streets somewhere, newly expelled from the inferno to gaze once more upon the stars, somewhere on this middle road of life, near destitution, paralysed though restlessly mobile, waiting for something, perhaps acclimatising to being on the outside, more likely not getting used to it at all, blindly wandering alien streets full of undifferentiated noise and movement, all these bloody people all around him suddenly, and him still wrapped in prison stink, a bubble of bad smell, uncaring and unheeding, face like stone and glass, hour after unstructured hour, buying a pie and chips, not enjoying it, absently stroking a dug, scaring folk away with that monster stare of his, standing at the park gates gazing into the lost world of the playground, mothers hustling their little ones away.

0.2.3.4.1.1

All loss, he must have been, all isolation: a mad jakey, a middle-aged catastrophe, talking to himself, if he ever talked to anyone at all. You'll've seen them about.

0.2.3.4.1.1.1

The sudden shouters, the schizoid self-debaters, the mad, the flotsam, the casually beaten and set fire to, the socially excluded if you want to get governmental about it, the economically inactive, the internal exiles of the marketplace, hostile and fucking weird, ex-servicemen, ex-prisoners, ex-inmates, ex-humans, really, startling folk on buses with philosophical questions, peering into second-hand Yankee comic book shops, clashing their wrists together and turning into Captain Marvel ... that kind of thing. They're everywhere.

0.2.3.4.1.2

I think if you'd have seen Tommy then, you'd not have looked at him twice. In order to avoid some insane dialogue or aggressive begging or both, you'd have passed him by on the other side, and you'd've been wiser than you could have known, truth be told.

0.2.3.4.2

Yes. I think this was Tommy Hunter, that April, two weeks out of the slammer, invisibly prowling after himself, arriving at the door of some bedsit or other he'd got sent to by the probation service, run, as such establishments invariably are, by money-grubbing cunts of the lowest variety, in this instance of South Asian extraction, justifying their cupidity in the name of the *ummah* with the same defensive, self-righteous bitterness as the Humean natives do in that of enlightened self-interest or whatever the fuck it is we say these days: one Assam in this instance, he being the third and least academically able son of the proprietor, specifically entrusted in lieu of a career in medicine, law or pharmacy with the cleaning and maintenance of the family property, his duties being performed in a spirit of desultory incompetence — and also, much more successfully, auto-directed to provoke the tenantry at every opportunity. This exiled and unconscious scion of the Punjab now alerts our Tommy to the arrival of a package with his name on.

0.2.3.4.2.1

"Ah hud tae fucken sign fur this," Assam informs Tommy, contemptuously extending the communication with the aggrieved self-importance of Hermes on a jihad.

"So fuck?" says Tommy with his hand out, adding interrogatively, "Did ye look in it?"

"Naw, did ah fuck!" Assam continues in his grammatically challenged manner, but handing over the blue and red striped bundle without further demur, for, dumb fucker though he is, Assam knows better than to mess too persistently with this particular cunt. While therefore only pantomiming his defiance, he is nonetheless driven to playing up a bit, so as not to avow himself entirely dickless in the presence of the infidel.

0.2.3.4.3

Tommy doesn't grant the prick another glance, however, as, now raised to the status of human congress by the arrival of communication, he pushes past his landlord's agent and unlocks the door to his dingy room, dismissing Assam from his consciousness, shutting the door behind him without further acknowledgement or thanks.

0.2.3.4.3.1

Assam batters on the door — (just the wance) — and says a bad word.

0.2.3.4.4

Meanwhile, inside, Tommy roughly splits the envelope and pours the money on the bed, thirty-seven thousand pounds in used tenners, spreading like a sheet of possibilities on the duvet of no return, light in the gloom, hope in the darkness, glory spread thin upon the surface of the sordid world.

0.2.3.4.4.1

And his face doesn't change a bit.

That's what must have been the case, in my book. The hell with whatever is the case in your book.

0.3

However Tommy Hunter in fact acquired his fiscal equipage, and whatever message or instruction to stay away was included, tacitly or explicitly, with this windfall, the incontrovertible fact of the matter was that here it was he manifested himself, one wet dawn in April a few years ago, skipping his probation, swinging down from the cab of an articulated bone rattler in a lay-by at the very edge of Oor Wee Toon, long ago invented, employed and defined as a single, specialised but long since superannuated link in the supply chain of the motor manufacturing industry, and now solely delineated by the ironic, taunting motorway that cuts through it like a grey swathe, a glimmering path that leads through it and out of it and away from it.

0.3.1

Away! That first word we sucked at our mother's tit! Away! Tae fuck!

0.3.2

Tommy had been away all right, but now he had come back to the very break in the very stretch of fence of the very cemetery where the poor cunts who'd never gone anywhere at all had ended up, and as he swung his leading leg over that fence at the exact same spot he'd used to when getting off his bus from special school, and he'd set off striding uphill, through the dead and towards those as

1.0.1.2.2

A firm that later on, it so happens, took over the running of one of the privatised prisons that both Tommy and Joe — and even old Jack Webster — ended up in at one stage or another.

1.0.1.3

Anyway, willingly or no, this boy was in on it too. For despite his salaried presence on this weary, stony earth, and the solid further acquisition of a wife and wean, this Eric or Colin had retained an entirely reasonable wariness of his former school chums, who in some way or other had arrived at the determination of turning Colin's (or Eric's) social success to their own advantage.

1.0.1.3.1

In the manner of all criminals, they knew with moral certainty that their proposed redistribution was only right. It was only right, they felt, that Eric (or Colin) should share his access to the world of banking, however tenuous and circumstantial it might be, with them, despite the fact that he was only on four-fifty an hour or some such pish, and could not realistically be held to be a major shareholder in the institution whose old notes his firm were transporting for disposal.

1.0.2

So, like I say. There were the four of them and Colin (or Eric) in on it, Tommy himself with Frank and Joseph Wheen being the core of the musketeers, with the now-to-be-named-fourth being Jack Webster, a gentle soul with a gift for the sourcing and exchange of dodgy articles — who had come up with the shooters and had scored the motor — as their helpmeet.

1.0.2.1

A lovely man, Jack, and not without aesthetic leanings, as a silver-grey Merc did seem excessive for the job, but Jack had liked the colour and felt that a certain resonance of much beloved episodes of *The Sweeney* was called for. So he'd nicked it and turned up with it.

1.0.2.1.1

Frank had rolled his eyes when he saw it. Frank liked to think of himself as a practical fellow.

1.0.2.1.1.1

Hunter had smiled, an enthusiast for other people's enthusiasms.

1.0.2.1.1.1.1

Joe didn't say anything.

1.0.2.2

Joe was more of an A-Team Ford Transit kind of a guy: all intention and no class. But no pragmatist either, as brother Frank could readily testify. A bit obvious, if you catch my drift.

1.0.2.2.1

Joe was the one who was obviously going to use the shooter once he had it in his paw. Practical Frank and the others should surely have anticipated that. Because once he had Eric (or Colin) and his fellow employee helpless in the woods with their van opened and the two of them forced inside to disembark the contents, there was no way that Joe wasn't going to succumb to the temptation of so readily available a cinematic reference. Knowing Joe as they did, the rest of them should really have seen it coming.

1.0.2.2.1.2

Joe had indeed, quite predictably, and without any provocation or even much malice aforethought, released himself to the trigger's explosive temptation, splattering Colin's (or Eric's) colleague all over the inside of the van — and making himself permanently deaf in one ear, incidentally.

1.0.2.2.2

And they all had understood immediately that now, obviously, they had to do for Eric (or Colin) as well.

1.0.3

Erin (or Colic) had begged and screamed and soiled himself. Jack Webster had sat on a tree stump throwing up, haunted now and forever by his glimpsing and momentarily scenting the inside-out horror of what was already on the walls and floor of the van, while the musketeers had just shouted at each other — Tommy, as had been customary all through their school and army days, finding himself the weathercock in the gale of resentment that blew between the Brothers Wheen.

1.0.3.1

Frank and Joe had always hated each other. For the very

good reason that being as close as they were, they knew everything there was to hate about each other.

1.0.3.1.1

Which was loads, obviously.

1.0.3.2

Frank will have argued on the basis of logic and operational security that it was now Tommy that was obliged to execute their soon-to-be-former co-conspirator; whereas Joe would have appealed more abstractly to sentiments of solidarity and general precepts of manhood in support of the same conclusion.

1.0.3.2.1

So they both would have went at him at the same time, Tommy's face sweating under his IRA balaclava.

1.0.4

And Tommy will have ended up doing it — murdering Choleric. That was never actually proved, of course. The bizzies found no powder burns on Tommy. Practical Frank had had all of them gloved and shoed and zipped in disposable cagoules.

1.0.4.1

You could argue, as Frank later did, that these strictures had vindicated themselves in operational terms, in that only Hunter out of all of them, after all, ever did any time for robbery and murder, though it was well known about the Toon exactly who had pulled off the blag, hours of speculative banter being wasted (in my opinion) in the intervening years as to exactly who did what to whom, when and why?

1.0.4.1.1

It was Tommy that had pulled the trigger on what's-his-name. I'd stake my narrative reputation on it, because it's the only way the sequence of events on his return fourteen-odd years later makes any sense.

1.0.4.1.2

Bang.

1.0.5

Now, everyone who knows anything will concede that Tommy Hunter, in his latter days, incontrovertibly occupied his allocation of the universe quite uniquely. But I'm saying here and now that even then, at that virgin time, he felt something more than a generalised guilt at having just taken part in a robbery where two poor fuckers on minimum wages had been quite unnecessarily slaughtered.

1.0.5.1

I say here and now that pulling that trigger changed him, all of a sudden, from one kind of cunt into another kind of cunt entirely.

1.0.5.1.1

Other sources may argue that he only arrived later on and in the course of his long stretch of incarceration at his fully evolved ontology. But I'm a simple soul, and I say that it was at the exact second when Tommy eased springs and turned Eric's head into a stump that Tommy Hunter quantum jumped from one kind of existence into another. From then on, he was just getting used to it.

1.0.5.1.1.1

Okay. The moment before he committed the murder he was still one of us, already a recklessly unreflective sort of cunt, I grant you, but recognisably of our weft and weave. But the moment after, and without measurable transition, I believe, he began to experience himself as other, as a prodigy, a stranger — a Gnostic of repentance, if you will. The world instantaneously inflated outside him like a landscape and inside him like a gulf, and now he knew himself, catastrophically, to be at odds with everything else that ever was or ever is or ever could be, and he suddenly had to learn to breathe in an atmosphere entirely different from that to which his former adaptive suitability had accustomed him. That event beyond time or space or good or evil emitted a new universe, and Tommy precipitously came upon himself already mutated into another order of being, like the big baby at the end of Stanley Kubrick, looking down on the rest of us with a stunned amalgam of bewilderment and rage.

1.0.5.1.1.1.1

It was the rest of us that stayed the same.

1.0.5.1.1.1.1.1

Apart from Colin (or Eric), obviously.

1.1

Whatever the Mendelian mechanics of the matter, the DNA inside of Tommy Hunter had set itself off in a phenomenal recombination of which he himself was unconscious, but which was, by contrast, immediately apparent to his comrades, who themselves now shared an instant, unspoken and unspeakable epiphany as to the irrevocable erstwhile-ness of their association with the once upon a time "Tommy Hunter".

1.1.1

He glowed. He gave off an unearthly light. That's about the size of it. And they were sore afraid.

1.1.1.1

Because they all sort of knew, all at once, how the story was going to go, in the fullness of time. That this wasn't going to be the end of it.

1.1.1.1.1

No. This was just the start of something for which their culture held no conscious precedent and offered them no guidance, but was something fundamental nonetheless to the way the world is. (Or was now, or had suddenly become.)

1.1.1.1.1.1

They were now and forever a destiny one unto the other. Life had a meaning and Time had a direction. The Future was a destination in the direction of which the events of the present were to be interpreted as comprising an itinerary. They were conjoined now in a teleology of tyrannical certainty. They were on to a loser. They could feel it. They could feel destiny's cold hand reach up into their trousers, grab hold of their testicles and squeeze.

1.1.1.1.1.1.1

Call it fate or kismet. Pick one and cough.

1.1.1.1.1.1.1.1

Apart from Tommy himself, it was probably Frank who actually caught on first, him being the brains of the outfit. Even in his newly blasted state, Tommy thought he caught Frank looking at him funny.

1.1.1.1.1.1.1.1.1

That was about it for the moment. Nothing overwhelmingly conclusive, I grant you, but something definitely passed between the two of them that permanently defined the parameters of their future relationship.

1.1.1.1.1.1.1.1.1.1!

Anyway, though it was Frank that was the first to give the feeling a thought, I'm sure they all knew now that which it seemed had always been there to be known, that their fate was now rewritten but as if from the beginning of time in their testosterone and bad haircuts, and that there was nothing to be done right now but to get their arses in the motor and think about it later.

1.2

Tommy came home to Janice and the kids that night

drenched from head to foot in gore. The Wheen boys had dropped him off at home, retaining the spoils for later distribution, as, they now argued, had been planned all along, and as now more than ever seemed providentially prudent.

1.2.1

Joe had threatened him, and Frank had made him promises, the brothers severally enjoining the positive and negative arguments for silence. Old Jack Webster had still been throwing up out of the rear passenger window.

1.2.1.1

When he was out of the car and standing by a puddle of Jack's sick, and when the Wheens had hissed their final admonitions at him and had driven angrily away, Tommy had stood alone for a contemplative moment in the battered street and sudden quiet of night.

1.2.2

Maybe it was the silence that changed him. Maybe it was then that the silence got into him and changed him. Who can say?

1.3

It was Agnes, his grandmother-in-law, whose house it was he lived in then with Janice and the kids, who had had to let him in. Tommy'd dropped his house keys in the woods beside the burnt-out armoured van — which turned out to be a matter of no little significance in the short and intense police investigation — and which particular carelessness went no way towards reconciling his newfound beatitude to his colleagues, let me tell you.

1.3.1

Perhaps from an excess of karmic enthusiasm for the closed circle, there are even some who are persuaded by the idea that Tommy left the keys not out of stupidity or shock as his co-conspirators variously later alleged, but in a moment of clarity as to how the rest of the story was meant to go — but I think that's overthinking things.

1.3.1.1

And it was only Eleanor, Frank's wife, who'd read more books than the rest of them put together, that could have really thought that logic through, and that was only years later, actually, when she told Frank that there were no such things as accidents. Positivistic, Freudian wee tart that she was.

1.3.1.1.1

(Eleanor'd never liked Tommy. She'd always thought he was what her daddy had called "a loose cannon".)

1.3.2

Agnes had never liked Tommy either. Not when Janice had left home with Gerry and had come home with Tommy with one kid in tow and another on the way — from Germany and Cyprus and South Armagh in succession, just to get that on the record. Her opinion of him had not improved when Ronnie had been born when Tommy was in Saughton doing six months for punching someone, losing both his pub job and his council tenancy, so that Janice and Janette and newly born Ronnie had all had to move in with the bitter old bitch. Then when Tommy had been released to crowd his monstrous personality within those same four walls as well, some familial tension had been well-nigh unavoidable.

1.3.2.1

The tin lid on it for Agnes was Tommy arriving home that night and waking her up — and her having to open the door to him standing there with a weird wee smile on his face and bits of somebody else's brains in his hair.

1.3.2.1.1

"Couldnae find my keys," he said, which was the kind of thing he always said.

1.3.2.1.1.1

Understatement in the face of the apocalypse was Tommy's rhetorical style, and it made you feel wild inside, it really did. He was a rush to be with sometimes. He seriously was. But Agnes wasn't his audience at the best of times.

1.3.2.1.2

Agnes did her banshee impersonation for him, and then there was a rush of wife and children into the hallway and a lot more screaming and recrimination for the next couple of minutes. Janice had known that Tommy was going out robbing, of course, and had wholeheartedly approved that he was finally making an effort to better himself, but the reeking thing in her grandmother's hallway calmly insisting that it was time to take a family holiday could not, on this occasion, work any of its charm on her.

1.3.3

Tommy adored Janice. You'll need to understand that as well. Janice was a privilege for him, an unbelievable bless-ing, as were the two children, miracles in half their genes as far as Tommy was concerned. None of the rest of us quite saw Janice the way that Tommy did. She was horny as Jezebel, and dolled up in a certain light was often mistaken for nice-looking, true enough. But to Hunter she was his intimation of a unified theory of everything. Touching her, he touched the infinite. In her eyes and smile he found his forgiveness and his evidence of God. In the possibility of her love was justification for the past, purpose for the pre-sent and eventual happy synthesis for the future. Janice was his eschatological hump.

1.3.3.1

The family he had with her was the one good thing he'd ever had. And he'd never managed to take them away anywhere. The prospect of a wee holiday trip with the family at last had been what had tipped the balance in favour of taking part in the robbery in the first place.

1.3.3.1.1

So Tommy took his baby son from her arms, then took his daughter's hand and smiled his infinite love for Janice in her face.

1.3.3.2

"Aw that fucken BLOOD" she was screaming at him as she followed him outside.

1.3.3.2.1

"Where's the fucken MONEY?" she went on as Tommy strapped wee Ronnie into his booster seat and Janette cried and cried and cried.

1.3.3.3

He thought they'd go up North, he said.

1.4

Tommy and the family never made it much past Pitlochry. He and the kids got trapped at the gate of the Drumochter Pass, severe weather warnings and a cassette of Walt Disney Sing-Along-Songs having offered them no protection from that happenstance. Or at least, that's where the country bizzies picked them up, out of petrol in the black mountains, sleet streaking the windows, Janette holding wee Ronnie on her lap as he slept, Tommy catatonic with shame and loss on the passenger seat as "I Wanna Be Like You" pumped out at a volume that distorted the what-passed-for-speakers that they fitted in motors back then.

1.4.1

No Janice, though. No sight or sign or spoor of Janice.

1.4.2

Tommy sat bereft. Of speech, of expression, of response. He never even looked at the constable from Coupar Angus as the flashlight played across his devastation. And to the subsequent loss of his children and his freedom, no trace of reaction crossed his features, as they took him away and the keys found in the woods were found to fit the house and the tale was told.

1.4.2.1

The keys had been found, incidentally, by then Police Constable Daniel "Danny" Boyle, who even as a poor plod of a bluebottle constantly plagued his superiors with theories and interpretations of the mayhem he so enthusiastically examined. Boyle was one of those souls in the public service who thought of knowledge as something one should act upon, rather than as something one should avoid so that all responsibility could be evaded if anyone should ask you later on.

1.4.2.2

Tommy never said a thing to "Danny" or to anyone. Not his lawyer, not the judge. About what had happened to Janice or about the van he had robbed. Or about the double murder. Or about the inside man. Or about either of the Wheens. Or about old Jack Webster.

1.4.2.2.1

Nothing. Never. Nada.

1.4.3

He spoke not a word as they sent him down, in his own defence or by way of incrimination of those others unnamed but universally known to have been his confederates in the dreadful, callous crime. "Yes" to his own name and "Guilty" to his own sin was all of Tommy's song. These were the only words anyone heard him say before they found him on the floor of his High Court cell on the morning of the verdict with his throat raggedly and inexpertly cut, and Tommy Hunter was sewn up and remanded for psychological evaluation before sentencing.

1.4.3.1

Not another word.

1.5

It was five years four months and eleven days before he asked anyone for anything.

1.5.1

A Bible, as it happens. He'd had a lot of thinking to do and now he was going to check up on a couple of things.

1.5.1.1

His catatonic silence had landed him in Carstairs by then, where the chaplain, an ex-army Episcopalian, had responded to Tommy's croaky request for the Good News with an enthusiasm heightened by the satisfaction that his professional rivals, the Reichians, Jungians, Kleinians and all the rest of their atheistic, atomising breed had drawn no response from Tommy to their chemicals and cant, while Jesus, it now seemed, had battered his way into the heart of this most lost of all lost souls with his siege engine of redemption. Not that it entirely escaped the chaplain's notice in the succeeding three years that Tommy breathed in his forgiveness and breathed out his hellfire, that what Tommy seemed to have found in Jesus Christ was not so much a personal saviour as a personal equivalent — a being alike extraordinary in his alienation from earthly appetites and as uncompromising in his holy, angry joy.

And it had been the chaplain, in fact, who had retreated from Tommy's revelation, and taken early retirement, his arteries prematurely furred by a fear he could not bring himself to name. It was shortly thereafter that Tommy declared himself theologically and intellectually satisfied and never opened another book of any kind again.

1.5.2

Eight more years of relative silence followed as Tommy quietly wore away the time that had been given to him on earth. Keeping himself to himself, his nose clean, out of bother … out of all contact of any kind in fact, as far as was possible, given the overcrowding … his aura discouraging camaraderie as well as intimidation from his fellow inmates, while he remained unvisited, also, from the outside.

1.5.2.1

For in all of that time, the endless fucking deserts of it, no single cunt once braved the journey down to Carstairs, or to any of the progressively less astringent institutions for the engineering of the soul through which Tommy descended like a rock through wet layers of bureaucratic tissue paper, inexorably heading towards his freedom and the manifestation of whatever frightful change all those years of silence and solitude had wrought in him. Not one.

1.5.3

None of us ever heard anything from Janice either. Nobody could say what had happened to her. Ronnie had been too wee, and Janette had testified that Mummy and Daddy'd left the car together somewhere en route, and that her father, sad, had returned to them alone. That was it. And of course the bizzies had kept at him for a while, before the trial and after the sentencing. But there is inertia in all things. There was never a corpse found. And Tommy was saying nothing. So he was never charged with Janice's murder. Even though we all knew he must have murdered her. Where the hell else was she otherwise?

1.5.3.1

There are Hunterologists who to this day put the cart before the causational horse in my view when they argue that Tommy offed Janice and consequently went catatonic. I think that's too obvious and doesn't take account of the previous murder he'd committed. At least, in my opinion. And anyway he got the postcard. And I'm coming to the postcard.

1.5.3.2

(see 1.6 and 11.3.2.2)

1.6

When the postcard of Night on Calgary Beach arrived for him at Shotts (with a Tobermory postmark), thirteen and a half years after his conviction, it sat for four months in the prison sorting office, as the screw in charge had assumed that Hunter 47931 had died, or had been transferred or something, as Tommy'd never received so much as a pamphlet in the post since his brief and intense period as an evangelist years before had occasioned him a flurry of hating literature from across the pond. Besides, the postcard was itself an eccentric communication, with only Tommy's name and a previous address "Care of Her Majesty" being written upon the reverse of a retouched and frankly improbable rendering of a picturesque Inner Hebridean strand by exaggerated moonlight.

1.6.1

The meaning of the message, if indeed you could infer from it any meaning at all, was as cryptic as the Gospel of Thomas, and provoked a brief twitch of interest and exca-vation from those of the Boys in Blue who were still pro-cedurally piqued at the non-appearance of the loot from that now ancient and obscure but irritatingly unresolved Episode of the Exterminating Van, the details of which they kept on file, and the sights and sounds and smells of which must have been stored too in Tommy's inner eye and ear and nose and throat, blasted forever on to the surface of his corneas, ringing in his ears, choking off his sleep, a constant waking nightmare, silently guiding his every step.

1.6.1.2

For what to the powers that be was but a troubling loose end must have remained to Tommy an existential impera-tive, compared to which the threats and cajolements of the indefatigable now Detective Sergeant "Danny" Boyle and his colleagues were as the distant song of birds on the new landscape of his vision.

1.6.1.2.1

Tommy did glean from his fresh interrogation by that assiduous official the potentially useful information that his two children, Ronnie and Janette, had been removed from Agnes's custody some years ago, when Agnes's alco-holism had precipitated Ronnie's absence from school for just six months longer than had been deemed acceptable, and that both kids had then been taken into the care of the Local Authority, neither natural parent being in any way available and nobody else being interested.

1.6.1.2.2

Tommy had not visibly reacted to this intelligence, which had been intended, I imagine, to torture rather than to inform him — and DS Boyle had sat back astounded once again at the moral nonchalance of these bloody people, and concluded the interview, tucking his complex of resentment, ambition and rectitude away for another day.

1.6.1.2.2.1

(see below)

1.6.2

After some bureaucratic perseverance on Boyle's part of no mean order, a party of our local filth, led by up to and including DS "Danny" Boyle, having got the police authority to cough up a grudging furball of expenses, had subsequently spent a fruitless week up north, attempting to establish some connection between Tommy Hunter and that remote West Highland locality.

1.6.2.1

They did some digging, literally, in the landscape, and figuratively, among the locals, and came away with nothing more than hangovers and a confirmed distaste for the countryside. They did not see what Tommy Hunter saw in that sentimental seascape where he'd never been as far as they could tell, and they unearthed no inkling as to who might have sent him it or what might have been its import.

1.6.2.1.1

While Tommy, for his part, back in his cell, gazed now through an interior window for hour after hour, searching in his mind that same never glimpsed or previously heard-of location, all the time becoming more and more confirmed in awful certainty as to the provenance and import of the disputed communication he'd been sent from it.

1.6.3

So it was this unsigned postcard from the Country of the Moon, dubious in its origin, worn and yellowed with the damp breath of his withered prison lungs, and the cold fingers of his perpetual holding and staring, faded by the friction of his gaze, it was this thin promise that sustained Tommy Hunter in all his five hundred remaining days and nights of purgation, so that when the time at last came for his release, and the confluence of that long solitude and a vision of the Moon merged with thirty-seven thousand pounds nestling at the top of a swinging carpet bag, it might well be said that as Tommy Hunter emerged from the town cemetery and hesitated for a moment to search his memory and to confirm his direction, and headed into an undistinguished scheme of semi-detached houses, that he knew exactly where he was going.

1.7

And a bell rang in heaven, and the seventh seal was opened, and there was silence for the space of half an hour.

2.0

A greater man than me once wrote that money is important in a human story in the same way that honey is important in a story about bees.

2.0.1

(The late Kurt Vonnegut Jr, if you're asking.)

2.0.1.1

So you're probably wondering by now what the money from the van had been up to all these years since it had been saved from incineration and returned to general circulation. You're probably speculating as to what role it had played in the economy meanwhile?

2.0.1.1.1

Even if you're not, I'm telling you anyway.

2.0.2

In theory they'd all four of them had an equal share of the scratch. In practice it had been Frank, unsurprisingly, who of the Musketeers had been the most successful in translating the loot into something like sustainable prosperity. He had been thrifty and shrewd with his tranche, washing it through pubs and taxis into a bank account or six, and had then persisted, overriding some protest, in housing his young and growing family for the succeeding three or more years, in a four-roomed housing association flat, while he strategically parlayed his growing pile into the field of age management.

2.0.2.1

Frank had read the papers, and the papers told him that property and senility were where a sudden cash injection best belonged in the middle 1990s. So Frank bought a terraced house for old cunts to live in — you could still do that round here for thirty-odd grand in those days — and filled it with cast-offs from the geriatric wards of our local hospital (itself not long for this world) at four hundred quid a Pop (or Nan) paid regularly from the Social.

2.0.2.1.1

That's each. Every week.

2.0.2.2

And what with this being only a Wee Toon where officialdom is comparatively cheap, and with very few questions getting asked if you can lift a few names off the waiting list for any damn thing, and what with needing to spend only so much on minimally suitable staff on minimum wages, plus laundry, strained fruit and wheat flakes, Frank had the big house and garden for himself and his family soon enough. And then some more. And then some more on top of that.

2.0.3

Joe, by contrast, had shot his wad on drinking, snorting and fucking, all inside of six months, and, returning to his uppers, he thereupon, without Frank's knowledge, leave alone prior approval, turned over a post office in order to maintain the lifestyle to which he had become accustomed. Making an utter cunt of it, Joe got himself sentenced to a seven-year stretch, dragging, as it happens, the dragooned Jack Webster down — and into prison — with him.

2.0.3.1

On his release after serving four and a half years, Joe had gone to work for Frank in one of his (by then) five asylums for the gaga.

2.0.3.1.1

By the time Tommy turned up, Frank owned or part-owned mebbe fifteen properties in the towns and hamlets of the county, plus there were the pound shops and the taxis and the share portfolios. This was plenty to weather any kind of seizure in the secondary accumulation of investment income that might be precipitated by a burst balloon of easy credit — the poor, as ever they would, needing some-where they could fuck off to and die.

2.0.4

Old Jack Webster had moved on too, since his release, or at least he had since he'd moved away to the Big Toon and thus avoided the company of Joseph Wheen. Having put a bit of his own share of the aboriginal accumulation in a sock in a drawer at his mum's best pal's house, Jack had been heretofore, and was even now, circumnavigating ruin in the used car and dodgy firearm trade of the nearby metropolis.

2.0.5

As for Tommy Hunter, be it on account of his long years of silent contemplation or of his original transformative experience, all that the money did for him was to conceal in a magician's cloak of financial transaction the fact that Tommy Hunter's arrival back on earth was more apparent than actual. That he had some money on him may have accidentally made a certain level of communication with the rest of us possible, but this could not alter the necessary and superior truth that was the case, which was, and I'm aware that I'm repeating myself, that Tommy Hunter inhabited another universe from the rest of us. Money was incidental to his being, a means and not an end. A word, and not a thought. His wealth made him not a whit less extraterrestrial.

2.0.5.1

To Tommy, you see, "the world" was a place where everything made sense, where everything was connected to everything else, where every experience coalesced with every other experience into a comprehensible unity imbued with purpose, meaning and direction.

2.0.5.1.1

To put it another way, Tommy Hunter was insane. And nobody from the real world was in any position to help or hinder or understand him. Even your narrator's exceptional insight can offer only an approximation, rather as in the Cloud of Unknowing, wherein one discovers the truth only by excluding everything you first thought of, and then everything else you might ever think of, and then what's left when you're exhausted and can't think of anything, is God.

2.0.5.1.1.1

What was left, in this instance, when you had abandoned judgement, or it had abandoned you, was Tommy Hunter.

2.0.5.2

Tommy's "life" in Tommy's "world" — was a story that was never interrupted. He told himself this story every moment that he woke, and he dreamed it every moment that he slept. No one else could tell him anything, and he still wasn't talking. He knew no contradictions. Solitary by nature, his prison time had merely confirmed his mastery of all existence. He understood everything.

2.0.5.2.1

No. He really did. He was one of a kind.

2.0.5.2.1.1

Good thing too. If everyone was like that, we'd be extinct in a fortnight.

2.0.6

You and me, unlike Tommy Hunter, despite the best efforts of philosophers and religious teachers, we've all of us (or almost all of us) always known, really, what life is all about.

2.0.6.1

We know, for instance, that every time we get an idea about anything, it's already doomed to failure. We know from birth the sheer humiliation of waking up every morning, of showering without hope and blearily reaching for a towel and a story to wrap around our helplessness. As soon as we're dressed up as ourselves, we pass the rest of our waking time in the fruitless attempt to distract ourselves from the terrible trap we find ourselves in. We seek for unconsciousness, if we're lucky, in work, in culture and in love. All too aware of the futility of living, we go on doing it anyway, not even dreaming of recovering Eden any more, knowing all too well that knowing things never made anything any better.

2.0.6.1.1

Look what happened to Adam and Eve, we say to ourselves. We *are* what happened to Adam and Eve. And who wants that?

2.0.6.1.1.1

We are fallen and we've always known that we are fallen. We've known there was something terribly wrong with us ever since we started knowing anything.

2.0.6.1.1.1

And yet, despite it clearly being an evolutionary liability, we carry this curse of consciousness all through our lives, despite the coffee and the telly and the shit music and the shopping. Nothing we can do about it, no matter how rich or drunk we get. Our consciousness is always there, perversely trying to make sense of it all, uselessly trying to make a picture of things within which we can include our own self-image without it being too fat or thin or young or old or just plain manky.

2.0.6.1.1.1.1.1

We already know, too, even as we paint these unreliable pictures, that our renditions will always get insulted by the amalgamated millions of alternative and equally unreliable pictures of "reality" that every other bugger is painting or projecting on to the mere accident of being, projecting their egocentric and inaccurate world orders, inevitably coming into conflict with our own efforts to evade the acknowledging of entropy. And then let slip the dogs of war.

2.0.6.1.1.1.1.1.1

"Chaos has come again," we say to ourselves, more in weariness than anger, as, every night, we crawl unfulfilled and weeping into our scratchers, seeking again in the womb of night, some little, palatable intimation of escape, while knowing all too well that soon we'll have to get up and go through the whole ghastly rigmarole once more; that the cosmos will once more stare balefully upon us from the empty heavens and from the unsympathetic eyes of our fellow sufferers, and demand, without pity or expectation, who the fuck do we think we are?

2.0.6.1.1.1.1.1.1.1

Although we can't answer that question, we can more or less survive the asking of it. We can get through life. Of course we can. Of course we do. What else is there? What, other than a grateful dive under a speeding train, is the alternative to this always renewable ritual of humiliated accommodation to the way the world is? And to ourselves the way we are?

2.0.7

Tommy Hunter is what alternative there is. No doubts, no pain, no need for entertainment, no possibility of distraction. No curiosity, no weakness. No comprehension that the few people up and about at this early hour on that Tuesday morning were all looking at him like that — staring at him, walking into lamp posts — because he was so absolutely terrifying, so terrifyingly absolute. They balked at his stronger existence, like he was a band of purple light walking up the pavement, brighter and more terrible even than the world itself, like Rilke's angel, staring back at them with empty, indifferent eyes, seeing them for what they were, annihilating them, destroying everything by understanding everything and caring nothing about it.

2.0.7.1

Real Life — into which Tommy Hunter was inserting his horrible clarity — this is the place where you and I live, where things only make sense for moments at a time, where some cunt will always come along to scribble their name over your masterpiece, trip your melody with an inappropriate rim-shot or giggle at your halting pentameters. Tommy knew with crystalline certainty exactly what he was doing and why. So there was no way for Tommy Hunter to cope with real life, or it with him.

2.0.8

He was so far away from us that he couldn't even see us. But we could see him.

2.0.8.1

Tommy Hunter, in the real world, was as sudden as a tiger and as disconcerting as a snake.

2.1

Mrs Elspeth Dewar of 31 Balmoral Crescent had no thought that morning that she'd shortly be opening her front door to the Creature from the Black Lagoon. It was still, in that particular suburb of humanity, very early on. Her son Donald lay asleep upstairs. All unconscious of what was going to happen to her in a minute, or in the days to come, she herself was drinking her second sugary tea at her kitchen table and rasping on her third cigarette, scolding herself half-heartedly for those indulgences, when the doorbell rang.

2.1.1

Oddly enough, though only forty-one, Elspeth already felt that she had seen too much and lived too long. Widowed at twenty-four, even the pity of her neighbours and the solicitude of randy, married men had faded to indifference in the intervening years. In the meantime, she retained sufficient self-respect to leave her cigarette burning in the ashtray when she went to answer her door to whatever the world had brought to offer her this morning.

2.1.1.1

Big mistake.

2.1.2

Swathed in a yellow dressing gown lifted slightly by a puff of underfloor heating, suspecting nothing, she opened her front door. The smiling, shabby, middle-aged man in front of her in his old coat carrying a carpet bag and some days' growth of beard caused her no immediate surprise. There are still Wee Toons like Oors where itinerant craftsmen and other panhandlers, some with skill, most without, as yet ply their trades from door to door, and will wash your windows and buff up your Flymo for the price of a breakfast. There was, however, nothing Elspeth Dewar wanted cut, cleaned or sharpened that morning, and she made to close the door with a muttered, "No, thank you," only to find its swing impeded by a wet, badly shoed foot.

"Mrs Dewar?" the man enquired politely, his voice still gravelly from disuse. "Mrs Elizabeth Dewar?"

"Elspeth," she corrected without thinking.

"Elspeth, I'm so sorry." He smiled then, this husky and well-mannered stranger. She stared at him for some sign of familiarity, deeming it unlikely that so ragged a figure might be here on District Council or other official business. The voice of a teenaged boy intervened sleepily from upstairs.

"Who is it, Mum?"

The man renewed his smile and took half a step into the hallway.

"I'm sorry to disturb you so early, Mrs Dewar. Might I trouble you for a moment?"

There was something practised and deliberate in this gentility that sped her negative reply.

"I'm sorry. It's not a good time. I don't want anything."

Once again, she attempted to close the door on him. But the stranger was persistent, and again her effort was frustrated by that interposed, leaking sneaker.

Tommy spoke again in his voice like broken stones, measured and insistent. After all, he had rehearsed all this endlessly in his cell, and he wasn't going to be deflected from his performance just because nobody wanted it.

"Mrs Dewar, forgive me. But would I be right in thinking that some years ago, you suffered a tragic loss?" he said, like he'd started copping his dialogue from Henry James or some such cunt.

Elspeth's heart lurched and dipped suddenly. She pulled the robe more tightly about her ample yet still not ungainly figure in recognition and resentment at the stranger's inappropriate knowledge of her affairs, as well as the excellent grammar which contrasted unnervingly with that mineral, gutter voice and tramp's appearance.

"Who is it, Mum?" the grumpy and now all too vulnerable boy from on high inquired again, more fully awake now.

"Who are you?" she echoed quietly, now on the defensive, lower tummy squirming.

"I want you to know," Tommy said slowly, his voice aching with the truth of his testimony, "that I am sorry for your trouble."

There could be no question of not believing this assertion, and no knowing from what district of hell it might originate. This avatar was undoubtedly sorry for something. But her suspicion kept her mute and guarded.

"Have you ever thought about forgiveness?" the voice was saying now, as if in need of forgiveness itself, while the face was still grinning unaccountably.

Now in the months and years following her husband Colin or Eric's murder in the killing van in the woods, Mrs Dewar had found herself both plagued and consoled by the kindnesses of strangers — sexual and religious strangers, sometimes both. But such attention, as aforesaid, had waned and died as the shock of her loss had faded from collective memory, and she in turn had lost for others that talismanic frisson that attaches to the tragic in general and the very young and newly widowed tragic in particular. Besides, none of those preachers and vagabonds had spoken like this oracular hobo, this gruff soothsayer. Her sense of something alien it was that prompted her precipitate rejection of his unsettling and unasked for, but not in and of itself unreasonable, solicitude.

"Just fuck off, will ye," she said ... and a strange light lit in the stranger's eye, and she was suddenly very scared.

"Your husband was murdered by unrighteous men." He said this with the level certainty of knowledge.

"Mum!"

The voice of her wee son was on the stairs now, and, thoroughly nervous for the both of them suddenly, Elspeth attempted physical persuasion, actually pushed at the man's body. And he did not resist her, only repeating as he retreated, "Have you ever thought about forgiveness?"

Reassured a little at his docility and, dimly, as through a glass darkly, recognising the word "forgiveness" as having had something to do with church when she was wee, she tried for the moment to believe that this was merely a return visit by some God-bothering bureaucracy or other she'd forgotten which just happened to have her name on a database or something, so she demurred again with more confidence: "Just leave us alane, I'm tellin ye. I'm no' interested."

Still he smiled. The stranger still smiled. Understanding nothing in the doorway. So she got a wee bit more aggressive, and defined her rejection of whatever he was offering more expansively.

"How dae you bloody people find me anyway? I've said I'm not interested. Just leave us alone, why don't ye?" she shouted at him hopefully.

And for the first time, Tommy now blinked, his smile failing and his expectations now confused. He'd lost the place and so improvised momentarily, went off his script, and then all was lost. He said this ...

"Elspeth ... I'm sorry ..."

... and shut himself up almost as soon as he'd spoken, actually putting one hand over his mouth and pulling the carpet bag over his crotch, as though he'd exposed himself.

There was a pause, and, hearing the pain and regret in him, she inclined her head to one side, as if to see him from a different angle.

Then she couldn't see at all suddenly, some awful dawn blinding her, till she got used to the light. And then she saw who he was, she saw what was happening. She looked into those eyes into which she'd last looked at the furthest extreme of her experience, and in that sudden reseeing, her veil of compromise and forgetfulness fell from all of her senses at once. She could smell again the stale sweat and old clothes in the courtroom, hear again the murmurs and whispers as the life sentence on Tommy Hunter was announced and he'd turned and looked at her sorrowfully from his pale, devil eyes.

That was all it took to bring her from her world for a moment into his. So now it was Tommy who had to watch as Elspeth's face melted in front of him, draining, aging visibly, turning grey as breathed-out smoke. And he knew that she knew him. And that she was helpless with that knowledge. She was struck dumb by her horror, by her hatred and her grief and her fear, and by only she knew what other griefs since.

2.1.2.1

He was never going to know. She was never going to tell him any more than she just had. Nothing was going to be shared between them. There was no forgiveness here. She was telling him nothing. There was nothing he could tell her to make it better. There was nothing he could say. Nothing she would hear. Nothing to be done. And thus, for the first, and by no means the last time, Tommy's narrative collided with real life and fell to pieces in front of him.

2.1.2.1.1

She fell to the floor and wept, and he lifted her left hand and sorrowfully pushed a sealed white envelope into her open fingers. It was, as we'll discover, his fail-safe or default gesture of recompense, and luckily Elspeth was too deranged with shock to reject it.

2.1.2.1.2

She said, or she told Frank later, that when she'd shut the door, or when he'd allowed her to close it on him … that she thought she'd heard him say "I'm sorry" once again.

Anyway, right now, Donald, fully descended in his boxers and a knock-off Jimi Hendrix T-shirt, saw his mother on the carpet in helpless, lonely tears.

"Who the fuck was that fucking guy?" Donald asked her, and getting no reply, pushed past her, his seventeen-year-old manhood surging through his PJs, and opened the door again even as she found her voice and screamed at him urgently please not to.

2.1.2.2

But Tommy Hunter was already walking away, not quickly and not slowly, mind already set on his next appointment, and he scarcely heard the yelling boy behind him, busy in reflecting rather, that barring Elspeth's emotional collapse, the first necessary preliminary to the fulfilment of his epic destiny had gone more or less as well as it might have done. He'd made his first delivery, after all.

"You! Hi! You! I'm talkin tae you, ya cunt!" a boy's voice was yelling behind him for some reason, but soon faded out of earshot as Tommy turned the corner into King Edward Street.

2.1.2.2.1

Donald, son of Colin or Eric, whose resemblance to his dead father might well have tweaked a pang of memory from his father's murderer, had said murderer been sufficiently distracted to turn round, Donald, with his bare feet sore, obviously, and realising also from the wind that froze the tip of it, that his willy was hanging out, tucked it back in and turned himself back towards his widowed mother, who now stood in the open doorway of her house holding in one hand a torn white envelope, and in the other what seemed to the young man to be the largest sum of cash he had ever seen in anybody's hand.

(Three grand it was. Thirty-four left in the carpet bag, if you're counting, as you surely should.)

"Who the fuck was that?" asked Donald. And watched as his mother's eyes turned to him, tears stopped up, blank as stone, implacable as war.

2.2

Meanwhile, Tommy Hunter strolled on into Oor Wee Toon, his mind quietly blazing in the quiet of the breaking dawn and looked across to the rainy hills, vaguely unsatisfied. Perhaps he had hoped to exchange words or regrets, tokens of shared humanity with Elspeth, as well as to deliver his token of repentance. But perhaps not. What he'd just paid her, after all, had been no more than Colin or Eric's agreed share in the original enterprise (or one-fourth thereof). But at least he'd done that much, perhaps he now consoled himself as he descended the hill into the brown haze of home.

His gesture had been his sole and sufficient purpose, I'm speculating. How his gesture had been received, as indeed would be the case for all of his future gestures, was not strictly speaking his business. He was not in the business of meaning, but only, in the words of Lowell George, of being willing to be moving. He was on the essentially private road to wherever he was going, and probably attempted to cheer himself with that thought or some approximation thereof. But he maybe felt a wee bit deflated as well, to have gleaned so soon some inkling of the inconsistency of the world and its purposes with his own, mad construction of it. It might have been the weather, too, which wasn't very good.

2.2.1

And ours, let's face it, is a townscape, even in its occasional sunshine, that few if any can return to without some feeling of defeat. The heavy grey and mocking orange of the buildings in the High Street, such as it is, are ugly even in comparison to each other. Our architecture sits on the soul like a weight. Even the best of us comes home, even at the best of times, even those few of us with money and accolades from the wider, better world to cheer us, even we arrive back here somehow with our tails between our legs. Even if we actually have done quite well for ourselves and we're only back to see our grannies, we feel like failures to be back here. Even if we return as kings, we still feel shame that we were drawn back here at all. Even if we aren't defeated, the very fact of our being here, being back here, makes us feel that we must have been. Our London or Hong Kong or New York eyes fall down quickly on the pavement where they belong, as if even the best of us are ashamed at presuming to have escaped.

2.2.1.1

We belong here for good and ill, for good and all. You'd think we'd be used to it by now.

2.2.1.2

Tommy Hunter's promises had only ever been to himself, and he was unclouded by illusions of worldly success as he pursued the familiar directions he'd so long contemplated and envisioned. His head was still held high, he was still defined and delimited by his antic purpose, still talking only to himself, still true to the lines on his internal map. The very rain seemed to part for him. He at least seemed to know where he was going which is more than you can say for most of us. And he stayed on his intended itinerary. What else was he going to do?

2.2.1.3

He paused, mind you, outside Saxone, the shoe shop in the High Street (just opposite the bell tower which not even the original architect could have thought was anything other than hideous), and squelched a moment, uncertain. His feet were freezing. But Tommy knew now that he could not afford to improvise, no matter the state of his feet, and he pressed on. First things had to be first. There was no other way to hang on to himself.

Besides, the shoe shop wasn't even open yet. Now he looked, he saw that there was nothing open yet. And he remembered, with a shock, that shops had hours, that people had jobs and bought things and sold things in prearranged orderings of socially contracted time, and he was momentarily panic-stricken at his own forgetfulness. He was out of practice in a world where people had such structures, however uncomfortable and annoying, in their lives. There was so much to remember, and there was nothing he just knew about, instinctively, not without thinking about it, not any more.

2.2.1.3.1

If he ever had just known about such things the way we're all supposed to. And it's not just his growing up in care, then being in the army and then in prison almost all his life. In the depths of an experience that had either been wholly policed or wholly chaotic, there had always been something deliberate about Tommy. Something self-directed and inscrutable. Unfeeling, some thought. Autistic, some psychotherapist had even diagnosed, and it is true that he had always had to consider carefully every step he'd ever taken. And that he was a poor judge of character. But that was because, deep down, he trusted the universe, and also himself. So he tended to trust other people. And who is to say he was wrong about that, ethically speaking anyway, in the long run?

2.2.1.4

He stood in front of the hotel now, which, being a hotel, was, to his relief, open and serving breakfast from the buffet bar in the William Wallace dining room. He breathed deeply a few times, and went into reception, still talking to himself, steeled for the next exchange. Whatever would be would be.

2.2.2

The receptionist on duty, as it happens, was a Polish lad called Miroslaw, which didn't faze Tommy in itself, as he already had to dredge up his dialogue in English from a distant memory, but Miroslaw having an accent like that might not have been thought to be helpful.

As it was, Tommy was pouring sweat well before he reached the desk, his long preparation of every step already hopelessly out of kilter with the perpetually surprising world. That he found himself faced with a nice young chap with an unimagined Krakovian accent was the least of his perturbations. He himself was a child again, and far more foreign to this locality, and younger in its mores, than Miroslaw, for all his Polishness, could be.

Besides, a commercial transaction can always admit of eccentricity more easily than can communication with the widow of a man you'd murdered getting on fourteen years ago, and so with cash paid for a night in advance and a false name and address murmured (both inspired, incidentally, by his sole attendance, with his own hitherto and ever-after absent father, at a professional fixture of Association football in 1988), Tommy Hunter, perspiring like a horse, found himself in possession of a small plastic card (which he nervously accepted, after some persuasion, was in fact a key) that opened up the minimal beige requirements of the weary business traveller. Having mastered the momentary vertigo of being given a key that wasn't a key, and, once at the door, being shown by a Somali maid how to work the thing, he stammered his further thanks and entered Room 417 and collapsed, fraught and shaking, into the nostalgia of finding himself settled until further notice into a small, institutional cuboid.

He got up again for a moment to shut the curtains and complete the homecoming, then he lay back on the bed in a twilit state of weeping, near collapse, his chest heaving as he shrank the world back into proportions he could handle and predict. It would be an hour or more before he could move. And that was to go for a piss.

2.2.3

The hotel records as later sequestered by DS "Danny" Boyle showed that Mr Greenock Morton made just two outside phone calls and had had no meals in his room. He didn't go out and had only one visitor until he left. Which was on the Wednesday.

2.3

Which hiatus allows me to cheat a little, and to narrate briefly the first of the cascade of unlooked-for consequences of Tommy's unlooked-for return. That is to say a phone call made by Elspeth Dewar to Frank Wheen within minutes of her son Donald's departure to the wee job at the supermarket (which had been secured for him by his Uncle Frank — uncle in the sponsoring rather than familial sense).

2.3.1

Frank Wheen, as aforesaid the brains of the old outfit, was by now a highly regarded figure in Oor Wee Toon, because, having invested his ill-gotten gains right wisely, he had also maintained the necessary incuriousness of a number of folk, constabulary and otherwise, as to the origins of his seed money by spending some of it on them — and distributing other forms of influential largesse in their interests. The list of these personages naturally included Elspeth Dewar and her wee Donald. Elspeth had been, before and throughout the debacle of the van raid, entirely conscious of Eric (or Colin's) role in the whole mess. And she had kept her trap shut all these years in exchange for an initial bung, followed by regular emollients.

2.3.1.1

In this initial communication, Elspeth omitted any mention to Frank of the further compensation for her loss that Tommy Hunter of his own free will had given her. Her self-discipline in this regard led her at this stage to restrict herself to merely deflecting a portion of her own trepidation on to Frank, informing him of Tommy's appearance at her door, you may be sure withholding no detail of the oddness of his behaviour, excepting only as aforesaid the financial gesture, which she didn't see any earthly reason to suppose was any of Frank's business anyhow.

2.3.2

The intelligence thus transmitted, Elspeth felt she was safe now, and had no further part to play in this narrative, an impression of which she would be shortly and, let me recoilingly confirm at once, forcibly disabused once the paranoia latent in Frank's social position and in any case embedded in his personality came into play. Let alone what might happen if Crazy Joe ever got to hear about it.

2.3.2.1

Indeed, the foremost consideration for Frank at this first news of Hunter's return was as to precisely what he was going to tell his fucking nutjob of a brother, presently not all that gainfully employed as a handyman for the string of care homes for the elderly which were still Frank's primary business interest. But whatever his fraternal trepidation as to Brother Joe, you may be sure that Frank no longer considered that the man-management of a non-familial nutjob like Tommy Hunter was any part of his portfolio, and was equally all too aware that man-management of a specialised variety was right up Joe's apples and pears, and that the same Joseph Wheen, once activated, was a hard man to control, even, or even especially, if you were his smarter, younger brother.

2.3.2.1.1

Frank was to remain — fatally — undecided for some days, about how much was the working minimum he had to tell Joe about this and other matters, and on how best to employ his (Joe's) talents in this tooterie situation. The fatality aforesaid being that Joe, once apprised of that situation, would apply those talents at his own terrible and indiscriminate discretion.

2.3.2.1.2

To be fair though, and smart though he was, there's no gainsaying that Frank had some tricky and time-limited considering to do that morning before accepting even his own role in the saga; a role which, he already felt certain, no matter what he did, and no matter what he did or did not tell his wild-souled sibling, would precipitate unpleasant consequences leading towards what he rightly feared might be no happy conclusion, even if he now turned Buddhist and did nothing, and even if he could somehow refrain from bringing his volatile predecessor of the maternal womb into the equation at all.

2.3.2.1.3

Which he couldn't. He knew that. Some cunt was bound to tell Joe something. Some cunt always did. So better if it came from him in a considered fashion so there might be some minimal possibility of damage limitation. He'd have to tell Joe right now that Tommy Hunter was back in town. Right now. He knew that fine. Nonetheless, Frank poured himself a cheeky wee malt, and indulged in the illusion of free will for another three minutes and forty-four seconds.

2.3.3.

Let us leave Frank for that period, then, in his discreet brown study, and transfer our attention to the party of the second part, Joseph Wheen, who, in that same short span of time, was enjoying some desultory sexual activity, the precise details of which I'll not be going into, thanks, with Joan MacHutcheon, a nursing assistant at one of the care homes aforementioned, taking advantage of the temporary absence of Alec MacSwiney, normally resident therein, but happily away in Motherwell today having his cataracts seen to.

2.3.3.1

When the reluctant call from Frank came through to his mobile three minutes and forty-four seconds into this activity, Joe had only just got hard, and it was the opening chords of "Purple Haze" that were his coitus interruptus (or preventus) and the fanfare of all that now followed. Not that Frank at this stage divulged any detail as to what his "fucking problem" might be in answer to that enquiry. At this stage Frank as the senior brother in income if not in years, and his elder brother's employer, merely requested the immediate pleasure of Joseph's company, of his "getting his arse round the house" at his earliest convenience. Something, he said, had come up — a consummation that, for Joan MacHutcheon, was devoutly to be wished.

2.3.3.2

After Frank's interruption, Joe did his best for some time to carry on in that regard, thrusting manfully in support of his diminishing and embittered equipment, but his old resentment of his brother distracted him, as did the realization that he and his lady-love had all this time been observed by a grinning, toothless harridan, one Frances O'Hagan, chuckling with inane nostalgia in the bedroom doorway, holding her purple toothbrush to attention. Joe said for her to fuck off, but the proximity of death or the memory of life made her stay to watch his pounding, joyless buttocks. Frances had herself, in times past, been notorious hereabouts for her waylaying of car workers on payday (when there were such people and such days around here) on their way home to their spouses. Perhaps she was smiling at the evocation of those simpler, happier times, rather than actually mocking the courting couple, but however that may be, Joseph Wheen found himself unable to continue with his lovemaking, and, as he pulled his trousers over his dwindling, damp erection, he loudly and colourfully evinced his confirmed and recurrent Weltschmerz.

2.3.3.3

Fucking Frank. Who the fuck did fucking Frank think he was fucking talking to?

2.3.3.3.1

Etcetera.

2.3.4

Frank, meanwhile, assuaged his own disquiet by means of telephoning and berating the most senior of his numerous sources within the local police service as to why the hell was he being taken by surprise by the unwelcome intelligence of Tommy's arrival? What did those cunts think he was paying them for?

"I'll meet you at the golf club tonight," came the enragingly complacent reply from Superintendent Bellamy — the bane of the aforementioned DS Boyle's existence and vice versa ... of which, again, much more to follow.

2.3.4.1

To reassure himself still further that he remained, as yet, the master of his fate, Frank slammed the phone down on his bland interlocutor. Then sat himself down and had himself another sloppy dram of Bowmore from a heavy-bottomed Caithness crystal tumbler, sitting in his big front room with his big bay windows, looking out on his big back garden, facing south in the pissing, filthy rain, the sounds of his happy family home all around him already stained with tenuousness, their voices now echoes in a cave, the expensive whisky poison on his tongue, as he anticipated loss with every fibre of his bloodstained being.

2.4.

In summary, then, this was the condition of our principals, including the money, most of whom have now been, or are shortly about to be, introduced into the narrative. Frank had his garden, his golf, his children, his VAT returns, his investments, his Meissen, his carburettor problems, his Rotarian meetings, his charitable contributions and his wife Eleanor to contend with, and with each of these he had an ongoing, complex but largely predictable relationship. Joe had his mates and his speed and his women and his wee bets and his anger issues and his probation officer to contend with on a similar footing. Eleanor had the precarious management of the house and the school and the universe likewise under her control. Even wee Ronnie and Janette, Hunter's children, after their fashions, had stuff like work and school and walking and talking and bus fares and the weather to deal with along with all the other stuff that life had already had the time to throw at them, and succeeded in so doing, by and large. So too did old Agnes, though her world was now tightly circumscribed by her angry routine of aches and serial diagnoses of some or other fucking thing in her body that was trying to kill her ... as well as a certain amount of cooking and her crossword puzzles and going down to the Paki shop for bread and milk. Ronnie's social worker Padraic had the various mispronunciations of his name and the pretended optimism of his weekly reports upon his juvenile charges to occupy his waking life. Even old Jack Webster had his fear and his negotiations and his seeking out of this and that to keep him from the frightful vacuum of space-time impinging itself too much upon his consciousness.

2.4.1

Only Tommy Hunter had nothing. Nothing nothing

nothing. Apart from thirty-four thousand pounds arranged in envelopes in a carpet bag, he had just himself and his own howling, crouched like a stone wolf in a hotel room with the blinds down, eyes closed, feeling it swirl about him, this vortex of uncertainty in which he was a singularity. Only Tommy Hunter lived within the event horizon of himself, inside the black hole, his gravity sucking down light. Only Tommy knew the truth, the elemental, world-ending truth. And its gravitational pull was off the scale, its other-dimensional topology all-circumscribing.

2.4.1.1

The rest of them, Frank, Joe, Jack, Agnes, Ronnie, Janette and the rest hadn't yet been drawn into that crushing, stretching orbit. That's why they were still part of the sky. Even the remaining thirty-four thousand pounds now neatly bundled into packages of various amounts tucked neatly in the folds of Tommy's carpet bag, however large and decisive a role it might play among the inhabitants of the strange sphere he was visiting, was inessential, as far as Tommy was concerned.

2.4.2

Only Tommy Hunter was free. You could look at it that way as well if you wanted to.

2.5

But now there was a knocking at the door, a rapping through the empty chaos of Tommy's liberty, making him blink uncomprehendingly. He had a visitor. His first in fourteen years. And he was free no longer. His negotiated re-entry to our common bondage was upon him. There was, and is, only one way that ever ends for anybody.

2.5.1

Tommy sat up, cleared his throat, said, "Hawd on," adjusted his crotch, approached the door, and opened it, exhausted, each successive action costing him decisions, as if he'd been remembering the rules of chess.

3.0

I never actually met Ronnie Hunter, but let me tell you something that happened to me on a bus once.

I was sitting thinking about something else with my eyes facing front when I hear this mad wee tune going on somewhere behind me. Kind of a humming in a wee sing-songy voice, and a hollow clonking noise, quite gentle, keeping time with "Wonderwall" or some such shite ... this was a few years ago now ... and I couldnae help myself, I had to turn round to look, and I saw this horrible wee ned, pattern of a cup and ring shaved into his baldy, singing this horrible wee song, horribly tapping a half-empty bottle of cider against an old man's skull. Keeping the beat. Nice and slow. He wasnae hurting him or anything, but by Christ, he could have if he'd wanted to ... kind of thing. And I don't know if this thin old guy had been a POW in Burma, or had liberated Europe once upon a time, or was just a retired tube fitter with a dodgy lung or whatever, but he was pale as imminent death at being traduced like this, at discovering that all he'd ever been in his life to whoever had loved him was now reduced to the shame and humiliation of being at the mercy of this poisonous, anonymous gnome whose voice hadnae even broken yet, tapping a rhythm on his napper, gently like, just like that, just because he could. Singing out of tune as well.

There was no way, there is no way, that an old guy like that, with a story, a history of marriage, military service and employment or whatever, could cope with the degree of shapeless, consequence-careless threat that was bonking a bottle in time to its own psychosis on his tired, tired skull. The old man's lips were moving, silently voicing something ... disbelief, terror, I don't know. He was talking to me silently. I don't think he was asking me for help, but. He was past help. We all are.

Then, of course, psycho boy caught me looking at him in his theatre of shit. He stopped his singing … and now he looked straight at me. Now I was his audience. He started talking to the old guy's cadaverous, tufted earlobes, but he kept on looking at me.

"Jew no like me?" the wee fuck was saying, "Jew no wanni be friends wi me?"

And what did ah dae? Ah did fuck all, didnta? I turned back round and looked away, hair erect at the back of my neck. Sure I did. And I wasnae the only one.

This was a bus full of adults, men and women, you understand. And maist of us could have had the wee cunt, even the women. He was only skinny … five foot nothing and half-cut as well. But not one of us did anything. Whether by calculation or animal indifference, we had all handed our moral compass to a nasty wee shite who wouldn't know what to do with a moral compass if you stabbed him in the face with it.

We were all so degraded as to actually be relieved when a fat boy from a posh school got on the bus and Frankenstein Junior decided to go and talk to him for a bit. He started telling this Bunter character in graphic detail all about him diddy riding his bird … or some such pish. But we didn't care. The posh kid had a violin and everything, and deserved whatever was coming to him.

Aye, him, we all said silently. Have a go at him.

Then I got off. Me and a guy in overalls wi a tool bag, we both did. We didn't even look at each other. We had seen the future. And there was nothing about it we wanted to discuss.

3.0.1

Like I say, I never met wee Ronnie myself … but I think that was the likes of him. None of that inchoate tribe of lonely wee monsters varies in the slightest degree from any of the rest of them in my experience. I remember thinking about the boy on the bus later on when I heard about the summit conference held by the Wheen brothers with Ronnie Hunter at the Dryry Street hostel where Ronnie was housed at the time.

3.0.1.1

Not quite sixteen years old by my reckoning, Ronnie must have been panting for his freedom by then, which was gonnae be short-lived, of course it was. If there ever was a boy with "Property of Her Majesty's Prison Service" tattooed into his genome, it was Ronnie Hunter, third-generation parentless, his only male role models an absent father reputed to have done for his mother, and of course, those slightly older exemplars of immediate energy, his peers at school and various hostels, who had been torturing the worthlessness of everything into Ronnie's flesh every waking and sleeping moment since he left Janice's lost womb, giving him general and specific evidence of the universal rule of casual violence, till he had a PhD in the random science of tomorrowless existentialism. Which creed is surely definitive for the likes of Ronnie, abandoned and forsaken multitude that they are, a future-robbed creature made of thousands of limbs and a thousand heads all with a single thought: Trust No One. Never. Not yourself, not your friends, not your social workers. And you'll not be too disappointed when they betray you and lock you up for the good and safety of those incomprehensible others with their families and lives and ambitions and legal ownerships of this and that. Ronnie was of that lost, dangerous tribe.

3.0.2

It could be worse. There's places in the world where wee cunts like that are the Polis.

3.1

They didn't have a lot of visitors except the Polis in Dryry Street. Once in a while mebbe, a drama worker came in to exorcise his or her bourgeois guilt preparatory to running back to Mammy and a proper job. That was about it. So when Frank and Joseph Wheen swept up in a BMW 3 Series that Monday morning and got out wearing suits, you'd have to call that an event. There'd be nothing else worth talking about till Tommy Hunter manifested himself a couple of days later (also in a suit) and turned the world properly upside down.

3.2

Frank thought about his own kids while he and Joe surveyed the rancid hallway, you can bet he did, and he warmed himself with his accomplishment of their rescue from places like this. But it wasn't Frank that anybody was looking at. They knew who Frank was of course. But they were all looking at Joe. They'd heard his legend, and they were poking their heads round doorways for a noisy, shushing glimpse of his grey face and his white scars and his polished nails. They bathed in the once and future violence he so thrillingly embodied. He was, after all, and despite the best efforts of our tolerant and inclusive and endlessly self-deceiving culture, their ideal. Even Padraic Macreesh, their genial and troubled superintendent (who would unhappily also be on duty two nights later), couldn't help looking at Joe while he spoke to Frank. He was only human. He knew who they both were, of course (it's only

Wee, Oor Toon), and that Frank was a power and a presence in the parts of the world that Joe's lumpenproletarian charisma couldn't reach (as well as vice versa), and that between the two of them, they represented practically the full possibilities of the social elite of North Lanarkshire, but Mr Macreesh too had a title and a set of regional and national parameters to bolster his self-worth, and he dodged behind his statutory obligations in an effort to seem relaxed about this unwonted interest from these local celebrities in one of the most anonymous and hapless of his unlucky charges.

"Perhaps you'd like to come in the lounge, Mister Wheen," said Padraic, with the confidence of his stewardship.

They all sat in the encouragingly postered games room, the social worker protected by a pocket file. "I have informed Ronnie that his father has in fact been released, but I have to tell you, we've had no contact from him, either through head office or directly. Not in all the time Ronnie's been here, in fact. It's a most unusual history …"

"Is Ronnie here now?" asked Mr Wheen, interrupting respectfully. Padraic hesitated. Frank went on. "As you know, we've looked in on Ronnie and his sister from time to time. Just to see how they are."

"Yes … Mister Wheen … might I ask … what is your relationship with Ronnie? You're not down here in the file as being family …"

"We grew up together … Ronnie's father and us … We served together in the army, Mister Macreesh. "

You did, didn't you? Thought Macreesh … you pounded up and down the streets of Newry stomping your Scottishness into my already Jock-afflicted Isle … and now look at you … and look at me … you bastards … but all he said out loud was:

"Then, perhaps, you're in a better position than …"

Frank sat forward. "We don't know where Tommy is. But we do know that he's dangerous."

The social worker blinked his dark Irish eyes at them. Dangerous Scotchmen were something he and his ancestors knew a lot about.

"Do you think he might be dangerous to Ronnie?"

Joseph interjected. "He killed his fucken mother. He fucken killed her. What dae you fucken think?" Mr Macreesh decided against offering a measured judiciary caveat to this assertion.

"What are you suggesting, Mr Wheen?" he asked instead.

Frank sat further forward, and, in a tone of quiet concern, said: "We'd like to know where Ronnie's sister is. And we think that Ronnie ... should be moved ... until ..."

"Mr Wheen," attempted Mr Macreesh, "Mr Hunter, I understand, has been released in Glasgow on condition of weekly parole attendance, and according to my information ..."

"He'll miss it," said Frank. "He's been seen ... here ..."

"But you'll understand ..."

"We'd like to talk to Ronnie now. Alone."

"I'm afraid I can't sanction that, Mr Wheen. Ronnie is in the care of the local authority, and I can't ..."

"We understand," lied Frank with a glance at his brother. "Stay if you want ..."

Macreesh stood. "Excuse me," he said and left the room.

In answer to his brother's unspoken question Frank answered to no one in particular.

"I want this under control. I want this done right."

3.2.1

Macreesh returned, leading a barefoot, tangle-haired, chewing youth in a donated orange sweatshirt and blue pyjama bottoms, smelling of armpit and calamity. Not looking at anyone, Ronnie Hunter gave his bony arse to gravity, sat down, feral eyes shaded under an unfashionable auburn mop.

"D'ye remember me, Ronnie?" said Frank, as gently as he could. Ronnie chewed to himself behind his hair.

Frank glanced at Macreesh, who declined to prompt the boy into responding, looking straight ahead of him, just like I did on the bus I told you about, declining to compromise the meaningless autonomy that served Ronnie as his parodic set of human rights — here, as so often in the arena of our social relations, generalised indifference to the many manifesting as respect for the individual.

Frank persevered in his own pretence, trusting to Ronnie's experience of the jungle to identify the threats and promises behind his careful choice of words.

"I want you to know you can call me … anytime … if there's anything bothering you … Okay, son? If you need my help." He put a card on the table with a twenty-pound note. "That's my number. And a wee something for yourself. Okay?" He thought maybe Ronnie graced him with a glance. "I wanted to … eh … get in touch with your sister too. See if maybe I can … help her out as well …"

Macreesh leaned forward. "Now, Ronnie, you know you don't have to answer any questions if you don't want to." Macreesh smiled legalistically. Ronnie knew very well he didn't have to answer to anybody. And his communication of that understanding was no more verbal than the grubby paw that scooped up the card and the twenty, only looking at the purple note derisively so that Frank could see that, yes, an understanding had been reached, before flopping from the room as silently and untidily as he had entered. Macreesh too smiled and stood.

"Will that be all, gentlemen?"

3.2.2

Moments later, outside, Frank and Joseph returned to Frank's still intact Beamer, Frank uneasily conscious that it was Joe's reputation that had protected it in a postcode where they can strip the wheels off a bourge-mobile in seventy seconds flat.

"What the fuck did ye dae that fer?" asked Joseph, referring to Frank's earlier donation to Ronnie.

"He's deprived," said Frank as he opened up the driver's door.

"I'm fuckin deprived" opined his brother without irony. Frank sighed as he buckled his seat belt. Everyone troubled him with their grievances. It was a cost of being himself he factored into his days.

3.2.2.1

With a scatter of gravel the visitors were gone, pink faces watching, pressed against mesh-covered windows. Macreesh stood at the threshold of Ronnie's dorm room respectfully talking to a headless heap of farty blankets. "Tell me if anything happens, won't ye, Ronnie," he offered, as yet another of the lives he had touched slipped between his generous, decent fingers and fell a little further into the valley of the shadow.

3.3

Hell, despite the Frenchman, is not other people. It is ourselves as we are constituted, alone as we are, forcefully confronted every day with meanness. All objective enlightenment as to our singular and collective condition is the same thing as despair. As witness another of our wandering souls, Agnes MacHutcheon, who, though no longer in loco parentis of young Ronnie and his more capable older sister, and thus free of all extraneous responsibilities, was yet as afflicted as Sisyphus with the pointless stone-heaving of it all. At her advanced age, she had come no closer than her grandson to the Vedic acknowledgement of her own weakness and stupidity that might alone have saved her. She believed that people should be strong and wise and good, and, hence, finding herself wanting in all three of these admirable and illusory qualities, she struggled continually uphill into a thickening cloud of self-reproach, itself formed of a condensation of categorical imperatives, hefting a sack of moral burdens which she no more than the Pope could either raise to an acceptable height, nor yet slough off and let tumble down the hill again, despite their being, actually, on the level of ideas, a useless bag of rocks. Our not fitting into the world that we are forced to inhabit is not a soluble anomaly of social and philosophical origin and therefore capable of ameliorative thought or action. I am rather convinced as to the fatality of our evolved state. Perfection is not our possibility, therefore our faults are not faults exactly, rather features of our ineluctable incompleteness as creatures trapped in continuing evolution. Let me say a stoical "yes" to all there is, like your German man. That would be my song. But then, I've always gone pretty easy on myself, for all the good it ever did me.

3.3.1

Nothing was ever easy for Agnes any more. Not walking or breathing or seeing. Stubbornly independent, she refused all offers of health visitors or daily women, leave alone being sequestered in the tender care of one of Frank Wheen's "care homes". She had spent a month in one of them once after an operation, and had taken the presence of old people there as a personal insult. That was not for her. Rather, her path was a routine of rising and drinking, smoking and walking, once a day, to the Paki shop four hundred and thirty-seven increasingly painful and now nearly impossible steps up the slight but tyrannical incline round the corner and on to the main road. She didn't observe anything on this, her only remaining perambulation on any day other than her own feet. She hated the television. She didn't understand the radio. She had elementary crossword puzzle books piled by the hundred around the only three downstairs rooms of the house that she lived in any more, of which both the kitchen and downstairs lav were blackened nightmares, and the front room was so thick with dust that the mites had given up on excreting any more. But as long as her existence was cyclical and eventless, it was bearable. Even her slide towards death was tolerable in increments.

It took her an age to get to the shop each day — but, then, she had an age to get there. Mr Iqbal was always friendly and solicitous and she was always astonishingly rude in return. It took a longer age to get back, as she balanced two blue bags containing luncheon meat, Milanda and the milk and sometimes teabags and a new puzzle book (once a week) in a precise cantilever of minimum social entitlement. She'd not look up at sudden noises and occasional insults. She knew every crack in the pavements, and noted the growth patterns of the lichen therein with an approximation of interest. She walked on knives, her hips shrieking at her almost enjoyably. She wasn't dead as long as it still hurt. As long as nothing interrupted her, as long as nothing in her life spoke to her of sequence, consequence or change, she could say she was okay if anybody were ever to ask her, which nobody ever would. She was rotting on her feet and made no complaint about it. Had she started complaining she'd not have been able to stop. She would have howled the last of her life away in protest. So she kept quiet. Today — Tuesday — was like every other day. Wednesday would be different. She'd be dead by Friday. Which only goes to show.

Returning now to Tommy Hunter on that Tuesday lunch-time, he was standing at the door of his hotel room, holding his breath without realising it, so that when he opened up to admit the tailor (see 2.4.1), he breathed out in a somewhat startling fashion. But then he was himself startled at what he saw. His first visitor in fourteen years looked to be made entirely of something like butter — round, a face of broken capillaries, balding, wisps of white hair transparent to his head, itself like an old tomato balancing on a brown suit, a white moustache just visible, a film on a blood-swollen upper lip.

"Mr Morton?" The sound came out without him moving his mouth, the chap! Tommy stared, and the flesh-enfolded eyes, perfect dots, fled from his own in a flicker to the suit bags draped over what must have been a limb at some ancestral evolutionary stage, and thence to the bags of pants and socks and shirts and shoes that dangled from the sinister paw.

"McIvor" came the voice from nowhere, brisk and comfortable. "Ross and Dean."

He only seemed to speak in names, this fellow, and Tommy was still a number. So, he hesitated. The sphincter in the middle of the boobling fruit before him again widened disconcertingly.

"Gentleman's outfitters for Mr Morton. We spoke on the phone this morning," the mouth said, before once again regaining itself, pursed.

(In fact, Mr McIvor was anxious not to show his teeth, misshapen and discoloured as they were by years of pipe smoking and the later penitent sucking of Barley Sugars and Stripey Minty Balls. An extrusion of noise from an impossible source in any event.)

Tommy remembered then that he was in disguise as a human being and coughed "Aye" and let the stranger in.

And now Mr McIvor of Ross and Dean was all busy-ness, all bustle and chunter, rapid observations of the weather splicing into a bewildering commentary on local and national affairs as as a charcoal-grey suit was laid out and displayed with some pride on the bed, two boxes of shoes at the bedside, and the bag of shirts, socks and boxers equally well placed at the foot of it, too neat and quick for the eye to follow, talking too fast for the ear to hear, Tommy standing back the while in bleary amazement, only roused to wariness by the sight of this wee man suddenly standing still and seeming to protect himself with a white strip of plastic stretched across what must have been his chest, held lightly but firmly between the doughy lumps on the ends of what were, in fact, now he looked more closely, arms. The tailor had also stopped talking, having covered his available material in a matter of heartbeats.

What's this?" Tommy asked him.

"It's a measuring tape, sir. It is awfully dark in here."

Tommy reached behind him for the desk lamp and could then make out the numbers on the tape. "What fur?" he asked, genuinely mystified. Mr McIvor chose to take this as a joke, expelling three short puffs of breath and spittle.

"Why to measure you, Mister Morton. My conscience, we can hardly have you buying two suits from us without my confirming your measurements."

"Naw," said Tommy, in a rising flush of panic that uprooted his scalp, "yer aw right."

"When was your last fitting, sir?" said McIvor, almost scolding in his emphasis, blind and wise in a very small universe.

Tommy felt sweat sting his eyes as he tried to remember ever having been there himself. "Nineteen … eighty something … I think …" he managed, the taste of vomit in his mouth.

He told himself he was going to have to get used to this. He overcame the dizziness by force of will.

"For heaven's *sake*, Mr Morton ..." McIvor tutted, itali-cising, and then, unbelievably, started towards Hunter, actually came near him, oblivious to the surely prover-bial danger of a man getting near to another man without prior, expressed permission. Tommy stumbled backwards in shock. "Sir?" asked McIvor, almost crossly, unknowingly close to the sudden death that Tommy in his crowded mind had already inflicted on him, opening his face, stamping him into a vivid carpet of guts and clarified fat.

Tommy bit back the vision and submitted, eyes closed, his arms outstretched to accept his crucifixion.

"On ye go, then."

He suffered then, Tommy Hunter, in a way that only those who have been abused, and have learned to prevent any further abuse with frightful retribution, can suffer, as he allowed this little man to touch him, probe him. Against every instinct he suffered, as this parody of inva-sion took his inside leg.

McIvor, miraculously still alive, stood then saying: "I think, perhaps ... sir has put on a little weight ..."

"How?" demanded Tommy disbelievingly, opening his eyes and grabbing the measuring tape.

Mr McIvor puttered at him. "A matter of an inch or two on the waist ..."

Hunter recovered himself from fury and accepted the evidence, handing the tape back to the tailor, forgiving him who knew not what he did. "Right," he said, and looked straight at him.

Did McIvor glimpse, in that moment of eye contact, the whirlwind he had come so precipitously close to reaping, him and his Urizenic measurements? No, he did not. He just stood there not knowing what anything meant. By means of rescue for the both of them, Tommy gave him an envelope from the bedside table. Still uncomprehending, McIvor took the thing and wondered vaguely what it was and what he was supposed to do with it.

"£298.96. That right?"

McIvor looked at the envelope in his hand, and slid a podgy finger in the aperture. Tommy, insulted, and maybe even with irony, turned up his own vocal expressiveness just a little.

"Ye no gonnae *count* it, are ye?"

Penetrating the fog to which an unconsidered life had reduced his vision, a light went on somewhere inside Mr McIvor's medulla oblongata. Never dreamt of such a thing, it told his sluggish forebrain, while simultaneously driving an adrenal jolt of flight into his legs (that had to struggle past the cholesterol, right enough), but having succeeded, a pulse of unaccustomed circulation rattled the coins in the package in his hand. Startled by the sound, obeying the better angel of his nature, McIvor of Ross and Dean, Gentleman's Outfitters puttered again and giggled like a small girl and as he left the room backwards, the door seemed to shut in his face by magic.

3.4.1

When he had gone (not daring to open the envelope till he was well outside, as he later told DS Boyle), the tailor found the money to be correct. So, more or less right with the world, he went back up the road to tell young Mr Dean all about it, while Tommy, by contrast, back up in his hotel bedroom, looked balefully at the slightly too tight trousers on the bed and the slightly gappy shirts in the bag. "Fuck," he said. The universe had let him down again. Without another thought, Tommy sat on the floor to do some exercise.

3.4.2

Hour after hour after hour of press-ups, sit-ups, prison calisthenics, pausing only to place his single other recorded call to a phone box in Carntyne at a prearranged time, never communicating with anyone in any other way than the peculiar rhythmic thumping his exertions evidenced in the surrounding rooms, which no one thought twice about, even when they heard them. No one complained, according to the hotel day or night books. Again, according to the hotel records, as examined by DS Boyle, Room 417 never had a meal brought up until "Mr Morton of Greenock" checked out next day, in a well-fitting suit, carrying a carpet bag containing his second suit and a second pair of shoes, three shirts, two pairs of pants and socks, and £33,611.04, having paid ninety pounds for one nights' bed and breakfast, getting no discount for not having had any breakfast, and having slept, apparently, on the floor … if at all. His sheets were clean of his DNA. He was positively identified in the police lab by the towels and discarded clothes he'd left in the bath on the Friday morning.

3.5

The night before Hunter's egress, Joe had stopped by brother Frank's for a bite to eat with Frank and Eleanor, which was by no means a regular occurrence, let me tell you, especially on a Tuesday. Frank's oldest, Katherine, was upstairs busily preparing for her Advanced Higher English exam in two days' time, rereading *Miss Jean Brodie*. The younger of the offspring, Curtis, was plugged into YouTube like a sphinx, re-editing classic cartoons with swear words and screaming noises under the soubriquet of Badluckcrow. They were both for keeping well out of the way of Uncle Joe, whose thunderous demeanour had never, for them, unlike for Ronnie and his fellow inmates in another world, held any glamour. They'd had left over chicken earlier anyway.

Downstairs over dinner, and after, in the drawing room, the conversation hadn't flowed so much as belched from time to time. Joe had got redder and redder listening to the pair of them debating the merits of the universities whose open days they had recently attended, turning over his plum and couscous salad like a forensic vet examining a turd. Now Eleanor, whose sartorial as well as culinary tastes leaned to the near and far oriental, draped herself and her flowing dupatta across the chesterfield, looked between the brothers with languorous superiority and asked the questions it hadn't occurred to either of them to ask.

"What does he want? What did he actually say to her?"

"Who?" asked Frank. Joe looked at him with suspicion. It didn't take much.

"Elspeth Dewar. What did he SAY to her?"

"I don't know. Does it matter?" asked Frank, puzzled.

"Why did he go and see her?" Eleanor had a way of asking simple questions that made everyone feel like a dick.

"Has he talked to you? Have you seen um?" Joe demanded of his brother. Frank ignored him for the moment.

"I'll go and talk to her," he conceded, gratefully, to Eleanor. Frank was no fool. He knew Eleanor was smarter than he was. He turned to Joe, who he knew wasn't.

"What about you? Any word?" he asked, knowing the answer in advance, deflecting further questioning of his own prior knowledge.

"A'd uv fucken told ye, woodenta?" Joe answered truthfully as Frank had known he would. Joe sank deeper into an Italian armchair that was worth much more than him at any reasonable estimate, hating his brother for knowing him so well, feeling vaguely he ought to ask him something else and not knowing what.

"He's getting ready for something," said Eleanor. "He's going to show himself eventually. When he does, we'll know what he wants."

"We spoke to Ronnie, we're meeting Bellamy. I think they'll both let us know if they hear anything."

"Who else might he talk to? What was her name? The grandmother. Janice's grandmother?"

Frank shook his head. "She'd not tell us anything, even if Hunter had been to see her. Not without ..." Frank glanced at his brother. Eleanor felt safe enough to tease them, reaching for a chocolate.

"What are you afraid of, both of you? He's just out of prison ... he doesn't want to go back." She settled back and popped her praline where it would do her most good. Joe snorted with contempt. Eleanor flared her eyes at him, her voice even. "What?"

But Joe said nothing more that night, just looked pityingly, provocatively at his brother and sister-in-law for the rest of the evening. Expert in such matters, he'd not honour her by replying that she'd never understood anything, and that his brother seemed to have forgotten everything he'd once known.

Look at them, he thought. They think they have it all. They can't see that they are not safe but only enclosed here, the two of them, in illusory security — that the thickest walls are but thin and permeable, that old reputation offers no current protection. He looked at Frank's dull face and thought how old his brother looked.

They'd used to tan houses just like this one, the two of them, just for laughs, just to show they could, when they were kids, stealing without discrimination, laying a shite in the piano, wondering, like Loyd Grossman, what kind of cunt would live in a house like this? So what made Frank think now that his alarm system and Eleanor's expensiveness and a degree of education for their children made them safe? Children that they actually talked to when they came in to say goodnight. They talked to their children, like people in films. He snorted at them again at that thought, and they stared at him.

3.5.2

Mentally, every time he came here, Joe was torching the place, gleefully, bitterly raping them all, killing them all, leaving them all to burn. And as he looked into their hateful, healthy, intelligent faces, he knew that they were the helpless ones in this world, that he could protect them or turn on them, just as easily, with an alike impulsiveness, that he could choose to save or lay waste to their universe, just to show them he could. Just like Tommy Hunter could.

And Joe smiled at them, almost lovingly. They recoiled from him as if he'd lifted his leg and farted.

3.6

Meanwhile, in his tiny room, all night, Tommy Hunter sweated himself into fitting the clothes that he had ordered. He'd no time for alterations; no alterations were conceivable except in himself. These, after all, were likely the last clothes he'd ever wear. He had already decided his appointments.

3.6.1

The register recorded that he checked out at half past eight. He was at the barbers on Dundas Street before nine, and at Agnes' door just on quarter to ten.

4.0

Having conquered her daily Everest that Tuesday, and having attained the summit of her doorstep through a painful mist, as she now automatically inserted her latch-key, Agnes scarcely saw the hand that took her shopping for her, or the other hand that came around behind her to give her door an encouraging wee push. It wasn't Sherpa Tenzing, but she couldn't have been more surprised; it was all so sudden and unexpected, seeing Tommy there again, and seeing him too this morning as she'd never seen him before, not even on his wedding day, scrubbed, suited, his hair just cut, shaved and shiny, smelling of talcum and cologne. He'd never looked so good, bar the shiny scar where he'd cut his throat. So happy to see her. So much the kind of man she might have wished for her grand-daughter that he'd walked her into her house before she was fully conscious of his actually being there.

4.1

Tommy closed the door behind them and stood in her hall-way, filling it with an unaccustomed radiance of prosperity and self-control. Wordlessly, and having looked him just the once in his face, Agnes shuffled mechanically ahead of him towards the kitchen. He followed her slowly with her shopping in one hand and his carpet bag in the other, past the little stacks of bumper crossword collections, bright paper islands in a sea of grey dust.

"Ah'll jist pap this in the front room," he told her, nipping behind her to do so, his carpet bag disturbing the little sandpiles of dead skin on the carpet beside the sofa, making silent little clouds.

Stepping into the front room, Tommy, knowing he had

to, glanced up, seeing as he knew he would, the photo of Janice, when she was aged fourteen in Seamill, still in its silver frame upon the mantle. His hungry little miracle. She smiled at him, enjoying his attention all over again. He turned away it hurt so much.

When he re-emerged from the front parlour, choking a little, into the hallway, Agnes was still shuffling, just a little further on into the kitchen, head slightly bowed, heading for the kettle. Without turning round, she asserted without interrogation or emotion: "Ye'll be wanting yer tea in the front room."

He stole in front of her with her shopping, it being the work of but a moment to take in the blackened filth around her bath and toilet bowl through the open door of the cludgie; the mingled reeks of old Spam and Tuna and the growing things around the rims of badly washed out tins on the kitchen table and sideboards; the crowns of dirt on the inside and the outside of the tops and the bottoms of the windows; the empty light fittings and the tray with the doily and the teapot and the single cup and saucer — and the work of only another moment to appreciate that for all his years of custodial solitude, he had managed to inhabit the world more fully than this robotic old woman, her brown eyes squinting at him, her face grown into a resigned mask of suffering as she came towards him in the musty stench that seemed all of a piece with the reluctant light that had penetrated this far into the gloom.

"That'd be nice," he said, smiling.

Her face and her movement never paused or altered. "It'll be through in a minute," she told him.

He watched her lift the kettle from the range, then he did what a man was supposed to do. He left her to it, and returned to the sitting room in silence, noting that although things had decayed here, they'd not changed in any other way since he'd first come here (unsuccessfully) to ask Janice out, when they were both just sweet seventeen. He'd stood waiting on this same carpet, looking at these same patterns on the same wallpaper. The same pictures. And of course, *that* picture, which was still where it was the first time he saw it, and which was the single clearest image he retained in his mind of her face. He looked again at her, in the picture on the mantle, at her aching absence from his life. She was still smiling at him, like she always had, from that picture taken a year or more before he had even existed for her, from within a tiny, fading world of primary colours, in front of sand and windbreakers, on a beach on the Clyde coast sometime in the eighties. She'd already been dark and wicked even then, and there she still was, frozen on a summer beach, still endlessly amused behind the freckles, in a red one-piece swimsuit, goosepimples on her forearms and there, budding beneath the damp fibre, her childish breasts, nipples stiff with cold. He felt himself growing erect even as he mourned his immeasurable loss of life and joy, and spoke quickly through to Agnes in the kitchen, to distract himself from the lost world within the silver frame.

"I want ta see ma kids, Agnes. That's what I'm here fer. I want tae dae somethin fur them. If I can." He listened. Waited. There was a clank of fetched pottery, the low roar of gas and heating water. "Ah know it must have been difficult for ye," he continued, loudly and deliberately. "I'm grateful tae ye fer aw ye did." Wandering as he spoke, he counted, beside her armchair, six empty bottles of Smirnoff. Generously, he continued. "I'm no blamin ye fer anything. I'm no saying I didnae dae things wrong masel." He hesitated. Could she hear him? Could she understand? "Agnes?" He popped his head back through to the kitchen.

4.1.2

She was rooting now in the kitchen drawer for some reason, hands blindly searching. He stood in the doorway, watching her, hearing her babble to herself as the water in the kettle rumbled and began to boil. "I want to make things right," he said, as the kettle began shrieking and Agnes turned, having found the bread knife, the blade catching a little light as she flew towards him in slow motion, her face writhing and tortured, features melting in the heat of rage. She moaned in grief as she tried so very, very hard to kill him, kicking at his shins, a toe breaking on him as he held her by her tiny wrists. Her shoe came off. "Have ye heard from her at all, Agnes?" he asked her, as if she'd offered him a scone.

She screamed then, finally, ripping it out of herself, the loneliness, born again. "I never hurt her, Agnes," he tried to tell her over the noise, as if saying her name would calm her. "Mrs MacHutcheon," he attempted, remembering both her married name and his manners. She screamed and gulped suddenly. Her dentures fell out, shattering, and a breath of hell washed his face.

"I've heard from Janice," he said, taking advantage of the sudden, comparative silence.

4.1.2.1

Her attack slackened for a moment, just long enough for him to gently give her a shake and disarm her without breaking anything else. The knife clattered on the lino. He kept holding her, smiling, full of good intent. Her screaming at him slowly degenerated into a groaning from the diaphragm as she came back to herself and became gradually aware again of pain, not just in her foot, but also in the fossilised muscles she had torn in her frenzy. The floor yawned at her feet, nauseating her.

"I got a postcard," he told her, suddenly aware he had to hold her up to keep her from collapsing entirely. He took her childish weight and she hung her arms around his neck, and like lovers, they held each other close as he walked her backwards into the sitting room and sat her in her armchair. He nodded, smiling still, and went through to the kitchen to turn the kettle off. She breathed painfully, chest hurting. Returning, he went on, having taken the postcard from his pocket. "She sent me it," he said, pushing the yellowed moonscape into her fingers. She held it there, unseeing, spent. "I'm gonnae take the kids up North," he explained uselessly. She never even looked at him. "Are you okay?" he asked, this latest absurdity finally drawing her attention for the duration of a brief, ironic stare into the face of his impossible innocence.

He took the postcard from her. "I wanted to look in on ye so I could tell her yer aw right," he said with renewed confidence, reaching into the carpet bag for a single white envelope inscribed with her name. "This is for your trouble," he told her, and smiled again as if he'd sold her something. A funeral plan. That's what rose into her head, and she laughed at him quietly. In her pain and distraction the shock of his presence receded from her consciousness to regain the mere agony of memory.

Glad to see she was more cheery, he asked if there was anything he could do. She waved at him vaguely. "I think I might do something about that toilet," he said, and removed his jacket.

4.1.2.2

Agnes was asleep and breathing thinly in her chair an hour and a half later when he left, three thousand pounds lighter, his obligations that much more discharged, to keep his next engagement. He seems to have borrowed a thermos flask to help him with the engagement after next.

4.1.2.2.1

£30,611.04

4.2

Old Jack Webster was leaning against a gravestone on Kirkyard Hill, dressed too young, mebbe, but was still as charming as he had always been, even when he actually was still young, reluctantly here now to keep an old promise, already regretting it, even before he saw the juggernaut of his mortality bearing down upon him in an off-the-peg suit and carrying a carpet bag.

"Tommy! How's the boy?" he attempted. "Been ages. How ye keepin?" He even danced a little, just to show his happiness. He had on a welcoming face. But Tommy Hunter was close now, and he felt himself go pale and sick at being back in that unholy presence. He'd thrown up a lot, Jack, you'll remember, that time long before, and it was sense memory as well as common sense that garred him grue.

The wind whistled at him as Tommy Hunter stood and faced him, looking down on him, inscrutable. "Je get everythin ah asked ye fur?" said Tommy among the whistling wind and the dead. "Sure, sure ah did … nae bother," said Jack, to mollify the blouster.

4.2.1

He wasn't a bad man, Jack. I want that on the record. He always did his best. He always did what he said he'd do. He had a certain sense of honour, even though dealing principally with thieves, and his reliability wasn't all just market positioning. He had his principles. He looked out for his maw, and his cousins and his nieces and nephews, when he could.

He couldn't help one of his eyes being funny. Or that he was only wee. He always had been. He'd never had the option of being intimidating. He hadn't the furnace of rage in him that Joe Wheen had, or even the slow burn that

Frank had, let alone Tommy's volcanic propensities. He'd always got by on a wink and a smile. He saved up jokes and stories. He was a salesman, born to it. He liked it. He liked people being pleased with the things he got them, being pleased with him. And they were, mostly. People liked Jack Webster. And the truth was that he liked them back. He was a man who was capable of love and of being grateful for love. He even loved Tommy Hunter. He thought of Tommy as a friend. He appreciated his idiosyncrasies. He thought he understood Tommy Hunter, and that he was appreciated and thought of fondly in his turn.

So that when the first contact between him and Tommy had been made after so many years, fourteen months back, when Tommy had appeared at his shoulder one day in the lunch queue at Shotts Prison, he'd been really, honestly pleased to see him, pleased to know that Tommy was still alive, bursting with joy almost that Tommy wasn't dead like everybody thought. Tommy had not long been transferred at that point, and Jack had turned to see him with genuine warmth and a sense of rightness, that the only one of the old gang who Jack had always liked, enjoyed and admired, even, had survived against the odds.

So he had been hurt, then, in the dismal clatter of the prison cafeteria, at Tommy's emotionless and immediate demand that he get hold of some gear for him when he got out. He'd said yes, of course he would, and he did ... he'd got Tommy everything he'd asked for, confirming the matter on their prearranged phone call to the phone box round the corner from his mum's the day before, but he'd been disappointed nonetheless. Of course he had, he was only human. He'd been hurt at Tommy's lack of human interest. That all Tommy'd told him after all these years was that when he got out he'd be needing a motor and a shooter and could Jack arrange that for him? "Aye, of course I can, Tommy ... God, man, but it's good to see you," he'd said, standing there in the queue for prison burgers, where human warmth, being so rare amid the broken souls, was so precious … and he had felt his heart break with an actual snap when Tommy'd turned away from him and walked away to eat alone and look at his postcard without another word.

And Jack's heart was broken all over again now, curse it, curse his optimism, as Tommy didn't (of course not) ask after him or his family, but only asked him for the gear. Just like that. As if it hadn't been near two years ago since they'd spoken face to face, as if it hadn't been twelve years before that, as if they hadn't … as if HE hadn't … as if all that … it … he … meant nothing to Tommy. And it was as if he meant nothing to himself, to anyone, as if Jack deserved this contempt.

He felt it, he wondered if he did deserve it, he was hurt and upset. That's the kind of guy Jack was. He offered love, and felt guilty and weak for his neediness when it was rejected.

He should have known better, he knew that. But it was to his credit, I'd like to think, that Jack Webster felt the way he did. Just my opinion. But I did want to say.

4.2.1.1

So, humble and hurt, Jack handed Hunter a heavy paper poke from which Tommy drew, in full view for fuck's sake, a Browning Nine Mil, a monster of a gun; fifteen rounds rapid could take the door off a house or the face off an elephant.

"Hi, Hi, Tommy, Holy Fuck!" said Jack, appalled.

Hunter stuck the big black beast back into its bag. "Ammo?"

"Five Hundred," Jack said, wanting to smoke. "In the motor."

"I'm not looking for any trouble, Jack," said Tommy, implausibly.

Jeezuz. Was that a fucking THREAT? Or what was it? Jack made like he understood that Tommy's intentions were obviously entirely conciliatory, despite the hardware he'd just handed over.

"Naw, Naw!"

"I'm not."

"Yer okay!"

Jack swivelled his eyes round at his possible escape routes.

"Course yer not, Tommy," he said sincerely. "It's a dangerous world."

Hunter looked at him, evenly, as if considering saying something more. Almost as if he thought that Jack might understand if he explained. But then he didn't.

The two of them stood there for a moment. Hunter spoke first, almost gently, prompting him.

"Where's the motor?"

Jack, back to business, and cars (which were, along with human relationships, his passion), became almost secure again, dropping into a role that somehow bridged the emotional and the pragmatic — that of a salesman with something good to sell, something that he genuinely thought was good. "Now there I think you'll be pleased," he said hopefully.

And he found himself bowing to Tommy, arm out, palm up. Tommy walked in the direction thus indicated, and Jack straightened, thinking, What the hell is it about this guy anyway? Jack thought about that as he caught up and as they walked up the hill together, like a couple of old pals.

4.2.1.2

And the motor was a classic, right enough. The same minute Jack'd saw it, he'd lifted it, sweet as a nut. It had caught Jack's eye as just the thing for Tommy.

"1974 Racing Green Mercedes SLC," he gushed, and ran his hand with a pleased squeak across the finish. "Got a split new V8, reconditioned gearbox, automatic fuel injection, Bosch electronics, CD player, air conditioning, automatic windaes, the lot ..." He sniffed back his emotion. "Somebody LOVED this car," he said, moved at his own pitch. He took a step back, almost tearful, stood tall and pointed. "That," he concluded with some authority, "is a beautiful thing."

"It's all right," grudged Tommy.

Jack bridled. Who did this guy think he WAS? He was a nothing, a con, a lag, breaking his parole, wanting wheels and a shooter for whatever stupid, doomed reason, paying way over the odds, on the nail, on the barrelhead, up front. Cos he fuckin had to. Cos he was a cunt.

With the generosity of dudgeon, Jack went on, swallowing disappointment, trying to forget who he was talking to, thinking of the money, but sales pitching to himself, really. Therapeutically.

"Got ye some vintage sounds in here for no extra charge. Tae go with the period theme. Average White Band, Little Feat, bit ah Graham Parker. Chronologically coordinated wi the motor. Just the old songs. Nothin but the best."

Jack dug the keys out from his coat. He tried to reach out emotionally again as he reached the keys over to Tommy's open hand.

"So where are ye off tae, then? Cos if yer lookin fer any work ...?" He tailed off like a dick. The pale blue eyes bore into him from out of that face, that silence. He could have been speaking Dutch for all the good it was doing either one of them. So he stopped, still holding the keys out, like a statue, Tommy's hand staying there too, like they were posing for a photograph.

And as they just stood there, the two of them, Jack thought maybe it was occurring to Tommy too, now, just how far he'd come now from where he'd been. How far away and lost he was. How impossible. Jack looked at him again. Was that a tear? Was that a tear that gleamed in the corner of a granite eye? Or just a trick of the light?

"Holiday," said Tommy. "Ah'm gaun on holiday." He made it sound like he was casually looking for the Grail.

Tommy held his hand out further for the keys, took them when Jack dropped them, then opened the door. He indicated the poly bag on the passenger seat, seemingly immune to the intoxicating smells of old leather that wafted like complicated wine through Jack's olfactory organs.

"Them the shells?"

"Aye, uh huh," confirmed Jack. "The handcuffs are in there as well."

Hunter tore the bag apart and, putting the cuffs to one side, opened the first box of cartridges, already knowing what happened next.

Jack, not knowing, not wanting to know, said: "Holiday? Aye. Why not? That's great. But efter, I mean … I mean, folk are gonnae know yer out, and if yer available … I mean … I could point ye …" he hesitated. Tommy turned in the silence. "What's yer plans, Tommy? For after ye get back? From yer holiday?"

Tommy turned his back on Jack to load the clip. Click. Click. Click.

Jack shuffled and looked down. Click. Click. Click.

"What about ma kids?" Tommy asked, not looking round. "What d'ye hear aboot them?" Click. Click. Click.

"That kinda information's no sae easy tae come by, Tommy." Click. Click. Click.

"Fourteen years," said Tommy at last, a great wrath within him, not easily contained, so he repeated it. "Fourteen years." Click. Click. Click.

And then Jack did know what happened next. So he tried to run away.

4.2.1.2.1

Tommy had anticipated this, of course, and tripped him on the first step. Then Jack was down, sprawling, tarmac scraping the heels of his hands, pants immediately full of warm piss. And Tommy was over him, weapon ready, safety off. Fifteen rounds ready. One up the spout. In Jack's face.

"Get up, Jack," he said, as though it were that simple.

Scrambling, trying, Jack said: "Agnes, the old lady … she's an alky, Tommy … nae way Frank could've gied her nothin fer the kids wioot it bein aw roon the toon … Frank said …"

Tommy gave him his arm. Jack rose and stopped talking.

"I know," said Tommy, almost kindly. For to know all is to forgive all. Not that Jack knew anything about the things that Tommy knew.

"In the car," said Tommy. "Put the shells in the back."

Jack's first thought was for the leather. You'd never get the honk of piss out of the leather.

"You are a fuck face bastert," he said. And got in.

4.3

When they had been driving for some minutes, Tommy smiling at the purr the engine made with every gear change, Jack said, "Tommy, c'maun tae fuck. What is the fuckin problem, Tommy?"

Tommy glanced at him, still calm, still easy, and turned into a side street. Jack scented hope as well as his own wee wee, and risked being a touch more aggressive.

"Tommy, c'maun … stop the fuckin motor, will ye. Stop the fuckin motor, Tommy."

And Tommy did as he was told, swung it into the kerb, parking smoothly, turning off the engine.

They sat then for a bit, not looking at each other. Jack

breathed through his teeth, trying to anticipate the next situation. The street was quiet. Nobody about. Cleaning a cream leather interior like this would be a nightmare if Tommy shot him here. He didn't think he would. He wouldn't. So he didn't move. Didn't look. Tommy waited, not looking at him either, the pistol cradled lightly in his hand.

"I heard yer boy plays pool," offered Jack, finally.

"At the Keys?" Tommy asked him, half turning. Jack nodded, thinking he might live. Tommy looked at him, right at him, his face almost human all of a sudden. "He any good?" Jack felt his own tears now, in his stomach, surging upwards like puke, tightening his throat, filling his eyes.

"He's a chip off the old block. Yer lassie's up North somewhere. S'all I know.," he managed, before his shame and helplessness won an unequal contest with his dignity. He crumpled. He sobbed and hooted, heaving in his seat, stinking, his piss getting cold. Tommy let him cry. Then he offered him one of his new hankies, still stiff from the box. Jack looked at him, knowing he was safe now, perhaps. He took the hanky angrily and blubbered the worst accusation at Tommy that a man could think of under the circumstances.

"You and me are meant tae be pals."

Tommy said nothing. But he looked like he almost remembered what that meant.

"Aye. I know," he said sadly, finally, "but I've got stuff tae do. Ye know?"

Jack mopped his face cursing him inwardly, then held out the hanky.

"Keep it," Tommy said, promising Jack eternal life. Not a promise he could keep, as it happens. "Can I drop ye off somewhere?"

"I'm fine here," said Jack, and opened the door. Tommy's hand was on his arm.

"Jack ... Nothin ... okay? Nothin tae nobody."

That last remark was uncalled for in the circumstances. Jack was offended.

"I'm a fuckin church mouse. I'm a fuckin professional, Tommy."

The grip tightened on his arm.

"I'm not. Ye understand?"

Tommy didn't care. That's what that meant. This wasn't professional. Whatever this was, it was a calling, a vocational thing. Tommy didn't care what happened to him in its service. That's what he meant. He could do anything at all in its name, untempered by consideration of his own, or anyone else's, safety. That's what Tommy was telling him, and the fear was back in Jack's tummy. Fear for his friend, as much as for himself. Tommy blinked at him, and a shared understanding of shared fatality whispered itself between them. And here was that funny light about Tommy again, playing round his face through the windscreen ... that light he'd last seen ...

"All right, Tommy," Jack told him, suppressing the memory, telling Tommy he understood, though he could have scarcely said what "it" was. Tommy was going on holiday. And that was that. That was the world which was the case. Tommy reached into his jacket for a white envelope.

"This is for your trouble," he said. "Count it if ye want." Jack didn't want to count it. It didn't matter if it was right or not. It wasn't going to be enough for his trouble, anybody's trouble. Nothing Tommy offered anyone would ever be enough for anyone he offered it to.

And besides, Jack knew now, this service he'd performed, that he'd been asked and he'd accomplished, had been a tribute, not a transaction. Whatever he did for Tommy was what he had had to do. It was what had been his portion, ordained since time began. And he found he was obscurely grateful that he'd had the time to do it.

Jack forgave Tommy. And forgave himself, too, all at once.

He got out of the car and slammed the door. Even that sounded good. Solid. Ker-chunk. He leaned in at the window. Tommy slid it down for a last benediction. Jack squinted at him wisely, succumbing to a generous impulse despite himself.

"Tommy," he warned him with real concern, "you should get yersel a new line ae patter. Naebiddy does this demented fucking shite any more."

Tommy almost laughed. Jack almost laughed as well. The window slid up, and Jack could only see his own reflection in the glass.

4.3.1

He could have sworn, later, if anybody'd asked him, that as he drove away, Jack's very last sight of Tommy Hunter was of a man with a song in his heart, and a smile on his puss. Hunter turned the machine beautifully at the top of the road and he was gone.

Jack shook his trouser leg, four and a half K in profit. This was gonnae sting. Maybe he'd get a taxi on the High.

4.3.1.1

£26,111.04

4.4

Tommy must've drove around for a couple of hours, just getting used to the feel of the car. He put sixty miles on the clock before he stopped, so he must have been enjoying himself.

4.4.1

The brakes maybe weren't all they could have been,

admittedly. The cigarette lighter was buggered. There was a spidery crack in the passenger mirror. But the gears grunted and the engine growled and the stereo was terrific. Things had moved on a lot since the early nineties in terms of in-car entertainment. Hunter played *Sailin' Shoes* and *Cut the Cake* right through from top to bottom. First tunes he'd heard in a while, so it was probably more an endurance than a pleasure. An acculturation in 4:4 time. He wasn't used to the idea of sequence and duration yet, but he knew he'd surely get there, given time.

4.5

He'd had the passenger seat valeted somewhere by the evening. Still smelled a bit, but only when the heated seats were on. I'm assuming Jack gave him a full tank of petrol.

4.5.1

£26,091.04

4.5.2

He parked early in the evening in a vacant lot opposite the Keys around six and sat there to wait. He just sat and watched them going into the old pub. A lot of kids, like in the old days, like you'd expect. He can't have really supposed he would recognise his son when he saw him. Then perhaps he thought he'd know Ronnie by his attitude. Tommy'd grown up that way himself, shunted about, care home to foster parent, pillar to post, into the army, into the jile. He'd always thought it had left a mark on him, I remember, a readiness for insult, an anxiety to respond and reassert a doubtful dignity. Maybe Ronnie would have the same mark, exhibit the tell-tale twitches of the lost. So Tommy must have waited, scanning every angular, acned face. Besides that, he wouldn't have wanted to show himself too soon. Somebody might've recognised him. And he'd have known that by now the word would have been out that he was back. That the word of him would be spreading like bacteria by now. He was likely puzzled for a moment by the gaggle of smokers outside the door. Were they waiting for something? Then he observed that they'd go in when their fags were finished, to be replaced by other sets of tar-hungry lungs on legs. Did Tommy even know that you're not allowed to smoke in pubs any more, I sometimes wonder, dizzily. Did he have even the most rudimentary sense of history, that time had passed?

I never thought the smoking ban would stick; I thought there'd be some pubs in some places where it would have been a reckless landlord indeed who asked you to put that out. But it does stick. Seems to. People actually obey the interdiction. Gratefully, even. Shows what I know. Perhaps it means something about where our culture has come to, that we've accepted this policing of our own good so readily. Who knows?

4.5.2

It got dark around nine anyway. And Tommy headed then into the warm roar of the Keys, all familiar, down to the paintwork, bar to the left, pool hall straight up the stairs, like long ago. He'd not clocked his boy going in as it happens. So he'd have to ask someone.

5.0

INT. BAR – THAT NIGHT

Maybe eight pool tables, mobbed with kids, old guys. Air rank with old spilled booze. Loud music. HUNTER is at the bar drinking an orange juice, watching his son RONNIE playing pool.

5.0.1

£26,089.54

5.0.1.1

Kind of cocky and grim at the same time, Ronnie is smacking the cue ball about the table like he means it. A BOUNCER comes up to the crowd of boys, and Hunter watches with interest as pills and money change hands. He turns and speaks to the BARMAN.

> HUNTER
> That him? Ye sure? That's Ronnie Hunter?

> BARMAN
> Aye. Right wee pain in the arse.

> HUNTER
> Thanks.

He moves off from the bar to get a closer look.

5.0.1.1.1

Hunter approaches the table to watch his son admiringly as Ronnie gets everything but the eight ball away, but leaves his cue ball snug on the top cushion. Ronnie squints down at the shot. Then just as he's about to take it, a bundle of notes hits the baize. Ronnie turns. His unknown progenitor, Hunter, is magically at his shoulder.

> HUNTER
> Hundred says ye miss it.

5.1

Ronnie looks at his father. There's a glint of recognition. Not of the face, but of the genre.

> RONNIE
> Dae ah know you fae somewhere?

> HUNTER
> Balk left pocket, son. Hundred quid.

> FAT BOY
> (adoring)
> Gaun, Ronnie!

Ronnie grins, and takes the shot. Lots of top. The eight ball clatters in bottom left to the cheers of Ronnie's mates. But Ronnie waits … the cue ball is spinning dizzily towards the centre right … but seems to die almost on the lip. Ronnie picks up the money, grinning at Hunter. Hunter takes a ball from the top left pocket and puts it where the eight ball was. Silence falls as he replaces the cue ball. And counts more money on to the table.

HUNTER
Two hundred says ye cannae dae it again.

RONNIE
(in a manner to remind you vaguely of Audie Murphy)
Ah kin play that shot aw night.

Hunter looks at him. Every bugger in the room seems to be looking at him now. Everything goes quiet like in a film. Drunks look up from their sorrows, arguments freeze mid-insult. Had there been a player piano, that too would have been silenced.

5.1.1

As it was, the medley of awful eighties hits relentlessly kept going and Kajagoogoo were now uncomfortably audible. This is when I looked up from my drink, too … when everything went quiet, but I was at the wrong angle and didn't see what had happened.

5.1.2

Hunter watches Ronnie for signs of pressure, but either Ronnie is too stupid to care, or he has some nerve. Serious but steady, Ronnie gets ready for the shot, but before he can take it, the bouncer comes up, to be played in the movie, possibly, by Slim Pickens.

BOUNCER
There is no gambling permitted on these premises. That's you and your mates barred.

Ronnie and the others protest, a whining chorus from which Hunter's basso profundo rumble emerges.

HUNTER
All he did was take the shot.

BOUNCER
Whit?

HUNTER
It was me that put the bet on.

Hunter swivels slightly on his left hip, Jack Palance-like, head on a slight tilt.

Bar me, why don't ye?

The bouncer looks away, preparatory to attack. It's a very old trick. So that by the time he swings at Hunter, Hunter is well placed to punch the chap in the kidneys, very hard, and grab his hand, twisting it up at the wrist, bringing the arm round the back to smack the bouncer on to the table, right cheek down.

HUNTER
Now, you say yer sorry.

BOUNCER
Ay ya.

HUNTER
Naw. "Sorry … "

BOUNCER
… sorry …

HUNTER
Not tae me … arse face. Tae them.

He brings the bouncer up to face the boys.

BOUNCER
Sorry …

Hunter releases the bouncer. Hunter is shaking with adrenalin, with the potential for mayhem. The whole bar is standing up to see now.

5.1.2.1

And that's when I saw him. That's when I knew him. Tommy Hunter. I almost called out his name but something froze my tongue.

5.2

Ronnie takes the shot. It goes in, the cue ball not even close to dropping this time. Cool Hand Ron. A young and plooky Paul Newman throws the cue down on the table.

RONNIE
(to the bouncer)
We were gaun anyway. Yer bevvy's shite.

Ronnie and his pals move off. Hunter watches their backs for official or free-spirited intervention. All Quiet in the West of Scotland. Hunter makes for the door, following the gaggle of yobbos. Out of shot, I struggle to get past people so I can talk to him, so I can see him again. Meantime, the barman intercepts him with menace.

BARMAN
Ur you his DADDY ur somethin?

HUNTER
That's right, pal.

Tommy decks the barman with one jabbed punch to the
throat, and turns to face the bouncer who is coming at him
with a chair, but Hunter kicks the bouncer in the crotch
and he goes down vertically, the chair landing on his own
head with cinematic justice.

HUNTER
(admonishing the miscreants with the
official moral of the scene)
Those drugs are slowin you down.

He heads for the door, bold as Jesus, cool as Alan Ladd.
And everybody is asking all at once, Who was that
unmasked man?

5.2.1

£25,789.54

5.2.1.1

I knew him, I knew who he was. I struggled through the
uproar he'd left in his wake, as the upstairs bar at the Keys,
violence having been released in all of us, now went the
full John Wayne, opportunistic punches being thrown
everywhere you looked. Guys hitting the deck, hitting
each other, a sudden flash of blood across my vision as
somebody got glassed.
I called after him, "Tommy! It's me!" but he can't have
heard me or he didn't turn if he did.
By the time I reached the stairwell he must have already
been outside, because by the time I got outside, he was
gone. Disappeared. I haven't seen him since.

CUT TO:

5.3

Identification of his boy accomplished, logic tells me and imagination confirms that, Hunter could now follow Ronnie home from the car park either on foot or in his vehicle, depending on what seemed operationally appropriate. He chose to proceed on foot and became one with the shadows on the street.

5.3.1

Ronnie's cohorts were meanwhile cavorting, dissecting the improbable events of the evening, looking back apprehensively at the pub. Ronnie himself, not having the logic or imagination that would have allowed him to essay an interpretation of the evening's events, had done what we would all do in such circumstances: he had pocketed the cash and forgotten everything as best he could. He was surrounded for the moment by an electrified crowd of self-regarding youth, buzzing on the adrenalin of their expulsion, not yet consciously aware that their evening was already over, that their solidarity was a thing of moments. But gradually, Hunter knew from memory, Ronnie would become detached from these deprivation tourists that currently surrounded him. Sooner or later he'd get him alone. He knew that. The likes of him, the likes of Ronnie, are always left alone in the end.

When Ronnie moved off finally with around sixty per cent of his entourage intact, it would only be a matter of time. Hunter followed, keeping to the darkness, keeping his distance.

And gradually, right enough, the rest of them peeled away from him, in descending order of cool, till Ronnie was left with the fat kid. That's the way it always was. The fat kid had nowhere he wanted to go, though he clearly, unlike Ronnie, had a home he could go to, but Ronnie's tolerance, however temporary, was the nearest he could come to affirmation, just at the moment.

The two outcast boys walked together, the outcast man their accompanying ghost, as the houses around them got bleaker and darker, the street lighting more sporadic, the sudden noises of domestic strife more startling as a soft rain began falling.

Hunter peered as the two boys talked and walked, or rather, as the fat boy talked and Ronnie looked down at the pavement, face cowled in the dark, dangling a half-empty bottle, while his companion danced a slow-motion rondo of obeisance around him, chattering without response. Till they stopped.

Hunter drew his muscular, skinny frame close to a wall and didn't breathe. This was obviously fat boy's corner, and Hunter smiled to himself at his son's patience, then changed his mind about Ronnie's motivation for keeping company with such an obvious loser, and wondered, heart sinking, if it was loneliness that kept his son there to listen to the latest on something called YouTube, and he felt a strange pang of something that might have resembled shame or sympathy or guilt, and found that he too was growing impatient. He was on the point of interrupting when a shift in Ronnie's weight from one foot to the other told the fat boy that was that, and the fat boy left, presumably to go back to the parental home, whatever that might be like.

5.3.3

So Hunter and Ronnie, staggered by Hunter's surveillance technique, went together deeper into the scheme, into the desert of home. As they walked, Hunter dodged, and Ronnie tapped a rhythm on walls and railings with his bottle of caffeinated wine.

5.3.3.1

Ronnie turned the corner of the fence around his socially provided address, and Hunter, clocking the telltale green paintwork of collectivist days of yore, sped his pace and called to his son, his own face catching the downlighting of a flickering sodium lantern to some advantage, like Harry Lime in a doorway in Vienna.

"Ronnie," he said.

5.4

Ronnie turned around, showing no surprise, no fear, no welcome. His eyes were still shaded as Hunter took his own heart in his hands and told his son who he was.

"I'm your father, Ronnie."

He waited for an acknowledgement. And, eventually, Ronnie looked down at the darkening, wettening pavement, and said nothing. For a moment Hunter doubted that he'd spoken out loud at all, thought that the words he'd practised for so long had been lost in the rain somehow.

"I'm your father, Ronnie," he repeated, just to be sure he'd been heard.

"I heard ye," Ronnie noted, not looking at him, his body language cryptic. There was, mebbe, a new, jangled brightness to his tone. But now Ronnie was silent again, weight on his left leg, slowly swivelling his right foot on the ball of his heel. The concerned parent in Hunter wondered whether his boy was shy. But an older instinct told him that this guarded non-response to the appearance of a long-lost parent was a tactical opacity.

"Have you heard something?" he asked his son. "Has somebody been talking tae ye?"

"I thought you were a poof," Ronnie offered him, flicking him momentary eye contact from under his hair.

"Would ye like to go on holiday?" Hunter said.

Ronnie huffed a kind of laugh at the unexpectedness of this, weighing the bottle in the air now, testing the heft of it.

"Holiday?" he said, and swung at his father.

Hunter had anticipated the attack just enough to turn and bow his head, so that the bottle hit his shoulder blade as well as his skull, the impact sending the weapon spinning out of Ronnie's hand to smash on the pavement, adding a little poison to the rain that was falling quite hard now, as Hunter crouched in a posture to protect his head, throat, balls and kidneys from permanent damage, and Ronnie whaled on him silently, betraying a lack of art in the random order of his kicks and punches. Hunter took a bruising, right enough, but even as he went down, he could tell that his son, for all of his experience of the care system, had not grown up much of a fighter, that he was wasting energy on anger, that he'd be exhausted soon, bored even, if Hunter just went limp and rolled with it, confident that it was only if he left himself exposed in a vital area that the boy might actually do him harm of any more severity than his own penitence already demanded that he suffer. He didn't move when Ronnie stopped kicking him and stepped back for the valediction. Ronnie's voice was breathless, the air in his lungs heaving past premature smoke damage.

"You tryin tae make a cunt ae me? Ur ye?"

Last kick coming at the head, Hunter turtled it into his shoulders and just caught the edge of Ronnie's shoe. The pain was purple as his retinas were shaken.

5.4.1

Hunter lay there for another full minute after Ronnie had gone, tasting his own blood, concentrating on each area of hurt in turn, assessing it. His suit was fucked, but he had another just like it. He was fine. He sat up on the soaking street, and felt the cool water in his arse crack.

Meanwhile, Ronnie, a bit nervously, was ringing the doorbell over and over at the hostel further up Dryry Street, muttering to himself for Macreesh to hurry up and push the fucking door entry button, ya dick-brained Irish fuck, ye.

"Hello?" crackled the friendly doorkeep of the Western World.

"It's Ronnie," Ronnie said, and waited for the opening buzzer and pushed, with one glance back into the street. He saw Nothing. No one.

5.5

"Close the door, Ronnie," said his social worker with patient admonition. Ronnie, hands in pocket to conceal his skinned knuckles, used his foot. The iron door crashed and shook the whole place.

"For goodness SAKE!" said Macreesh, as Ronnie ignored him and walked past without a glance. Ronnie reached his dorm room door and opened it and shut it behind him almost in one movement.

"That's two demerits," Macreesh told his disappearing back. Macreesh tutted, something heroic in his insistence on thinking the best of everyone, in thinking that no one is without hope, in believing that things could change for the better.

That's what a hero is. One who still hopes, despite everything we all know to be true, and acts according to his hope and not his fear.

Frank and Joe, meanwhile, heroes to no one, not even to themselves, were sharing an overpriced drink at the Golf Club with Superintendent Bellamy, and in that Leisure Centre for the Suburban Bourgeoisie, Joe stuck out like a burglar's turd on the Axminster. He'd probably turned over half of these cunts in his time, he mused to himself sourly, doctors and lawyers and accountants and marketing men and therapists and the rest of their inexplicable, hateful breed.

Joe was not relaxed in this milieu.

Frank, who had persuaded himself that he was, was trying not to notice the sarcasm and condescension in the eye contacts he momentarily connected to, but was no happier at the flushed jollity of the Superintendent, who with a blithe disregard for the evidence remarkable even in a senior policeman, was telling the Wheens again and again that there was nothing to be worried about.

"If he doesn't report for probation tomorrow at 11.30, the Glasgow cops will pick him up. They've got his address, his description. You're worrying over nothing."

Bellamy looked at their angry, scared faces, and felt a certain professional pride at seeing the Wheen brothers reduced to this state of anxiety, like everyone else he ever spoke to on police business.

"You've done the right thing talking to Ronnie ... and his social worker. And to me." He gracefully allowed them that, enjoying himself. Having achieved no change of expression or diminished the angry tension in their faces, the policeman wittered on like a patronising arsehole: "I have to account for every hour of every officer's time, Frank. You can't expect me to send any of my men to go looking for any old lag, let alone make a request to another force, when there's nothing we know of he's actually done."

"If he cuts ma fuckin throat, will ye be interested then?" offered Joe, unasked, hands clasped, legs apart, his balls sweating with hatred.

Repressing the response that he'd be delighted more than interested at that eventuality Bellamy reached out his hand and patted Joe's knee in a palliative gesture of utter contempt. Joe stared at the hand disbelieving.

"I know it's uncomfortable," he sympathised, "but the past is the past, Mister Wheen. I don't think any of us want to revisit it ... even Tommy Hunter."

He looked at Frank meaningfully like some wanker off the television and sat back having delivered this cosy threat. Bellamy looked over to the bar past Joe's shoulder, where DS Boyle nursed a whisky and stared at their conclave with a hatred almost equal to Joe's written unsubtly all over his own righteous mug.

5.6.1

The Jesuits had done a job on "Danny" Boyle all right. If he hadn't been so angry all the time, he might have kept going with his studies and been a priest. As it was, he turned away from the Gomorrah of corruption that he saw personified in the Wheen brothers drinking with his senior officer to his own companion that evening, DC Maggie "Single" Singleton, and said it made him sick. She told him that she knew it did. She had long ago conjoined his Catholic discontent to her guilty Presbyterian conscience. She adored him. She wanted to help him. She had often told him so in her imagination if never in those spoken words.

"If I could just get something on that ... those ..." he said, and turned away again, obsessing, unable to speak the intensity of his thought. The arrogance of it, of those criminals being publicly associated with HIS ...

"I know ... I know ..." she told him.

"What are they talking about?" he asked the universe rhetorically, not looking at her yet. His not knowing the answer to things was always a personal affront to the tenacious DS "Danny" Boyle.

"I know … I know …" she said again, meaning only that she felt his pain. He looked at her then, his eyes and face exhausted by his years of unrewarded righteousness and perpetual discouragement. She smiled at him sadly, unworthy, she knew, of his love.

She was thinking as ever about that longed-for night when she would take him in her arms and legs, that night which had to come soon, or she would dry up like a purse. He was wasting his life and hers on this fretting. She knew that. He was eating himself when he should have been eating her, her white flesh offered like cake to that strong mouth, to those dark eyes and bitten fingers. She longed for him to turn his rage on her, so he could churn her into butter. He turned to her, not seeing her melting for him.

"There's something going on," he said. "There's something going on."

Nothing. There was nothing going on, Maggie moaned to herself in secret. She dropped her eyes, her pheromones flagging for the moment. Boyle looked back at Bellamy, and his boss stared evenly, complacently back at him.

"One day," he promised himself out loud. "One day, you'll fuck up. And I'll be waiting."

He looked at the bar and drank his Glenmorangie, bitterness swallowing the absurdity of his rhetoric. Maggie looked him, and wondered who'd be waiting longer.

"I'll help you," she told him, all procedure. "I'll draw the files."

"You're a good girl, Maggie," he said unnecessarily. She already knew what a good girl she was.

Around about then, four miles away and at the other side of the universe, Hunter, having dumped one suit and changed into the other, drew the Jag to a silent halt on Dryry Street outside of Bruar House. He put his left hand on the passenger seat. The handcuffs went in his pocket. He put on the ski mask. He turned off the engine and picked up the gun.

It was raining hard now. That would kill the noise, if there was noise. Sheets of it drummed on the roof and the wind whipped it at the windshield. No moon. Like that other night of no moon fourteen years ago, he might have remembered. He opened the car door and stepped out. The portent of what he was about to do throbbed in his bruises. He shut the car door and started walking slowly. He wiped the wet hair from his eyes and rang the front doorbell. He couldn't hear Macreesh's patient tutting as he approached the door. Just the rain.

CUT TO:

5.7.1

INT. BRUAR HOUSE – NIGHT

The buzzer is sounding. MACREESH is getting into a dressing gown, heading for the door. Several of his young, restless charges already have their heads outside their doors, bugging him, saying "Who is it?"

MACREESH
(walking towards door)
I'll just see, shall I?
(opening door)
Now who …?

Hunter's gun comes through the door first, the barrel going right up Macreesh's nose. Hunter backs him inside, bleeding into his ski mask. The younger children scream.

What?

HUNTER
(absurdly, to Macreesh)
Don't worry.

HUNTER
(to the rest of the kids, or those who remain)
Get back in your rooms.

SMALL BOY
Shoot him, Mister.

Hunter's eyes drift to Macreesh's eyes quizzically.

HUNTER
Tell them.

MACREESH
(to the kids)
Get back in.

No one moves. Hip to the nuance of the scene suddenly, Macreesh puts his hands up.

MACREESH
(to Hunter)
What do you want?

Through his mask, Hunter sees Ronnie (partially clothed, having pulled his jeans on) in a doorway. He pushes Macreesh back in that direction, not giving away his destination. He goes past Ronnie before shooting out a hand to grab his boy's T-shirt.

HUNTER
Come on, you.

RONNIE
(resisting helplessly, wondering briefly why if
this cunt has got a grip like this, why didn't
the cunt defend himself the last time)
Get tae fuck.

He smacks at Hunter's hand. Might as well smack at a building.

HUNTER
(strictly)
Ronnie … do as yer told.

Ronnie stares at the eyes in the mask. They stare back. Not to be argued with.

MACREESH
Ronnie … do you know this man?

RONNIE
(swatting with both hands now at the good left arm
that's near enough lifting him off his feet, thinking
dizzily: Christ, this cunt is STRONG …)
He says he's ma stupid fuckin faither.

MACREESH
(to Hunter, scolding gently)
Mr. Hunter! Really, now …

Hunter points the gun at Macreesh again.

HUNTER
You're comin as well. I'm takin both of ye.

MACREESH
(there being nothing in the handbooks
to cover this contingency)
Me?

RONNIE
I'm not goin anywhere wi you.

The small boy is now tugging at Hunter's sleeve.

SMALL BOY
Mister ...

HUNTER
(ignoring the child)
Ronnie ...

RONNIE
No fuckin way ...

MACREESH
Mister Hunter ...

SMALL BOY
(still tugging)
Mister ...

HUNTER
(finally, to boy)
What?

SMALL BOY
Can I come too?

Hunter looks at the boy for a moment. Tousles his hair. Then looks at Ronnie and Macreesh.

> HUNTER
> (explaining)
> It's just these two.

> RONNIE
> Away and shite.

The kids are starting to gather again, heads poking out of doorways. Hunter looks round. This is beginning to go wrong.

> HUNTER
> (in frustration fires a single deafening shot into the floor)
> Will you DO …

> HUNTER
> (firing another shot)
> … as you are TOLD?

The kids scream and run, some into their rooms, some out of the front door. The three of them are suddenly alone in a corridor of acrid blue smoke.

> Please?

CUT TO:

5.7.2

EXT. BRUAR HOUSE – NIGHT

Hunter hustles his captives out to his car. He pushes Macreesh against the car boot.

RONNIE
(reasonably under the circumstances)
I huvnae even goat ma shoes oan!

HUNTER
(to Ronnie)
In. Ye've seen a car before.

As Ronnie gets into the passenger seat, Hunter lifts the lid
of the prepared, open boot.

Sorry. Come on.

MACREESH
(looking to see there is a blanket, a thermos and
sandwiches in there, thoughtfully provided)
Please God. Please God.

HUNTER
(looking up to rainy, empty heaven)
I'm tryin, brother.

Hunter manhandles the babbling good man into the boot
of the Jag, and shuts him in. Now there is only the sound
of the rain. He looks up to see Ronnie open the car door,
and try to get away. He lunges forward, grabs Ronnie.

RONNIE
Ay ya, ay ya, ya fucker …

HUNTER
Behave yer self.

He turns Ronnie's wrist behind him, and reaches over him
to pull the handcuffs from his pocket. He cuffs Ronnie's
hand, then attaches the other stell band to the interior of

the car door, while Ronnie yells his protest.

Hunter gets into the car beside his son. He takes off the mask and starts the engine. They set off. Ronnie is keeping up a barrage of abuse.

RONNIE
(delivered in a monotonal screech, the
following a representative sample only)
No fuckin way you're dead I'm fuckin
connected ya piece a shite ye …

Hunter rams down his foot to engage the brand-new brake pads and the car goes from sixty to nought in two seconds. He jams the gun up Ronnie's nose.

HUNTER
I ruined your whole LIFE, didn't ah?

Ronnie has his eyes closed, expecting to get shot. Nothing happens. He opens his eyes.

I apologise. Okay? I'm really sorry.

Hunter starts the engine. He pulls the car away from the kerb. Ronnie is looking for something to say. Hunter lets him look for it. They turn left and set off towards the north.

RONNIE
Where are you takin me?

HUNTER
I told ye once.

They drive on in silence. After a while, the lights of the town are gone and they are in country dark, enfolding.

6.0

Leave alone intelligent life, from what the cosmologists are saying at the moment, it does seem that matter itself, and energy and space and time as well, is actually not what the universe is made of, mostly; that we can't actually see or feel or interact in any way with most of the stuff that *is*, because it's wrapped around and inside what *exists*.

The instantaneous transformations of quantum physics make sense, they tell me, within a universe whose dimensions and duration are zero in all directions, so most of the universe doesn't exist at all in any of our terms, and everything we experience, in any way, all four dimensions of it, are a freak of nature.

And if our experiencing the existence of space and matter and energy and time is an anomaly, then what can you say about solar systems on the relatively empty edges of galactic arms where the rocky planets are on the inside, and the gas giants are further out, for fuck's sake! That's unusual to the point of being downright bonkers, apparently, cosmologically speaking.

... and once you start factoring this being a rocky planet with a molten iron core and magnetic field at the right distance from the right kind of star to keep liquid the water that accidentally arrived here on a comet at exactly the right time, the water carrying some complex carbon molecules and remaining in the narrow temperature range where there can be such a thing as liquid water ... for 3.8 billion years continuously, for fuck's sake ...

... then factor in Jupiter being there like a gravitational hoover of the dangerous, planet-forming and destroying shite that's still whizzing around out there, and then add in that some agglomeration of the chemicals off the comet, possibly in a suboceanic volcanic vent, somehow became capable of ingestion and expulsion of other elements ... and then of reproduction, fuck's sake, leave alone reproduction with mistakes in duplication that sometimes turn out to be advantageous thus getting the whole preposterous business of evolution going ...

Then our being here at all is every bit as miraculous as anyone could wish for, and God, far from not *playing* dice, as Einstein put it, turns out to *be* dice ...

Nothing can ever be anything other than surprising and wondrous, can it? Even the existence of the Pet Shop Boys is inevitable by comparison.

6.0.1

None of this miraculous series of accidents was much joy to Ronnie as he awoke that unlikely morning in a location of unlikely beauty in an ice-sculpted corner of the unlikeliest possible world. He was well beyond surprise by then and had never learned to wonder. Like most of us, he took for granted that survival is best served by pretending that you know what's going on, when, frankly, he and we might find that confessing our incoherent, babbling idiocy might be a more pragmatic and honest response to the raw statistics of life.

Hunter and Son were parked by a loch of spooky stillness in achingly lovely predawn light, in a golden hour of as yet sunless loveliness, soft gold on the hills and heather, an unspeakably subtle arrangement of greens and browns and purples washed in the glowing cold. Ronnie heard the breeze caress the leaves of a nearby oak into whispering song, a skylark crying at the gorgeous possibilities of day. He was still handcuffed to the passenger door. He watched his father pissing in the long yellow grass. He sat up.

Ronnie saw his social worker too, released obviously, drinking steaming tomato soup from a plastic beaker, sitting on a tuffet. He could hear that his father was talking to Mr Macreesh, the unhappy fellow, but didn't care to search out words in the sounds that wafted towards him and away from him with the vagaries of the open air. What he did see and hear, oddly, was the ease with which the men were talking, or at least, his father was. Hunter was talking and moving easily as if he belonged here. With all the wind and sunlight and birds and shit.

Ronnie's neck was sore. He'd slept through the uncomfortable aftershock of his abduction, dropping off quite soon into his ordeal, oddly, though he'd not reflect on that. He stretched, as best he could, to get the crumples out of his limbs and back. He froze as his father turned and closed his eyes, pretending to still be asleep. He didn't want to be involved in whatever conversation was going on.

Hunter looked away, and Ronnie felt in his jeans pocket for the rolled-up card that Frank Wheen had given him, then said "Fuck" quietly to himself as he remembered that his phone was on his bedside table.

What Ronnie didn't know yet, of course, was that this table was smoke-blackened by now, and his phone a lump of melted solenoids and plastic from which even mazuma-mobile.com would find it hard to extract the minerals.

6.0.1.1

Thing is, about our actions and inactions in the world, given that it does exist, is that they are consequential. Events in time imply progression and duration, however unreliably. They start stories, steer them … sometimes end them. Which is why, like Ronnie, we should sometimes avoid them.

6.0.2

For example, the rest of the world reasoned that Hunter

must have had a story in mind. The forcible abduction of his son from the institutionalised indifference of society must have been part of a plan and had to be interpreted as the inciting incident of some premeditated narrative or other that it was now imperative for the likes of Frank Wheen and Joseph Wheen and DS "Danny" Boyle to read and to anticipate. So there were several conversations being had that morning, whose chronology was also impelled by the need for close reading.

6.0.2.1

First, an anonymous report of a fire at the Dryry Street hostel was placed at 3.19 on Wednesday morning. The last rain had already done most of the work of extinguishing the blaze by the time bright-red engines got there that morning, waking every bugger up in the whole scheme in the process, escorted as they customarily were to that uncivilised locality by the happy overtime earners of the boys in blue, among whom was the insomniac, self-lacerating DS "Danny" Boyle, his encyclopaedic paranoia having reminded him that Ronnie Hunter was one of the inmates of this latest local asset of collective provision to be stripped, burned and abandoned to the heat death of the universe.

Boyle learned quickly that Ronnie was missing, of course, but so what? So were most of the rest of them. But one small boy who had remained near the smoking ruins of what was, after all, where he had lived, did confirm to him that an incident had taken place the previous night – before the fire – that was itself of no little note; that is that Ronnie and Macreesh had been kidnapped by a masked man with a gun who said he was Ronnie's father. Boyle nearly exploded with long-repressed excitement. His lips started forming soundless words, his fingers fell to drumming on his trouser leg, his mind to racing.

Tommy Hunter had came hame, Boyle realised, and the pot of slow corruption that he'd boiled in all these years had suddenly, finally, been stirred. Tommy Hunter had retrieved his son, but he had also kidnapped a social worker. Boyle didn't know why, and for now, he didn't care. A crime had been committed. A line had been crossed. He had a finger in the pie and there was nothing that fat cunt Bellamy could do about it.

One thing nagged at Boyle a little ... puzzlement and the solving of clues being his spiritual meat and drink ... that the man described by the little ones as Ronnie's mental dad, had been, according to those same wee witnesses, possessed of a charcoal grey suit, as well as weaponry and transport. These were not items with which one customarily emerged from custody. So, Boyle reasoned, Tommy had to have a made a connection somewhere, and had to have some financial resources available to him. How and who could that have been?

Pondering these questions, DS "Danny" Boyle turned to look into space, his mind already floating out there, at 4.46, whereupon his happy peepers fell upon the haggard shape of Frank Wheen, who was stood there in the dawn, still with his jammies on under his camel-hair coat, shoes on and no socks, looking like he was the one who was suddenly homeless, looking like an irreparable catastrophe, like a motorbike on a blind corner had, without any provocation and entirely out of nowhere, smacked him one in the BMW. There was Frank Wheen of all people looking bewildered and insulted by what had just happened to him, like a stockbroker in a road accident. There was Frank fucking Wheen staring at the ashes of a social work hostel as if it was his own house that had fallen on him.

Boyle whooped. He actually whooped with joy at the sight of the disaster written all over Frank's face. Frank turned at the sound and saw his Nemesis grinning at him in the semi-darkness, and then Frank turned on his heel and went back to his Beamer driving off before that grinning fuck could make his morning worse.

As for Boyle, he now found himself in possession of the biggest, hardest boner his trousers had ever known. He had to go and sit down in his own car to hide it. Near delirious, his thoughts turned obscurely to Maggie Singleton and he had to go home to calm himself down before heading bright and early into the office.

Elspeth Dewar, who you'll remember was the subject of Hunter's first visit (see 2.1), was in turn awoken by her doorbell at ten minutes after six, and wasn't happy about it, let me tell you, and even went so far as to initially deny Frank entry. Now, for Frank, who knew that his reputation as implacable was the foundation of his name, took this as a further slight, and, unwilling to be so impugned, lowered himself further into the abyss by telling her loudly and in some detail what his brother Joe might do to her son Donald should she not see fit to reconsider, and by seven, weeping and terrified, her son Donald confined to the toilet, Elspeth had furnished Frank with an exhaustively detailed, if for the moment unenlightening, account of her encounter with Hunter two days earlier. After he'd struck her a few times, steeling himself against nausea, she'd even told him about the money, though you can be sure he didn't share that particular nuance of their pickle with his brother Joe when, on exiting the house, he called Joe from his slumbers at a quarter to eight. To add money to Tommy's disruption of the universe would have been precipitate. It would have meant abandoning what little leverage he may have been able to bring to bear on the situation. Not that he wasn't aware that his situation basically was that of a man flapping his arms around having already fallen off a cliff. He had found himself, even when he'd backhanded Elspeth a couple of times, sick and shaking. He was unwilling or unable to rouse the proper cruel spirit in himself, and he felt dyspeptic and old as he drove home.

By that same time, Boyle and Maggie "Single" Singleton were already together in the office, having pulled the old files from the robbery in the woods, and, over coffee and brioches that Maggie had brought in for them, were looking, among other things, for the last known address of Hunter's daughter Janette, who, Boyle was certain, was next on Hunter's list. Wherever she was, that was where Hunter was going next. (Boyle, being a creature of purpose and intention, read purpose and intention into everything ... it was another face of his psychology.) They didn't find an address. But they did have the record of where that postcard (you remember that postcard?) had come from, and they both thought that might count for something.

Even though they were as yet nonplussed as to exactly what to do next. Boyle was jubilant that morning, though unwashed, and Maggie, who was washed, very much so, ached with longing for him, and caught, maybe, just maybe, a hint of warmth from him, a hint of encouragement, of a positive attitude towards life, which she took almost as a promise, that once this was over, once this was done, once justice had been thoroughly, punishingly served, then she'd finally get her turn. He seemed to perceive her anew this morning, the curves and tightnesses of her, the little sounds and shapes her uniform made upon her hips and breasts. Once, she even thought she heard him smelling her as she bent across his desk to shift a glossy.

Anyway, like I said before, just after eight, Frank turned up at Joe's room in the nursing home and gave him his car keys, telling him that Hunter had somehow got a gun and had acquired transport, and left it to his brother to make the enquiries in the underworld (to which environment he recognised now more than ever that he was ill-adapted due to his years of complacency and near-legality) as to where these items might have come from. He'd get a taxi in town and borrow Eleanor's car if he needed to and she wasn't using it. He did not tell Joe that he himself had seen and been seen at the ruins of the hostel by DS "Danny" Boyle, and that therefore said official might well already be pursuing a parallel investigation. He knew he had to rely on Bellamy, Boyle's superior, to impede Boyle's enthusiasm. His brother Joe's enthusiasm, he knew, was his problem.

As if to prove that middle-sized minds think alike, Boyle and Maggie were just getting around to considering popping in to see Agnes after investigating a reported disturbance involving Ronnie Hunter at the Keys Pub and Pool Room last night as Frank himself got a cab to Agnes's house before nine, rapping angrily on the drunken old bitch's door and getting no reply though she had to be in at that hour. He tried to look in through the window, but saw nothing of any help to him. He caught himself then thinking that Joe would just have kicked the door in, and that thought of their reversed superiority enraged him yet further and he felt as hopeless and wretched as his brother, in their youth, had so often made him feel.

Frank's mind went numb and his eyes stung, his chest constricted. He leaned his skull on the closed door. He closed his eyes and memory filled him. His body was invaded by the sensations of childhood. The fears and the pain that Joe had inflicted on his body and all the pain and fear of the mind that he had inflicted on his brother in revenge ever since they were in long pants were bottled together inside him. He was filled by his whole past all at once. He couldn't think. Couldn't even come close to thinking. He wished he hadn't given up smoking.

There was nothing he could do but follow through this stupid story he was trapped in. Demeaned and made ridiculous by the banality, Frank found he couldn't even bear the thought of going home, of facing Eleanor, her furniture and aspirations. His children. His children! That lovely girl with her already assured entrée to some lovely universities ... that boy, that inexplicable wee boy who never left his bedroom except to collect food and defecate as far as he could tell ... these creatures were all aliens to him now, and unspeakably precious in their fading away from him. He couldn't face them any more because his intuition told him that even Elspeth Dewar's moment of defying him that morning had been an instance of incremental decay of his substance.

He was going to have to break into a house. For the first time since he'd been fifteen years old ... he ... Frank Wheen ... Rotarian and pillar of the community ... was going to have to break into some stinking old bitch's house.

Slipping, as the poet said, is Crash's Law.

As Frank reeled in the tumult of his collapsing certainties, Boyle and Maggie were telephonically checking hotels for unusual guests, and turned up almost immediate trumps at the Wallace. "Mr Greenock Morton? Paid in cash? Fuck's SAKE!" said DS Boyle, and got his coat, and actually smiled and winked, actually flashed Maggie an actual glimpse of his perfect teeth. Her insides sprang into warm, juicy life. She could hardly believe her joy.

So the universe is made and unmade in us.

It would take Joe another hour or so to locate and trap Jack Webster, and it was three hours after that before the Stirlingshire police found Padraic Macreesh wandering in shock on the road between Callander and the Port of Menteith. Frank, for reasons so shocking that we'll go not go into them until the next chapter, had spent most of that time in the bath at home, mechanically draining the cold water and topping up the hot, almost catatonic, and had slowly become a prune, purple and wrinkly on the outside, with a stone in the middle.

Joe came to pick him up around two in the afternoon.

Meanwhile, back in time, at 6.37 a.m., Hunter had opened the passenger door to unlock Ronnie's handcuffs.

"Huv a stretch," he told his son, and opening the back door retrieved a Morrison's bag from the passenger shelf. "There's rolls and sandwiches in there," he told Ronnie. "I didn't know what ye liked so I got some different wans. Yer pal's already had the egg mayonnaise. D'ye want some soup?"

Ronnie stood and stared at him, blinking. "I'll get us a primus stove when I get the chance," his father told him. "Then we'll have a proper picnic." Hunter tutted. "C'maun, Ronnie, get yer legs working. Ye'll need to get yer circulation gaun."

Hunter stopped talking, his head inclined, as if forgivingly disappointed at the inertia of teenagers. As if he was copying something he'd seen of fatherhood in some heartwarming American bollocks or other on the telly on a Sunday afternoon, forgetting, apparently, that this particular teenager had just been kidnapped at gunpoint by his own father — a man who, the boy had reasonable grounds to believe, had murdered his mother. That he himself was the kidnapper and the possibly homicidal parent in question seemed also to have slipped Hunter's mind. By the look and the sound of him, Hunter was now inhabiting, at some mad second hand, another genre of movie altogether. Something from the forties, maybe. Like Ronnie was Mickey Rooney in an Andy Hardy flick ... and he was the Judge.

"D'ye not want any breakfast?" Hunter glanced at Padraic for adult solidarity and put the bag of sandwiches on t he roof of the car. "Whenever ye get hungry," he said indulgently.

"Get tae fuck," Ronnie told him, having had some experience of the admonitions of foster parents, of cunts who presumed to know what was good for you, what you needed, what was best. Who wanted to make you happy, the cunts. He was reassured and relocated, in fact, by Hunter's solicitude, at being begged at by an adult for approval once again. They had all been the same, even the sadists and the molesters. All of them had wanted to be loved.

So Ronnie waited, knowing that he didn't have to say or do anything, that saying and doing was an adult's role, and grew steadily more sure of himself, sure that he could force Hunter into speaking again, into making him another offer he could then witheringly refuse.

"D'ye want me tae talk tae ye? D'ye want tae know what happened tae me? D'ye want me tae tell ye about it?"

Well ahead on points, his kidnapper clearly out of his depth, Ronnie pulled a non sequitur from his repertoire

"I huvnae goat ma fuckin clathes or nothin."

Hunter sighed patiently as though it had been Ronnie's wayward decision to have come out in his jim-jams.

"We'll stop somewhere," he conceded, "but Ronnie ..." he insisted, "me and Poor Egg (sic) have been talking. And we've agreed that place was no good for you. Playin pool and underage drinkin. Drugs. I know what that leads tae."

Ronnie somehow found the saliva and the scorn to spit. Hunter was smiling wisely and sadly at him, and pulled out a non sequitur of his own.

"Where's yer sister? Ye gonnae tell me?" To the accusing silence, he repeated, "I had tae get ye oot ae that place. You were driftin intae a life a crime."

"What is your fuckin problem?" Ronnie asked him, provoked a little now.

"Yer Mammy and yer Daddy. They're the ones that care about ye."

Ronnie, being unable to give an articulate response to the irony of this blithely conventional assertion, spat on the ground again. Hunter remained wise and smiling, telling him fondly, "It's been fourteen years since I've saw ye and yer still an awkward cunt."

He took the carpet bag from the back seat then, and turned from his son to the staggered, blasted figure of Padraic Macreesh, who had in his turn been reflecting on his own existence so far, and on how badly, on balance, it was going at the moment. A child of the Galway seminary, then of happy student protests against the twin oppressors of Church and Capital while at University College Dublin, Padraic, having served an apprenticeship as a housing activist in North Dublin and this having led him to taking a qualification in social work, and the Celtic Depression of the eighties having, in turn, led him to Scotland, first to Glasgow, and then to the wilderness of residential work in Oor Wee Toon, Padraic was thinking of all the faces of all the battered, battering little weans he had ever come across, at how few of them could really be saved, or even dreamed that they could be saved, at how glibly and lazily these days even his own once-committed and serious superiors seemed to not even pretend to care any more, and then he looked up at Hunter's mad, smiling face, and felt nothing but nausea at himself and everybody else, especially this smiling Scottish lunatic, this Black and Tan bastard with God knows how much blood on his hands. And he wasn't even afraid now, just sick and angry and cold. He was saying something, this thug … what was he saying now, him with that ungrateful, smug little sprog of his hanging back behind him there? Padraic shook his weary head and tried to listen.

"I'd like tae apologise tae ye," was what Hunter was saying.

"Not to worry," Padraic heard himself reply from some depth of gentility. It was shock at his own helplessness, at the helplessness of his and our condition in the face of unreasoning force that reduced him to politeness — that, to his credit, being his base condition, his default mode of dealing with the world.

Hunter sat down beside him, hand on his knee, man to man, adult to adult, playing a role of some kind for Ronnie's benefit, it must be, Padraic thought.

"Don't hurt me," Padraic said out loud without meaning to.

Hunter laughed lightly at the very idea and asked him seriously, "Yer a social worker? I mean you must deal wi faimilies in unusual circumstances aw the time."

"Yeah ... I mean, I do," Padraic answered meekly, without inflection.

"Mebbe you can help us oot, then," Hunter said, as if he actually meant it. Padraic blinked at him.

"Mr Hunter ..."

"Call me Tommy. After all, we're practically family." Padraic blinked again at him. Hunter seemed to be making this unbelievable statement in all seriousness. He was full of fucking surprises! "I mean, you're the wan that's looked efter them aw this time, while I couldnae," Hunter went on, then hesitated, awaiting a response. Padraic failed to think of one, so Hunter went on again.

"See, Padraic," Hunter said, again pronouncing it Poor Egg, "what I'm tryin tae tell ye is that I mean him, Ronnie, I mean ... ur ma daughter ... ur anybody ... nae harm in the world."

Head swimming, Padraic thought he glimpsed his landfall for a moment: a therapeutic port in the storm of the situation. He hardly dared to breathe. He leaned forward, and Hunter cocked his lug, expectant. Padraic did his best.

"Well ..." he essayed first, "Mr Hunter ... Tommy ... I think the first thing is maybe the three of us ... should go somewhere quiet and talk."

Ronnie stirred, wanting for some reason to play a part in this conversation, which was no good thing, Padraic thought. Ronnie addressed the following to his father.

"You killed my ma."

That was it, was it? That was what Ronnie wanted to contribute? A flush of rage at the foul boy's ignorant

130

fucking crassness seized Padraic by the roots of his greying Irish curls. But there was no answering accusation from Hunter, just a calm slow shake of the head.

"She's waiting for us," Hunter told his son. "I got a postcard."

Giving up trying to make sense of any of this, Padraic tried again to return this conversation to the more familiar territory of his own rituals, his own possible intervention.

"If we could just …"

Hunter turned to him, smiling encouragement.

"If we could just, you know, go and find somewhere we could talk."

Hunter smiled at him, and devastated his hopes.

"Poor Egg … I'd love to, honest … But I've goat a once-in-a-lifetime opportunity here tae bring ma faimily back thigether."

"What do you mean, Mister Hunter?"

"Twenty-five thousand pounds," he said.

Ronnie jerked his head towards Hunter like a rabid squirrel. That was the kind of money people talked about on the telly.

Hunter tossed the carpet bag on the ground, some of the money visible, tightly bound, bouncing out of the bag. Ronnie stared at it. So did Padraic. Neither one of them had any pre-existing interpretation for this eventuality. But there it was. There was the fact of it, like at the end of a quiz show.

"Holy fuck!" said Ronnie, who had seen a lot of telly, what with one thing and another.

Hunter, still sitting with his hand on Padraic's knee, turned to his boy.

"It's yours, son, and yer sister's. D'ye see what ah mean, Poor Egg? I wanni gie ma poor wee weans a bit ae a head start in life. More than I ever had."

And maybe for a moment, Padraic could see that this was something for which no categories of recorded behaviour could prepare him, that this man here was of an order of being that …

Padraic leaned towards him professionally, showing that he trusted him, like Hunter was a dangerous animal who might be tamed.

"I want to help you, Mister Hunter," he said, and he really did want to, at that moment. By way of thanks, Hunter took the gun from his waist band and pointed the barrel into Padraic's forehead and stood up, preparing to shoot him dead.

"Then tell me where to find my daughter," he said.

Poor Egg gave a strangled cry and fell on to his knees, the way everybody does when they are certain beyond hope that they are going to die, like his great-great-uncle Norrie had on that country road in the border country when they'd caught him running guns into Fermanagh in 1921, like the Jews did at Babi Yar, or the Cambodians did in the Killing Fields. Hunter turned to his son.

"Think, Ronnie. Tell me where yer sister is."

Ronnie shook his head.

"All right, said Hunter calmly and fired a shot that roared close past Padraic's face and burned his hair, sending him face down in the dirt to cool it down. He screamed, then screamed again, anger and outrage breaking past his terror.

"You fucker, you fucking fucker." He began to crawl towards Ronnie's feet. Hunter followed him with the snout of the pistol and spoke again to Ronnie.

"Ronnie … I asked you a question …"

He fired again, careless of his aim. The slug buried itself a foot from Padraic's head, four feet inside the clay. Padraic jumped a foot in the air and landed on his back like a pinioned fly, and screamed wildly up at Ronnie.

"Tell him for fuck's sake! Tell him!"

Janette is going to be furious, Ronnie thought, and hesitated, just for half a second, long enough for Hunter to loose off another round, this time into the air.

"She works in a hotel," Ronnie said.

"Ronnie ... PLEASE!" said Macreesh. "I can't think of the name of it."

"Some fuckin place ... I don't know what it's called."

"Kinloch Rannoch." Macreesh dragged from his unconscious. "Fuck's sake, it's in Kinloch Rannoch."

Hunter turned to him. Padraic turned his muddy face up to meet him. "She used to have a job in Kinloch Rannoch. I don't know if she's still there. She was in Mull or some fucking place before that, okay!"

Hunter lowered his weapon, eased the hammer and engaged the safety.

"Kay," he said, replacing the weapon in his belt. "Now, Poor Egg," he continued, businesslike, "You understand there needs to be a bit of a delay before I can have you talkin tae anybody?"

He helped the social worker to his feet, and was surprised to find the man was furious with Ronnie for some reason.

"Why didn't you fucking tell him, you fucking little shite. After all I've fucking done for you. I am so sick of youse fucking ..."

"Calm down," Hunter told him. "Time is a factor here, ye know?"

Macreesh was still on at Ronnie. "Were you just gonna let him SHOOT me? Jesus CHRIST!"

Ronnie turned away, not able to look at either of them. Padraic too looked down. Hunter left them to the wreckage, or perhaps clarification, of their past relationship, and practical as ever, went to retrieve the thermos from the car. Ronnie dragged his gaze away from both the landscape and the man he had almost seen murdered there to stare again at the money lying in neatly tied bundles in and around the carpet bag.

Hunter handed Padraic the flask. "There's a bit merr tomato soup in here. If ye go a coupla miles up that way, ye'll come tae a main road. Then it's about five miles tae Aberfoyle, aw right, ye know where ye are frae there?" He bent down then and took an envelope from the bag, with a glance at Ronnie, still staring at it. He handed it to Macreesh.

"That's fer yer trouble," he said. "I apologise again."

"What?" Padraic asked him.

Tommy patted his hand. "It's for yer trouble," he repeated, looking up at the sky. "I hope it keeps fine for ye. On ye go."

Padraic stared uncomprehending at Hunter, the envelope, and at his former charge, who still couldn't look at him.

Hunter told him, "I'll take care of Ronnie now." And with a good man's simplicity, Padraic Macreesh walked away from his statutory duty of care, no longer in loco parentis, thank fuck.

Hunter squatted down then and began to put the spilled money back in the bag, aware that his son was now looking at him differently. That the boy was now calculating, scheming. He smiled to himself.

"You've already got some," he said. "I gied ye it last night," he reminded him.

"I left it in the fuckin hostel, didn't I?" replied Ronnie. (Indeed he had, and his three hundred quid he won at the pool hall had burned along with all the rest of his possessions.)

Ronnie asked his father as if his loss entitled him to an answer, "Where d'ye *get* aw that money? Where did ye get that gun fae?"

Tommy stood, not looking at him, smiling.

"Get in the car."

"Is it from when ye robbed that van when I was wee?"

Like a puppy suddenly, eager, impressed, interested, a pack animal who had acknowledged the Alpha Male, Ronnie felt much better about everything.

Ronnie made gun noises in his cheeks as Hunter examined the AA Road Atlas he'd obviously picked up somewhere.

"Chceew! Wham bam."

He got in and buckled up, ready for the road.

"Were you really gonnae kill him?" Ronnie wanted to know.

"These hills here are called the Trossachs," Hunter told him now, as a kind of educational experiment. "This here is Rob Roy Country."

"Can Ah get a go wi yer gun?" Ronnie asked, buckled in.

"Mebbe later," said Hunter.

6.0.3.1

£24,776.04 (remembering to deduct £13.50 for the soup and sandwiches.)

Alas, poor Frank. Everybody knew him. It was the price of his status in Oor Wee Toon that everybody had a piece of him, owning him subtly even as he, more tangibly, owned them.

It is perhaps a throwback to our Serengeti-wandering days that human celebrity comes at the cost of sacrifice. It is maybe part of the natural balancing of the social order that to become visible is also to become vulnerable, and that this has been the case from the time the first hero stood up to a rhino (or the ancestral equivalent of a rhino), all the way to those bloodstained tossers on Reality TV. Both end up being eaten by jackals.

Whores of the Temple, trampled in the filth, worshipped as intermediaries in the great game of meaning, we ask a lot of people like Frank. We are both gratified and resentful when they go with our hopes for them under the terrible hooves.

Eleanor was outside the upstairs bathroom at a quarter past twelve, listening to the metallic drip of the water. She was listening to her husband's silence. She'd heard it before, of course. Frank had always had to steel himself to do the things he needed to do. His competencies had always been manufactured from his overcoming of his weaknesses. It was part of what had drawn her to him. He had had talent, but he had required polishing. His skills had needed nurturing, so he had always needed her, and she knew the power over him that gave her. But this was carrying his mood a little far, she thought. She sighed loud enough for him to hear, and walked downstairs with heavy feet.

He sat in his suds, getting cold now, knowing she was out there expecting better from him.

7.0.1

Brother Joe, his own grim heart lightened by secret knowledge, pulled Frank's car on to the gravel of Frank's driveway at 12.28. He went over that wee speed bump, and heard and almost felt the clunk of something heavy bouncing off the floor of the boot. He chuckled to himself. Eleanor heard the engine and the crunch of chuckies and looked out of the window.

At 12.31, Danny Boyle and Maggie Singleton, having interviewed the kids from the Dryry Street hostel, and punters from the Keys and the staff of the Wallace Arms Hotel, and having made an appointment to meet with Mr McIvor of Ross and Dean at lunchtime, were now stood at Agnes's door, about to see what Frank had already seen.

Having segregated Joe in the conservatory, Eleanor went upstairs and knocked on the bathroom door. Frank still gave no audible response, shifting uneasily in his tepid water. "Your brother's here," Eleanor told her husband at 12.32, trying to be factual, but with an edge of impatience. Still immersed, his toes going numb, Frank's heart ached for her to comfort him, all pink and wounded. But she was already going downstairs to put the new potatoes on to boil.

7.0.2

Frank had seen the dead before. He didn't like it, and usually tried to delegate funereal matters when they inevitably arose in the course of his role in the caring community. Things had usually been cleaned up by the time Frank got there. And when he had broken into Agnes's kitchen at 10.13 that morning, concealed by the back fence, there had been no premonitory warning of anything amiss.

He'd not seen her since he'd been a teenager, and back then she'd been a figure of some dread, one of those adults whose unpredictability had taught him his distrust. He knew she was an alcoholic. So he was a bit surprised to see the kitchen so neat, to see that everything in there, within the last day or two, had been washed within an inch of its life.

An unusual collection it was too, as if her kitchen were some pristine recycling station: cans were over here, plastics here, card and paper here, and a sparkling collection of empty Smirnoff bottles served for a centrepiece on the kitchen table. Something manic about it, he thought, but did not think to ask himself whose mania might have been the architect.

It was all clean, to be sure, but it had been done all at once, in haste, and left to dry. There were scummy accumulations of day-old soap that had found their way into the chips, nooks and crevices of the antediluvian Formica worktops.

"Agnes?"

He essayed a quiet call for her. He was answered by silence. There was a funny sour, not-nice smell he couldn't identify. He hesitated. Then, ball-footed, he stole into the hallway. The light was on. And he just knew that the light had been on all night and all morning and it would make no difference now to the illumination of the room even if he turned it off. The front room door was ajar too, grey daylight stealing through it to mix with the yellow wash from the light bulb and fall discouraged on his face. He realised he was sweating. There was that bitter smell again … stronger now. He held back before entering the room to see what was there (what was that stench?), not breathing. And, unusually for him, images from the past came unbidden to his brain.

He remembered seeing her once, years ago, Agnes … Agnes beating her granddaughter in the street, wee, dark hellion that she'd been. Janice had been about ten, and Agnes had just been at her, whipping her bare legs with a scrubbing brush, holding her by the hair, mottles coming up on the girl's thighs, and she'd gone on and on hitting her, Janice, till a crowd had gathered at the screaming of the girl, stunned at the persistence if not the fact of the brutality, and Agnes had just mechanically swatted her granddaughter again and again and again, no discipline involved in either the transitive or qualifying sense, simply a reflexive, randomly focussed, automatic hatred, a robotic loathing of all life that knew no shame, no context, no meaning beyond the exhaustion of whatever hellish energy had animated her anger in the first place, forcing her breath louder and louder, till she'd let the wee girl go, arm dropping from her hair and Janice, dirt- and tear-streaked, had run back in the house and Agnes had stood there, spent, chest heaving, looking at the neighbours like they were trees.

Startled at himself, Frank vividly remembered next him being wee-er still, keeping away from that house like his mammy had told him, walking quickly past that door, though sometimes glimpsing Janice, the wee girl who never went to school, staring out of the ground-floor window with grey-ringed eyes of hunger and depravity. He shuddered now, nearly forty years later, forgetting the growing stink, and in order to escape the intrusions of his own unconscious, walked into the front room.

Instantly, the smell that had been bothering him got much, much worse, and there was nothing he could do about that, now he saw where it came from.

Frank saw Agnes rooted to her armchair, smiling at him, her penultimate breaths gurgling past the filth in her throat, a set of broken dentures halfway out of her moving mouth, her tongue clucking dryly, her spit all mud, her eyes staring ...

... and there had been the sound of that breathing, Frank remembered in the bath, his eyes shut, as submerged as he could be in the perfumed bubbles, there had been the sound of that breathing ... and the smell had been everywhere, in everything ... cut into his skin, searing his brain like fire up his nostrils, clinging to his hair, it was still in his eyes and mouth and fingernails no matter how much bubble bath he used ... and he shut his eyes and saw again that greeny-yellow puddle of acrid awfulness that Agnes'd released from her bowels ... all round her feet and all around her bony arse ...

... and her arm had been extended towards him, holding him out a white envelope ... a last gift, a last revenge ...

His vomiting had been pure reflex, spraying through the web of his quickly lifted fingers, as reflexive and unconscious as Agnes beating at Janice's legs on the street had been all those years ago. As automatic as Agnes, he'd snatched the open envelope from her claw, seeing her name in Tommy's emphatic capitals written there. He knew he'd never be clean again, never escape the sight and smell of her, he saw the money ... and heard through the whisper of the notes he fanned the rasp as Agnes rattled her last curse at him and then froze, just as she was, arm still outstretched, talons still clutching, in an instantaneous rigor mortis and a last globule of something falling out of her nose. He dropped the money in the slowly spreading pond.

He had run, actually ran. He knew he'd never tell anyone about it. They'd never understand, for one thing. For another thing, to put the experience into words would have preserved its memory. So he didn't want to do anything like think that she was probably still like that and would be frozen in his mind's eye till the day he succumbed to Alzheimer's or died. He didn't want to think about it. On his way out of her front door he had wondered, uselessly, if he'd touched anything, his animal evidence already being all over the floor along with hers.

That's why Frank was still in the bath, listening to the gutter rumble of his brother's voice downstairs talking words he couldn't hear, not even daring to think.

7.1

There is another conversation you do need to know about before we get further into police procedure, or fraternal relations within the criminal demi-monde, or even explore any further the dance of intergenerational male bonding in contemporary Scotland as exemplified by Ronnie and his father. It's painful for me to have to tell you about it. But here goes anyway.

7.1.1

Joe Wheen had been washing his sore hands in the kitchen of Jack Webster's wee flat in Dennistoun at around a 10.45 when his phone vibrated and sang at him from Jack's bedside table. Stepping through the still fresh cloud of gun smoke and disintegrated eider feathers, and over the shattered corpse of his old pal and confederate, Jack Webster, Joe answered his phone and spoke to his brother with an uncanny calm. Together they discussed the testimony that Mrs Elspeth Dewar had provided as to the repentant nature of her interview with Tommy, and Frank, who had not long since left Agnes's house and was trying, vainly, to erase the memory of what he'd just seen … to get that smell out of his nose and that rattle out of his ears … fought against his own panic, fought to keep it out of his voice, fought to imitate the strength and calm he heard in his brother's voice, and promised that he would check in again with Superintendent Bellamy to see if he had heard anything new. Joe then reported that Jack Webster had confirmed that he had indeed been the source of the weapon and of the transport Tommy'd used for his abduction of his son. Jack had also said that Tommy'd told him that he was uninterested in a return to professional criminal activity and had expressed simply the wish to go on holiday, which expedition seemed now to include his son

Ronnie, and presumably also his daughter Janette, now living in Northern parts unknown. The brothers arranged to meet back at Frank's house at midday, and that they would head out in pursuit of Tommy Hunter after lunch.

7.1.2

Joe could tell when Frank got off the phone that his younger brother had been pleased with him. Information had been both lucidly and logically exchanged. He had also known that Frank had been lying to him and he was grimly satisfied that he had been able to conceal his own feelings from Frank so that the lying cunt wouldn't know what hit him when it hit him later on.

7.1.2.1

Among the things that Joe had not told Frank, any more than Frank had told him about Agnes, were that Jack, before Joe killed him (which he hadn't told Frank) had told Joe that Tommy had paid him in cash. Joe had requisitioned the envelope and its contents that Jack had showed him, you bet he had. But in my view, it must have been Jack who had then set what passed for Joe's mind working on the interesting question of who or what could possibly have been the source of Tommy's nest egg. And that with Jack's help, Joe had put two and two together and had come up with Frank.

7.1.2.1.1

Not that it really matters whether or not it was Jack that put him on to this idea ... possibly to deflect the tidal wave of violence Joe was crashing over him at the time. (He was no more successful than Canute.) Nor does it really matter whether or not it was actually Frank, who, for reasons of self-protection or in settlement of a debt of honour (!) had fulfilled the terms of the original deal and bestowed a quarter share of the proceeds from the robbery fourteen-odd years ago on Tommy now as a reward for his silence or as an admonition for him to get to fuck. What mattered was that Joe (I believe) now had the idea in his head, or in his heart or in his bowels or wherever it was he nursed his wrath to keep it warm, that his brother Frank had given that lunatic fuck that money instead of giving it to him, who really needed it.

7.1.2.2

Aye, ya cunt, thought Joe about his brother, as he pocketed his phone and looked down on the ruin of Jack Webster. Be fucking happy.

7.1.3

This brings me to what is perhaps the most intractable question in our whole study, one that I can no longer avoid exploring for the next page or so. I beg you to forgive me, but I really can't go on till I address the question: can or should we distinguish between the conduct of Tommy Hunter and that of Joseph Wheen?

Both used violence to achieve their aims, whatever those aims were. Indeed, challenged as we all are about Hunter's ontology, no two Hunter scholars I've ever met have ever entirely agreed as to exactly what Joe's motivation was in murdering Jack Webster that morning, in shooting him repeatedly the way he did, muffling the rounds through a succession of pillows, the folded duvet from Jack's bed and a cuddly toy Scottie dog. It may have been a fantasy of vengeance that Joe was indulging, for example.

But Hunter, though he hadn't murdered anybody for some years, had also forcibly involved a third party, Padraic

Macreesh, in whatever fantasy *he* was pursuing. He had quite deliberately terrorised an innocent, good man, as Joe had Jack. The fact that he acted in the name of redemption and had compensated the social worker with Heinz Tomato Soup and a thousand pounds may well be evidence of something, but it's hardly of moral rectitude. Hunter had been, even he would have admitted, distinctly unkind to Poor Egg.

7.3.1

Are we to allow sentiment to skew our judgement? Or snobbery? Can we be permitted, really, to dismiss Joe's behaviour as entirely predictable thuggery, simply because Hunter handed out little packets of financial penance after he did bad things? Can eccentricity stand as a defence of barbarism?

7.4

Joe murdered Jack and thereby ruined both his own and his brother's life. Can we really suppose from that being the consequence of his action that that's why he did it? That Joe was angry enough with his brother to have actually killed a third party as a rehearsal, as it were? That it was *really* his *brother* that Joseph had dragged through the doorway, forced on to the bed, and shot?

7.4.1

When Joe killed Jack, it seems that the murder weapon was inadvertently provided to the murderer by the murderee. Jack often had weapons for resale about the place. I think, then, we can rule out premeditation without having to stray into the "you say potato" territory of psychological profiling. Jack, poor proxy, had just happened to have a gun about the place. Joe shot him because a) he could and b) he found that he wanted to. That is about as deep as we can reasonably get down that particular rabbit hole. The violence itself had been its own reward, a positive step of self-improvement. Joe just liked being that guy.

7.5

My provisional distinction between the two men is hermeneutic, then, rather than phenomenological. Violence was, to Hunter, like the money, a strategic means for the accomplishment of a goal. For Joe, the commission of violence was an end in itself. The terrible harm that it was to do to his brother was a happy consequence of the murder, but not a cause.

7.5.1

Violence simplifies a complicated world, which explains its popularity among film producers, dictators and criminals. If you kill people, you don't have to talk to them. Your side of the argument becomes definitive. The argument has been won by death. By which all arguments are ultimately resolved.

7.5.2

For both of them, violence could temporarily silence both the voices inside them and those that opposed them in the outside world. But for Tommy Hunter, the violence his very existence implied was a confirmation of his solitude, of his already established silence. Joe wanted to make some noise. The difference between the actions each man took may well be limited to this nuance, but of what other than nuance can morality consist in a godless universe?

7.5.2.1

Discuss that one, why don't you?

7.6

See 0.0, above *et passim*.

7.7

Through that lovely, crisp spring morning, while all this ugly stuff was happening, Hunter drove with Ronnie into the glories of the landscape. He could feel his chest fill with the empty light and peace of it. From where they'd parked earlier, the map told him Kinloch Rannoch could be reached either by way of the motorway via Stirling, Perth and Pitlochry, or by the scenic route through Crieff or Lochearnhead. Hunter chose, happily, the Crieff road that would allow them a glimpse of the Sma Glen, then through Aberfeldy and over Schiehallion to Glen Rannoch, that place beloved of God, where the black woods meet the still waters, and the ghosts of stags clatter amid the birks through which the clans had marched to Killiecrankie.

It was a beautiful morning for the contemplation of history, for appreciating the complex sequence of accidents meeting desire. The roads wound through sheep and sward; trees dotted the horizons. Grey and brown mountains soared at every side.

"We'll need tae stop at the shops," Hunter told Ronnie. "Get ye somethin to wear."

Ronnie, having subsided from his temporary sociability, was playing with his fingers, picking the skin off.

"D'ye want some music on or somethin?" Hunter asked him. "There's CDs in the glove compartment." But Ronnie didn't seem to be interested in music any more than he was in history or the aesthetics of landscape. Hunter tried anyway. "Talk to me, son. Tell me what yer thinkin."

He was rewarded by a turn of Ronnie's head at least.

"Is it really for me?" Ronnie asked him. "I mean, half ae it."

"Aye … well … it's for you and yer mum and Janette. There have been some expenses, obviously."

"My mum?"

Tommy reached into his inside pocket and handed the postcard to Ronnie, who took it, confused.

"There's nothin oan it," he pointed out.

"My name's oan it. That's yer Mum's writin."

Ronnie accepted this, not having the expressive equipment to interrogate it. He may well have been mulling over the notion that his mother was alive, that he had now been as precipitately parented as he had once been orphaned, but you'd not have known it to look at him.

"Look at the view," advised his father. "I'd forgotten the sky up here." He hesitated, and decided, for the first time in a very long time, to say something emotional.

"I was inside for ages. The light in there made everything kinda green. Not good green like this. Like sick. I had a lot of time tae think. I made a lot of mistakes when I was your age. I want you and your sister tae dae better than that."

He fell silent. Ronnie gave him no indication that he had understood or even heard him.

7.7.1

They drove in silence through Muthill, the road winding past the pub and the post office. They had to drive slowly. There were children in the narrow, medieval street. There were parents in the houses or at work who loved them and looked out for them. There were retired people with careers and lives to look back on. There was a church where they gathered and sang. A graveyard where their memories were tended. There were trees and gardens. It was startling. Unbelievable. But it passed for normality here on earth. Neither Hunter nor Ronnie had anything to say about it as they turned on to the long straight road into the valley towards Crieff.

"This road is maybe Roman," said Tommy, trying again with the "inform, educate and entertain" meme that he'd inherited as a cultural notion of pater-familiarity from the century before last. But such was the profundity of Ronnie's deprivation, so naked his poverty of mind and body and spirit, that he still said nothing, owning no reference points to make sense of this or any other information, education or entertainment offered to him, not even owning his own ignorance.

7.7.1.1

Hunter, with his half-remembered gobbets of school, came from a different generation after all. It was only after Tommy's school days that the old ways of authoritarian hypocrisy had finally run out of steam, exhausted by not having an empire to play with any more, then to be further eviscerated by the mockery of the hip and self-satisfied. Once upon a time, within Tommy's cultural memory, the powers that be had also aspired to be the great and the good as well as the rich and the powerful, telling everybody what to do and why they should do it, imbuing them with only a handful of permitted ideas and a narrow, moralistic set of values to be sure, but at least telling them something. They may have been hypocrites, but it is at least arguable that hypocrisy serves society better than the open nihilism that mocks the very idea.

7.7.1.2

Once upon a time, after all, a mass workforce had been required by the economy, and a conscriptable proletariat had been required by the military. In short, it had been in the interests of those in power that the populace at large be at least barely literate, numerate, and acculturated to some notion or other of the common good. Not any more.

The population didn't need to be workers or soldiers now. The base requirement demanded of them was that they should buy things, that money should pass through them like pipes on its way to the Cayman Islands where it properly belonged. There is no requirement on consumers, welfare recipients and otherwise, that they are able to recognise the difference between fact and fiction or right and wrong, or that they should be capable of informed choice within a moral framework. Rather the reverse in fact. The more selfish, isolated, narrow and stupid people are, the better it is for the stock market. Rather in the same way that battery farms require that the blobs of fish-fed feathers that are stuffed into them be only genetically speaking "chickens", a human economy based on credit and imaginatively crooked investment packages has no use for any more than rudimentary human animals to keep the capital flowing.

7.7.1.2.1

Since the great and the good, in consequence first of their moral decline in the face of their own absurdity (in the seventies) and the sudden opportunity to make some serious cash (sometime around the mid-eighties), had long ago decided, well before the turn of the millennium, that getting rich was definitely more fun than pretending to give a fuck, the likes of Ronnie had been utterly abandoned (or "set free" according to the advertisements). Abandoned to the freedom of utterly uneducated desires, those desires in turn had been left to the whims of hatchet-hearted entrepreneurs, men who were properly evil, to nurture, define and fulfil.

7.7.1.2.2

So, even with his background of abuse and violence and the army and prison behind him, Tommy, at forty-three years old, with no paper qualifications for anything but mayhem, was Doctor Fucking Bronowski by comparison with Ronnie. The only pleasures Ronnie understood were narcotic. The only joy was to be found outside of himself. The only beauty was pornographic. The only understanding he had was that understanding anything was inevitably painful. In himself, perhaps, Hunter knew that whatever crimes he had committed, and had been committed on his kind, Ronnie and HIS kind, for all of their PlayStations and availability of hallucinogens of one kind and another, were victims of something far worse, of a neglect so deep and contemptuous that it made of them paupers of the spirit more helpless than any kid off the telly in Ethiopia.

7.7.1.2.1

We've been experimenting as a civilisation with being cultureless, self-directed monads, the hegemony of individual taste as our only moral and aesthetic compass. And the glutinous inarticulacy and undirected resentment of our society is the result, both for those with the comforts money buys and for those without. Tommy Hunter, with his diminishing hourglass of cash, and his limited conversation, was soon to be as inconsequential as any other non-participant in credit and consumption. He had only a closing window of financially defined significance left to him. It was his intention, before this window closed, to make what restitution he could for his own negative contribution to the human condition. The nobility of this, of what I take to be his purpose in dedicating what little remained to him of meaningful time to his destroyed, fragmentary family, makes me love him.

7.7.2

Tommy Hunter, nowadays it seems to me, was as great and as good as anyone could get. Which made it all the more regrettable that Ronnie had nothing to say to him, nothing to ask, not even the eminently practical questions he might have asked, given his own more-than-likely future, such as: "What is it like in prison?" Neither did Ronnie enquire about his mother, what she had been like. (Fearless, Tommy could have told him, the most fearless shoplifter he'd ever seen.) Nor did he offer his father any of his own experiences, or those of his sister. He could not imagine that anyone, even a parent, could have been interested in the good and the bad and the ugly of his memories of fostering, of his likes and dislikes in the fields of art and sport, for example. So atomised were father and son that they had no words to say even on the fluctuating fortunes of football teams, of manufactured celebrities and the like. So, bereft of even generic expressions of preference, leave alone the properly emotional revelations that Hollywood or its satellites would lead you to expect might have been occasioned by so unlikely a familial reunion, Ronnie could have quite truthfully answered (as indeed he did later, when it was all over, and he was being debriefed by DS "Danny" Boyle in the course of the latter's frenetic labouring to make something meaningful and advantageous to his career and to justice out of the whole wretched business) to the question, "What did you and your dad talk about after he kidnapped you?" — nothing.

7.8

Anyway, they parked expensively in Crieff and went into Miller's Outdoor Shop to try and get Ronnie something that Hunter called "suitable".

Ronnie would not normally have been seen dead in any of the pacamac big-booted self-coloured shite they sold in there ... the waterproof trousers and windbreakers and fuck off is that actually a HAT? Hunter had insisted, however, and had further diminished his stash by eighty-nine quid for a pair of jeans, two T-shirts and a green padded jacket that seriously wasn't Ronnie's style. They glared at each other like fathers and sons have always done throughout the ages all the way through the process, and were thus unremarked by the bejumpered middle-aged Staffordshire shopkeepers you inexplicably get in emporiums up there. The whole process of remodelling his son so that he looked like "some kind of a cunt" took almost twenty precious minutes.

7.8.1

Hunter was learning what may be a universal rule of parenthood that only immediate friction is expressible, that other matters of infinitely more weight will always be left till far too late, if ever referred to at all. Or maybe that's just in Scotland. I am nothing if not parochial.

7.8.1.1

£24,687.04

7.9

This was around about the same time that Padraic, poor Poor Egg, finally succeeded in flagging down some daytripper and got himself to the police station in nearby Callander, across the road from its excellent second-hand bookshop, where the proprietor will tell you of his summer spent as the house guest of Robert Graves on Majorca if you ask him. Padraic was in no mood to cooperate with anyone Scottish by then, and it was therefore some two and half hours before Frank and Joe saw him naked on the roof of the building in silent and eloquent protest against all that had happened to him and indeed had happened to anybody else at the hands of Ireland's Presbyterian cousins.

7.9.1

It took about an hour until even the news of Padraic's release from Hunter's grip was transmitted to Superintendent Bellamy, who then had to consider the news that Hunter was definitely out of town before deciding what to tell his increasingly bumptious subordinate, "Danny" Boyle, whose presence of mind in getting himself first to the crime scene of the kidnap and hence into leading the investigation officially had rendered more tricky than ever his removal from that into which he had no business poking his long neb.

7.9.2

The crucial further information that Mr Macreesh might have been able to pass on, that is, as to Hunter's immediate destination, both Bellamy and Frank Wheen missed for another hour and a half after that (due to Poor Egg's protest as aforesaid), which proved to be a gnat's bawhair too long to be useful to either of the interested parties. This information, which Bellamy and the Wheens did not learn till they themselves had got to Callander, as DS Boyle later testified at the enquiry, was never given to Boyle at any time at all, which was very naughty of Superintendent Bellamy. Very naughty indeed. And was featured as one among many other more serious naughtinesses that came to light in the course of the year-long later investigation Boyle led into Frank Wheen's affairs and Frank's own network of relationships with the highheedyins and officialdom of Oor Wee Toon and its environs.

7.9.2.1

That was all to follow. For the moment it was Eleanor who took Bellamy's call. Frank was well into his bath time by then. Confirming his already hostile opinion of her, she deigned to tell the policeman haughtily that he would need to call her husband back if he was going to be so obtuse as to withhold from her information vital to her household. Bellamy gave her his mobile number and after thinking for a moment about what a poisonous, stuck-up bitch she was, stepped out of his office.

7.9.2

Bellamy looked at "Danny" Boyle and at Maggie across the open-plan work environment, at the two of them with their heads together, animatedly cross-checking and comparing, speculating and hypothesising happily like a pair of pretend police off the telly. And the Superintendent wondered whether there was still a decent package available for voluntary redundancy in this day and age. Bellamy was deciding in his own slow way that playing both ends against the middle might prove to be the best policy in the meantime, but that the only really happy way forward was the way out. And it was this intuition that caused him now to put another nail in Frank's coffin and, without thinking it through properly, his own. That is, he went to talk to DS Boyle. For the first time that anyone could remember, he walked across the room to ask "Danny", nicely, quietly, if he had a minute.

"Danny" responded to this gesture of trust, this openness with predictable aggression, with peremptory demands that a forensic team look into whose sick it was that was all over Agnes MacHutcheon's carpet; that the sequential banknotes that he'd found on Agnes's floor and in the till of the Wallace Arms be traced back to their point of issue; that someone talk to the tailor who Mr Greenock Morton had telephoned and see if they'd been paid the same way and could offer a description of the clothes Hunter had bought; that a warrant be applied for to look into Frank Wheen's business records … in short that all manner of expensive specialists be hired from the internal investigators' marketplace, and finally that all known criminal associates of the Wheens (and here he passed a list under Bellamy's nose that had Jack Webster's name right at the top of it) should be brought in for questioning and compared to the location of the Glasgow call box the same Mr Greenock Morton had contacted. And Bellamy could plead departmental poverty if he liked, "Danny" told him, he was a terrier, he wasn't letting go this time.

"You're right," Bellamy told him. "This might open everything right up. This business with Tommy Hunter could be a blessing in disguise." Boyle froze in mid-harangue, suspecting that he was being outmanoeuvred — which, of course (temporarily and provisionally), he was.

"I'm taking this to Division," Bellamy told him. "I'm setting up a task force. It's about time we took another look at Mr Wheen. And I'm suggesting you to take the lead on it." He went on, before Boyle had time to think. "First, we need Mr Hunter's cooperation. I imagine he has a tale or two to tell."

"Aye, he …" Boyle managed before his superior confidently steamed straight over him. "I want you and Maggie on the road," he told him. "Hunter is heading somewhere with that boy and the best lead we have is probably going to come from a name on that list. I want you out there talking to people. I'll get the ball rolling here and pass on anything I get at this end."

"Danny's heading up a task force?" Maggie gurgled on her paralysed idol's behalf.

"Not up to me," Bellamy smiled. "See what Division says. But that'll be my recommendation. I'm proud of you Danny," he added improbably, believing his own bullshit for a moment, actually quite moved by it.

And before Boyle could think of anything to say, Bellamy had turned and walked away complacently.

Hardly daring to believe it, Maggie turned to "Danny".

"What do you think?" she asked him. But he wasn't ready to think anything yet. He looked right through her, not breathing.

7.9.3

At that moment that Joe was just minutes from pulling up the gravelled path to Frank's house, a devilish joy at the wee present he was secreting for his brother in the boot of Frank's expensive car warming his atrophied heart.

7.9.3.1

Having already passed Superintendent Bellamy's message on to the prune-like Frank, Eleanor was mixing a jug of non-alcoholic Pimm's.

7.9.3.1.1

Frank was still in the bath.

7.9.1.2

All of the above took place before one o'clock, by which time all manner of things had been happening, not the least which was that Hunter had met his daughter Janette again.

7.9.4

Back at 10.20, Janette, nineteen years old, another Pisces like Frank, was standing on the western shore of Loch Rannoch, her booted feet luxuriating in their grip upon the shale, staring at a swathe of pale blue sky meeting the black and green of the forests and the mountains, while the sound of a tractor on a forestry path, a mile distant, buzzed across the air, the loch gently lapping on the shingle, its surface a mirroring, blue miracle of cold perfection. Like metal, she thought to herself, metal with a freezing point miles below zero, thick water, syrup, quicksilver.

Janette was dressed just right for the weather, warm padded boots lined with yellow wool she'd found in a thrift shop in Pitlochry, an island-made jumper from the same source that smelled subtly of peat smoke when it rained … a pair of old jeans and a dark blue schoolie's rain jacket, her tout ensemble redolent of contentment, of fitting in, of being at home, of being happy in herself, as unlikely as that may seem in the familial and narrative context of hysteria into which she was shortly to be thrust. But Janette had parlayed her distressing experiences and memories into a journey towards herself, into somehow finding the hope in herself that her "self" was a place worth looking for. Her search was unhurried, not a quest haunted by loss or guilt or mortality in the way her father's was. Call her Ishmael, if you like, but this child of exile, though as abandoned as her brother, felt, in contrast to the former's grumpy hopelessness, at least at that moment, sufficient unto herself to surrender to what was around her, unthreatened by the songs of birds.

Janette, just nineteen two weeks ago, her thin brown hair blowing in the wind across the water, eyes open, felt no threat in the landscape, and actually wanted to understand everything, wanted to see the world, wanted to be more than she was. She was confident of becoming, given time, a person of some consequence, and not just because some parent or college or boyfriend said that she was. Her soul open to the elements, to the threads of richness in the smells and sounds the wind happened to send her, Janette Hunter, last seen aged five crying in the back of a broken-down car not too far from here, as it happens, without even glancing at her watch, knew exactly how long it would take her to get back to the hotel to start changing the rooms at checkout time, and that she had two more inexpressibly precious minutes to breathe and hear and see.

Look at this place, she said to herself, not for the first time. Just look.

The wind freshened, just perceptibly, and Janette looked up, feeling a tiny, almost weightless drop of rain from the one dark cloud overhead. She turned to go to back to work as the waters of the loch began to receive the cloud's tribute, and almost silently, almost invisibly, the raindrops stirred the placid water into circles.

7.9.4.1

The same rain had obscured the Sma Glen just as her father and brother drove into it from Gilmerton. By this time, Hunter had fallen back on mockery and wind-up as the default strategy for talking to teenagers, and Ronnie had this potentially glamorous adult pegged as just another self-deluding wanker with a mission to "engage" him. They missed the best of the scenery what with the low cloud and everything, but neither of them was looking at the scenery by then. Because they'd already picked up the hitcher.

Her wardrobe was a patina of cultural misdirection. So that when they'd first pulled over at that viewing spot near the Auld Stane Brig, Ronnie had asked his Dad "Yer no gonnae pick up a Paki, ur ye?"

There was just something about the sight of her, Hunter might have said. That she was stood there in the rain, the rain not touching her, like she was under an invisible umbrella. She was bright. Maybe she reminded him of something, intimated something. Maybe he was just attracted to shiny things.

A Palestinian scarf, a Laura Ashley skirt over purple leggings, a long coat of stars and a sacking bag stitched with symbols of the Lakota, straight brown hair in a bob cut, she swung out of the ether and into the back seat like the universe, a puff of Chance by Chanel and a soft South London voice, light brown skin and deep brown eyes, she told them Aberfeldy would be cosmic. She said her name was Denise.

Hunter became animated. Possibly just because she was young and female and she had a husky laugh. It had been awhile. Ronnie became catatonic for exactly the same reasons. She made the both of them feel more Scottish. That is to say, she confronted them with the fact of there being alternative possibilities to being Scottish. Could there really be a world where such un-Scottish creatures could exist? Might it even be *this* one? How is one supposed to deal with that?

Denise talked a lot in her husky voice, leaning between them, about a land occupation up north she thought she might get into, on an estate that had been intended to offer a hideously expensive Highland hideaway for the jet set but that had now been taken over by activists and squatters protesting about Scotland's uniquely iniquitous pattern of land ownership, then she talked about her father who'd fucked off back to Barbados first chance he got, she didn't even blame him any more with the racism he'd had to deal with from her mother's family, then she talked about her teacher training at Southwark College at the Elephant and Castle, and how that had been bullshit, and that she really liked kids but remembered just in time that she didn't like teachers and she didn't want to be one, then she talked about a camel festival she'd attended in Rajasthan and the red walls of Delhi and the observatory at Jaipur.

Hunter responded ... well ... by turning himself into a cartoon Scotsman, actually, rolling his "r"s, rasping the "ch" in "loch" and "Kinloch" and "Rannoch" like some emphysemic nutter in a kilt. He was play-acting. He was flirting. He was trying to be funny.

"Wir gaun tae Kinloccchhh Rannoccchh by Loccchhh Rannoccchhh tae visit Ronnie's sister. Then wir gaun on holly day."

Ronnie went redder and redder. Like a tandoori lobster.

Denise looked at the little ponds among the rocks as they reached the peak of the Ochils and said that she liked it up here. It felt like it was sort of, well, protected. Like it was safe up here. You know? She didn't articulate further what she thought it was safe from.

Hunter told her that he'd been to London a couple of times, and Denise asked Ronnie if he'd ever been. Ronnie made a sort of horsey noise and the tips of his ears went purple, which for a not-quite-sixteen-year-old boy from the West of Scotland passes for an articulate reply. Denise enjoyed it anyway. She gave them her full throated laugh again. Her eyes flickered knowingly between the two of them, and she offered Hunter an unspoken conspiratorial moment. That it was cute the way that his son was so shy, and that he himself was quite fanciable in a beaten-up old man kind of way. Hunter remembered that feeling of being flirted with gratitude, remembered that girls did that sometimes, made you a gift like that. It was good for him to remember — if one could forget the goal-oriented aspects of sexuality, and experience flirtation not as semaphore, but rather as an affirmation that life went on and was well worth living — and that this in itself was not nothing.

"Ah steyed in Camberwell the wan time," he said, and she said that was just up the road from Peckham where she was from. And he said he'd not got out much. Which was true. He didn't elaborate that he his fellow squaddies had done a dismal round of West End titty bars the first time, and he had stayed by himself in a pub in Brixton getting paralysed the second, miserable for reasons he had been too young to identify.

He told her he liked her clothes. And she said "Thank you" in the delicious way she'd come across by accident when she'd had a cold.

She enjoyed the attention, of course she did. And he was using her, of course he was. As practice for talking to Janice when the time came. When the time came that he had to talk to Janice again. Or not. Which I'll come to.

8.0.1

It's only twenty minutes from the Auld Stane Brig in the Sma Glen to the Auld Stane Brig across the Tay outside of Aberfeldy, a bizarre, single-lane, rather dramatically spired structure over which you drive into the town with its Birks and restored cinema and the Watermill, a rather good if slightly expensive coffee and cake and bookshop ... which was where Denise was heading with her flurry of bags and scarfs, to keep out of the rain. They dropped her at the lights on the High Street, and she was gone, easily accepting their brief acquaintance as just another happy thing in a happy life.

Hunter waved as they drove away, taking the road along towards the Loch, then making a right turn up to Fortingall with its ancient Yew. Observing that Ronnie was still rotating the colour of his face from puce to yellow and back to ashen, Hunter asked Ronnie a question about Denise, interested in his response.

"What did ye 'hink o' her?"

"How?" said Ronnie, like an unsure boxer, fists screwed up against his face.

"Ah think you should have got aff wi her."

"Ah thought YOU were gonnae get aff wi her!" said Ronnie.

Hunter tutted.

"Ah could be her Da." He thought for a moment. "Reminded me ae yer mither," he said. "At that age," he added.

"I fuckin hate hippies," Ronnie expanded.

"How d'ye ken she was a hippy?" Hunter answered, mockingly.

"Why the fuck are you talkin like that, onywey?"

"Like whit?"

"Like a fuckin fermer ur sumthin!"

"D'ye hate fermers anaw?" Hunter asked, making of country folk, as he had with Denise, an attempt to prise Ronnie from his narrow, schemey view of humanity. But Ronnie, further education declined for the moment, lapsed into silence. Hunter waited till his boy could think of something else to say.

Finally, he did.

"The road's windy as fuck. Makes me fuckin puke," said Ronnie.

"D'ye want these hills no tae be here anaw, Ronnie? That it?" Hunter said, swerving to avoid the grocery lorry that had just delivered vegetables to the Bide a Wee Hotel.

"What the fuck d'ye want fae me?" asked Ronnie, finally. "What are we fuckin daein up here?"

Hunter smiled.

"Wir oan holiday," he said. He smiled and made an unreliable promise, as fathers do. "We're collecting your sister and wir gaun tae see yer mither," he said.

8.2

"Okay, Maggie," said DS "Danny" Boyle so sexy, so strong, so purposeful as they left Mr McIvor all flustered with a nice cup of tea from Mr Dean and got back into the car and set off towards the M74 and Glasgow. "What do we know?"

Maggie looked down at her notes. She waited for him to continue, flattering him, encouraging him to enjoy his powers. He indeed went on, answering his own question in the way she knew he liked to.

"He stayed in the hotel for one night. The tailor was his first call, his second was to a phone box in the East End. That has to be where he arranged for the car and the weapon."

"So what does that tell us?" he asked, enjoying himself.

"He's got money."

"He's got money … but he waits a week from when he's let out of prison before he comes home. Why?"

"He was waiting for it."

He nodded as to an apt pupil, with maybe just the first faint glimmerings of awareness that she liked it and that it was fun to give her things she liked.

"He was waiting for the money." He smiled. "He was waiting for someone to send him the money. Who would send Tommy Hunter money? Except somebody who owed him money."

"Frank Wheen."

"Frank Wheen!"

They'd already talked about all this back in the office, of course. About what they were now sure forensics would report about the fingerprints in Agnes's house, and that the samples of still warm vomit he'd scraped from her carpet would turn out to belong to a third party, though that party being Frank himself would surely be too much to hope for.

But they were like a pair of excited kids, the two of them … working it all out, saying it out loud again to enjoy it again.

"It's lucky we've got Sally on our side," said Maggie, Sally being Sally Harrower, the girl from the CID who Superintendent Bellamy had bloody near assaulted at the Christmas party two years ago, and was consequently no friend of his. The thought of Bellamy made her wonder something else aloud:

"So what's Superintendent Bellamy up to? What's this task force all about?"

"Time. That has to be about time. He thinks that if this lot all cools down he can maybe get away with it."

"Get away with what?"

"He knows he can't stop an investigation, but he thinks he can limit it if he's the one who suggests it." Boyle turned to her, his eyes flashing with excitement. "But if we get to Hunter first, he can tie Frank to the robbery, and everything else will fall into place. There'll be nowhere for Bellamy to hide."

All concern, she turned to him, anxiety for his success in every sinew.

"But how?" she said. "Bellamy will tell Frank everything he knows … before he'll tell us."

"We know where Hunter's going," said DS "Danny" Boyle, thinking of the postcard from Moon Country. And he barked out a laugh that startled her. She nearly wept for joy.

They turned into the slip road that would lead them on

the motorway to the East End where the now empty theatre of Jack Webster's pain was waiting for them.

Poor Jack!

8.3

Her bottom was the light of Mr Lawrence's life. For the few
moments he spoke to Janette before she went upstairs to
change, Mr Lawrence, owner and proprietor of the sinking ship that was the Bide a Wee Hotel, couldn't wait to
stop talking to her face so he could see her bottom again.
He was obsessed with it. He had always said he'd come to
Scotland for the scenery.

It was an apple, a planet, a peach of a bottom. The cheeks
of it clung to his consciousness, enclosed him in their ripe
darkness. The shape of it made such promises of firmness
and smoothness. Mr Lawrence knew that he'd never get
closer to its texture than he was now, would never bathe
in the heat of it on his moustache. But it didn't hurt to
worship it as it went up the stairs, as it receded from him.
And soon it would be in that black skirt he'd bought for it.

There weren't many pleasures in his life.

The thing was that her face had just been telling him
that her bottom would soon be moving on. That she was
very grateful for the time she'd spent here, but that she had
been talking to some people about a job further north or
back out on the islands, and she was sorry, but she thought
she was going to go and would it be okay if she just worked
here till the end of the week, and maybe leave some stuff
until she got settled?

He wasn't listening. He was in mourning already. His
happiness was soon forever to be out of his fingers' reach.
He'd even stolen knickers from her drawer, the drawer in
the wardrobe in the box room upstairs where she slept —
clean ones, he wasn't a pervert — and had even thought
about putting them on, thought about joining the shape

166

of his bottom to hers. He hadn't done that, of course, they'd have stretched and she'd have known. So he'd just kept them, just for a day or two at first, and then returned them … but then he had taken another pair in exchange. This exchange of linen had become habitual, like her underwear drawer was a heavenly lending library. When he was alone, or, in bed, when Mrs Lawrence was in the bathroom, he'd take the latest pair from his pyjama jacket pocket, putting his thumbs at the sides, opening them out. So perfect. Then next day he'd put them back in the drawer so he could imagine her wearing them, filling them, picture them under her skirt, her jeans. He'd meant to stop doing it … he'd thought, more than once, perhaps she'd find out … and mock him … humiliate him. But that idea was quite exciting too. So he kept up his borrowing and returning so that both of them had a fresh pair every day. He even felt like he had her permission by now. That she thought of him fondly, even. As fondly as he did of her.

He wondered if any knickers she left behind for later collection would lose their charm when her bottom was far away from them. Would their promise age, as he was aging inside?

"I can't pretend we won't miss you, Janet," he'd said to her, mispronouncing her name the way he always had.

"I'll miss you too," she'd said. "Thank you, Mr Lawrence."

"Upstairs and do some hoovering and then get changed for serving," he'd said, his face engorging in anticipation of the sight of it working beneath her jeans as she ascended the stairs.

With her boss's eyes burning a hole in her posterior, and feeling a wee bit creeped out as usual when she'd been talking to him, Janette went upstairs to pack before getting changed. She was one of those women who rehearse their packing a few times days before actually having to pack. Which turned out to be providential.

For her part, Mrs Lawrence had fallen in love with

the Highlands from the start. That was why he — Mr Lawrence — had come here, because the missus had wanted to, from the very first time they came up here on their hols from Wolverhampton. It had been the estate agents who'd put them on to the Bide a Wee Hotel, and had talked about the excellent mortgage deals available for buying a going concern. And she'd always liked to cook, she'd said. And besides, she'd said, the region was an excellent source of locally sourced produce. Saying the word sourced like that. Twice.

The trouble was that Kinloch Rannoch's very special attractions also made it particularly reliant on a regular clientele, a clientele to be built quietly over a period of time, and whose loyalty had to be wooed, won and maintained. The main road from Pitlochry past Loch Tummel was, of course, achingly spectacular, with its banks of forest rising steeply from the waters, but, unfortunately, other than to Rannoch station, the road didn't go anywhere. So it wasn't the kind of place you'd come across on your way somewhere else. It was the kind of place you had to know about, which accounted both for its beauty and for its seclusion. And though Mrs Lawrence liked to cook, with the best will in the world, it couldn't be said that she was very good at it. Janette was an asset, of course, around the place, but they didn't really have the business now to justify even one full-time member of staff. And now she was leaving.

He watched her climb the stairs for perhaps the last time.

Her bottom, Mr Lawrence reflected as it turned the corner and went out of sight, could be considered as a religious object rather than an economic one. He blinked twice, his eyes stinging. And he jumped as he always did when he heard as he did every morning around now the sudden skirl of the pipes.

That bloody music booming around the bloody place didn't help. But Mrs Lawrence was of the opinion that their being in Scotland meant that everyone would enjoy the pipes and drums of the Cameron Highlanders playing a medley of their greatest hits. Loudly. All the time. That Scottish people would like it, and so would visitors of Scottish antecedence from the Antipodes and the Americas, and that even what she called "the continentals", their being weaned on translations of Walter Scott that frankly flatter the old boy's halting, lumpen prosody, would respond to the neo-Celtic romanticism that this music as played in march time by the British Army is mysteriously taken to exemplify. Even at breakfast time.

As a consequence, what had been a quiet but steady going concern was now, in inexorable slow motion, going down like the Lusitania, and all the Twittering and Facebooking and linking to websites in the world couldn't do anything about it. She didn't even ever put the Corries on for a bit of bloody variety.

Mr Lawrence looked across the wasteland of his dining room, the smell of overcooked venison burgers attacking his nostrils, just as the Cameronians went into a spirited rendition of "Hey Johnny Cope", this being at least doubly ironic since the tune celebrates the massacre of (largely) Camerons — by the Jacobite army which was in its turn exterminated by the regimental ancestors of the players. Unafflicted by the postmodern irony of it all, this Englishman abroad took his last pair of stolen Scottish knickers from his trouser pocket and sniffed them sadly.

8.4

Frank couldn't nail the moment of his crucifixion down exactly. He couldn't tell you exactly when and how he'd understood from Eleanor that she was relaxed about his coming sacrifice. That she didn't mind all that much. That he'd already served his purpose for her. That she thought that his loss was bearable to her. That his life was a price that she was willing to pay. For her life. For her peace.

It wasn't a surprise to him exactly. He'd always known she was a pragmatist. But he hadn't expected her to be quite so relaxed.

It was nothing she had said. It had been something in the ease with which she had agreed, over lunch, that, no question, whatever was happening with Tommy Hunter, whatever agenda he might be following, the consequences of Hunter's drawing police attention were potentially catastrophic. Frank was right. He and Joe had to find Hunter first, talk to him, find out what was going on. Evaluate the danger. Deal with it.

It was the way she talked about it with concern for him and not for herself … as if she were already safe, as if she'd already brought the shutters down, as if their destinies were already divorced. She wished him well and everything … but …

Frank had told Eleanor weeks ago about the money that he'd sent Tommy after Tommy's release. He had considered with her whether he ought to do that. Of course he had. In the world Frank lived in now, the fulfilment of contracts was something that was just supposed to happen, something that offered a hedge against chance. He had explained that to her. He had been afraid that if he hadn't paid Tommy his share of the robbery that had been the foundation of their fortune, Tommy would come after it. So having promised him the money when he went in, he'd paid it, as he'd promised, when Tommy came out.

He'd made that decision with her help and he still stood by it. I've no first-hand testimony available, but Frank must have got word to Tommy he'd do that. It was either that or he'd have to have arranged to have Tommy killed, which, what with inflation and Tommy's reputation, would have cost him almost as much, and besides, that wasn't really him. Not any more. He wasn't a gangster any more. He'd never really been a gangster, he told himself. It had just been circumstances.

A long time ago, understanding that money can only ever come of money, he'd accumulated capital in a primitive way. That's all. And just as she'd agreed to that action back then, to the blagging, I mean, so Eleanor, his entrée to a wider, richer life, had agreed to this now, agreed that the life they'd built together on whatever basis was now endangered, and that if the means to be adopted to secure the cultured life they'd built together involved him regressing to the uncultured methods of his past, to Frank's firstly making an undeclared payment to a criminal co-conspirator, and if that didn't work, to his risking his life by going up against the unpredictable force of nature that was Tommy Hunter, that was fine with her too.

It was a bit too fine with her, Frank now reflected, his kale salad sitting uneasily on his queasy tummy.

But he was clearly out of control, Tommy Hunter. If nothing else, Tommy's quite obvious madness, and the accompanying inevitability that Tommy would be caught eventually, and then questioned, made it essential that he get to him first. Eleanor could see that as clearly as he could. She'd calmly accepted that Frank had made an investment in Tommy's quiescence that had not paid off (a circumstance of which it was vital that brother Joseph should never learn, clearly), and that now, tits up, the situation had to be corrected, and there was no way he could do that without bringing his brother along with him. Muscle and risk were inherent in the attempt to secure peace by war. That had all made perfect sense to her.

He was a little sad about the fact that she'd agreed with him so readily, that's all.

She'd accepted everything he told her calmly, when the admission of his weakness and fear had cost him so much pain. Too quickly, too easily. Like she'd already thought of it. Like he was already lost. Like she already was thinking how she'd look in black. And thought that would be okay too. He himself was not essential to that which she was sending him out to defend. He was expendable. And if he was lost, well, that was too bad. He was extraneous to her good, comfortable life.

"Take care of yourself, Frank," is what she'd told him as he and Joe had left after lunch, and it had sounded so final. As if she was offering an occasional employee a disinterested farewell. He'd looked back at her before getting in the car, at her standing there in the driveway that curved past the Georgian porch and into the garden to the right that swept down the brow of the hill for nearly half an acre. She'd stood there in front of seven bedrooms, three public rooms, all with restored original features, like she was guarding all of it from him now, too, that whatever line the accidents of the last two days had meant that he had fallen across, he had already fallen so far away from her that there was no going back to the other side. He was dangerous to her now. To all she had. She was going to protect it, he knew that. She'd protect it, his children, their future, his achievement, from him, if she had to. That's what it had meant, that last half-sad look. It was goodbye. Just in case.

As they drove away Joseph looked fucking pleased with himself for some reason. That didn't help Frank's mood. The territory they were driving into was where Joe lived, he reflected, however novel the physical geography of the Highlands. Whereever they were going, he was entirely in his brother's power for the first time since the last time Joe had forced his head into the toilet. Unwilling to think too deeply about either his brother or his wife, let alone his past or future, Frank allowed himself to continue his bath time dwam, and Joe drove them in silence towards Callander, where Mr Macreesh was waiting on the police station roof, and where Superintendent Bellamy had said he would meet them.

While Jack Webster, dead, was wrapped up in plastic sheeting in the boot of the car, and his head bounced with a clonk every so often as they went over speed bumps or into potholes on the way. Frank wondered absently what that noise was? The car wasn't buggered as well now, was it!? That would put the tin lid on things. Then he forgot about it.

9.0

The following reconstructions do not pretend to answer every question every reader may have about them. In particular, the commentary around the words spoken must be admitted to being unreliable. The words quoted, however, assert themselves to be a true record.

9.1

INT. BIDE A WEE HOTEL – LOBBY – DAY

The picturesque Perthshire village of Kinloch Rannoch. Day trippers and tourists happily explore its range of amenities, with the notable exception of the Bide a Wee Hotel, where MRS MARGARET LAWRENCE is at reception, greeting some lamentably rare customers: a grinning middle-aged Scotsman in a suit, and a sullen teenage boy in a T-shirt and jeans from the back pocket of which he hasn't yet removed the price tag. Mrs Lawrence is the wife of the manager we encountered earlier (see 8.3). She is a round, floral woman from Oldham originally.

> HUNTER
> (smiling, finding that he is getting back the hang of this human contact business a bit now he's on holiday)
> Can we get a room?

> MRS LAWRENCE
> (pushing her luck, hoping he's bringing in a bus party)
> Lunch for two as well, is it, Mister ...?

> HUNTER
> (echoing her accent a bit, not entirely consciously, perhaps)

Is Janette 'unter still working 'ere?

MRS LAWRENCE
(pleased, overall, that the world is such a small place,
if also slightly disappointed that these guests aren't
here for her cooking — after all she tries so hard)
Do you know JANETTE, then?

HUNTER
(leaning forward, winning a confidence, in an
old lag's fashion, by giving a confidence)
I'm her father. This is Ronnie, her wee brother ...
and it's her BIRTHDAY, ye see ... so we thought
we'd give her a surprise and pay her a wee visit ...

He practically pours his criminal charm on the desk.

MRS LAWRENCE
(moving to the end of the desk, slightly disappointed
that it's that girl, who she doesn't entirely trust for
a reason she can't bring herself to fathom, who has
brought these good people here, but responding to
his charm's libation like a woman in the desert)
For heaven's sake, let me let her know you're here ...

HUNTER
(still leaning forward, his hand,
startlingly, reaching out for hers)
Oh, no, you're not to worry, that's fine ...
we want to SURPRISE her.

MRS LAWRENCE
Oh. Might you give me a credit card
to secure the accommodation?

HUNTER
(his smile fixed and disconcerting)
Would cash in advance be okay?

Ronnie looks dubiously at Hunter. Who still smiles warmly at his hostess. Who looks back at him with her face frozen in a funny position.

9.1.1

£24,607.04

CUT TO:

9.1.1

INT. BIDE A WEE HOTEL – STAIRCASE – DAY

A few moments later. Rather deafened by a spirited pipe-and-drum rendition of "Loch Lomond", Ronnie and Hunter go up the tartan stairs past the second-hand prints of second-hand sentiment, Hunter carrying the carpet bag.

HUNTER
(pleased at having met his daughter's protectress,
and that this party seems to be a cosy, decent,
sort despite a slightly strange sense of decoration.
Is that framed photograph there really of First
World War Prussian Uhlans on a tea break in
Belgium in 1914? Are there corpses of nuns
and spitted babies lurking just out of shot?)
What a NICE lady!

RONNIE
(without reflection, irony or any modicum of taste)

Ah thought she was a fat boot.

HUNTER
(a fond and conventional admonition, educationally
intended to encourage the good in his younger child)
Politeness doesnae hurt, Ronnie.

CUT TO:

9.1.2

EXT. BIDE A WEE HOTEL – BACKYARD – DAY

Mrs Lawrence has brought HER HUSBAND a cup of tea
out to the yard where he had been thinking about having
a smoke of his pipe. She has just told him whose father
has just arrived. His face has gone as white as a sheet.
His trusty briar hangs forgotten in his hand, loose tobacco
leaves spilling to the concrete.

LAWRENCE
(pushing the words through his tangle of fear,
guilt and remembered concupiscence)
Her father? Janet's father?

MRS LAWRENCE
(puzzled)
Yes, Bob.

LAWRENCE
(trying to be casual, forehead beading, his
penis unaccountably tumescing)
What's he WANT?

MRS LAWRENCE
(simply)

It's her birthday.

MRS LAWRENCE

LAWRENCE
(as if he didn't know that bottoms had birthdays)
Her birthday?

MRS LAWRENCE
(bewildered and slightly ashamed of the ways of
men, though without specific evidence or cause)
He seemed very friendly.

LAWRENCE
(turbulence escaping his intestine and venting from
his colon in a slow, thin ripple of hot, potent gas)
'Scuse me, love …

He goes indoors.

MRS LAWRENCE
Shall I leave your tea for you?

There is no reply. It being a shame to waste tea, sniffing
vaguely, she drinks from his cup, smacking her lips at the
sugar she doesn't take any more, but he still does, the silly
beggar. Well, that's what men are. They never go to the
doctor. One day she'll find him on the floor of the kitchen,
lips blue and tongue protruding … or maybe he'll just not
get up one morning, but sleep in forever and ever. He'd
like that. She'd like that. Her eyes glaze over peacefully.

CUT TO:

9.2.3

INT. BIDE A WEE HOTEL – BEDROOM – DAY

Ronnie and Hunter are now in a twin room in the hotel, furnished in heavy brown of assorted shades and periods, with uneven floorboards — in short, a room in the same uncertain taste as the hotel as a whole. The stuff in it could keep you awake at night speculating on its provenance. Hunter puts his bag on the bed. Ronnie shuts the door.

RONNIE
Dad …?

HUNTER
(suppressing the urge to whirl round and hug him … years of suffering dropping away, of loneliness … years of empty wishing … For Ronnie, who had been too young to call him anything the last time he saw him — his lost son — has just called him "Dad" for the very first time)
Uh huh?

RONNIE
(charmless, insensitive, greedy, inevitable)
Can I see that money again?

HUNTER
(a little hurt)
No. Ah shouldnae have shown it tae ye at all.

Ronnie has picked the gun up from the bed.

Ye gonnae shoot me now?

RONNIE
Naw. It's no loaded.

Ronnie sniggers, turns and aims the gun out of the window.

(gun noise)

Pcheuw!

We follow his gaze out of the window, where he is pretending to shoot hippies and sheep.

Pcheuw! Fuck ye …

Hunter snatches the gun from him. Ronnie turns to
protest.

Hi!

HUNTER
(struggling, as he has since their reunion, with an
impersonation of fatherliness for which he has no
personal model and which is therefore reliant on the
most tawdry and sentimental of cinematic clichés
on the one hand, and his instinctual and not to say
personally violent sensitivity to this latest slight to
his feelings on the other, thus suffering a double
repression, tightening yet further the internal knots
which seem sometimes to be all that is real about him)
Ye kin play wi it later.

RONNIE
(brattish in a learned manner, also at second-hand,
pouts and walks past him towards the bedroom
door, tossing the pistol on the bed as he goes)
Donwannit …

He reaches for the door handle, a simple glass sphere of
Caithness Crystal.

HUNTER
(as a stern father, finding himself playing the role in
response to Ronnie's impersonation of adolescent
strop, and perhaps in unconscious homage to

the early filmography of Sandy Mackendrick,
late of Canada, Scotland and California, and
thus, to the Komik, Katholic Kontortions of
Compton MacKenzie's postmodern tartanry)
You stay where you are, my laddie!

Ronnie opens the door. Turns to point a dirty fingernail at
the gun on the bed.

RONNIE
Tellt ye. That's no loaded.

He goes out and shuts the door.

HUNTER
Ronnie!

Hunter starts to hurriedly repack the bag, but runs out
before he's finished, leaving envelopes revealed, and calling again for Ronnie, setting up the forthcoming change
of POV.

CUT TO:

9.3

INT. BIDE A WEE HOTEL – CORRIDOR – DAY

JANETTE, all unaware of her family's proximity, is hoovering, humming to herself. She now becomes aware she
is being watched, and looks up. It's Mr Lawrence. It's not
the first time she's looked up, or round, or down, and
seen him staring at her with his mouth open, his tongue
flopped supine on his bottom teeth, like a tired dog. She
smiles tightly in anticipation of his furtive familiarities,
having developed a nose for the complex odours of male

wrongness at various junctures of her orphaned experience of her guilty and complacent nation which continually congratulates itself on its social conscience while as consistently crapping on its less fortunate citizens.

JANETTE
(over the noise of the hoover, posing a
challenge to the Foley artist were anybody
ever to actually make a film of this)
Mister Lawrence?

LAWRENCE
(likewise over the hoover noise, but at a reverse
angle, thus putting the putative engineer of
the soundtrack further on his mettle)
Ye've not told him, have ye?

JANETTE
(not hearing, and maybe not the only one,
if post-production standards decline yet
further into institutional indifference)
What?

She turns off the hoover and looks at her employer as the noise spirals down. He's even redder in the face than usual. His eyes are begging her for mercy. She looks away from them, and notes with astonishment that his trousers have made a tent to stand at right angles to the swell of his belly, and that a cheeky little patch of sparkly damp has formed at its apex.

LAWRENCE
(breathless at his own tension, blood pressure far
too high, beating at his neck and temples)
You've not been saying anything to your Dad, have you?

JANETTE
(genuinely mystified, or playing the line as if genuinely
mystified, who can tell the heart of maidens?)
What? What are ye talkin about?

Before Lawrence can reply, Janette is arrested by the sight
of her brother, impossibly, her brother (!) I mean fucking Ronnie (!) approaching her up the corridor. Lawrence
turns to look at what she's looking at. He sees Ronnie too,
blanches, and then bolts around a corner.
(to Ronnie)

What the f ...

Cutting herself off, she glances behind her at where the
hell Lawrence went, then back to Ronnie, and starts again.

What the fuck are you ...?

Ronnie walks straight past her, cutting off her question as
if she'd been nagging him for hours the way in his imagination that she always did, his older sister, who he hasn't seen
a lot of since she turned sixteen and escaped the compul-
sory attention of the state, having acted in the preceding
period as a kind of parental locum, perhaps even later as
a motherly interior voice arguing in favour of him looking
after himself and minding out what he smokes.

JANETTE
(pursuing him, grabbing at his arm)
RONNIE!

RONNIE
(as if, as above, he heard her voice every day and that
she was constantly making unreasonable demands of
his time and behaviour, which even may have been

true in a Jiminy Cricket kind of way — had she been
present to him as the personification of his superego —
which she may well have been for all I know)
Ach, fuck … get tae fuck, will ye?

He shakes her off and keeps walking.

Don't tell me what tae dae.

JANETTE
(still following him, and still straightforwardly
in search of useful information)
How'd you get here?

RONNIE
(pulling away still)
Ah wuz kidnapped …

JANETTE
(disappointed at so transparently spurious a defensive
witticism, ignoring it, letting him walk away from
her as punishment for his banality, and yet, in
contradiction, persisting with her enquiry, more gently)
Ronnie! Answer me …

HUNTER
(from behind her, OOV — if this was a movie
we'd see him out of focus over her shoulder)
Janette …

Janette spins to see Hunter, in full-colour high definition,
standing behind her. Her father! A man she's not seen
since she was five years old, who she recognises only from
old photographs — looking at her anxiously, beseechingly.
An unreadable, impossible complex of emotions start as
a hot flush somewhere near the bottom of her feet, rising

rapidly up her body like the way the mercury shoots up a thermometer in a Bugs Bunny cartoon, and explodes out of the top of her head in a nimbus of perspiration.

                    JANETTE
                    Aw, Fuck!

She shakes her head, dispersing the halo of her sweat.

                    Aw, Fuck.
          (to Ronnie, who has stopped to observe their reunion)
                    Fuck.

She pulls the hoover up the corridor towards Ronnie, and takes the nozzle of the hoover and WHACKS Ronnie with it on the top of his skull. Ronnie yelps in fright at his big sister.

                    JANETTE
              (demanding of Ronnie)
          What the FUCK do you think you're DOIN?

                    RONNIE
          (pathetic, hardly even objecting to this
           mistreatment, perhaps nostalgic for the
           renewed attention of an elder sibling)
                    Hi …

                    JANETTE
          (beating at him with something of the repetitive
           determination and force shown by her late and
           unlamented great grandmother in chastising
           Janette's equally absent maternal figure)
                    Bringing him HERE?

                    HUNTER
          (trying to intervene, but hamstrung by the emotion that

he is experiencing in seeing her again, recognisably his own wee girl, recognisably her mother's daughter from the crown of her dark hair to her having to stand on her tiptoes like that to keep whacking at her brother) Janette ...

CUT TO:

9.3.1

INT. BIDE A WEE HOTEL – STAIRCASE – DAY

Lawrence is hiding on the stairs, listening to the commotion from above and round the corner. Mrs Lawrence appears below him, startling him.

MRS LAWRENCE
What's the MARRER with ye, Bob?

CUT TO:

9.3.1.1

INT. BIDE A WEE HOTEL – CORRIDOR – DAY

Janette, Ronnie and Hunter are now standing in a Mexican stand-off, the two male figures wary of the female at the triangle's apex who holds them off, pointing the nozzle of the hoover attachment like a gun, alternately covering them both as she retreats.

JANETTE
Keep the fuck away fae me!

HUNTER
I just want tae talk tae ye ...

Janette throws the hoover nozzle at Ronnie and runs.

Janette!
Pursuing, Hunter trips over Ronnie and the machine as Ronnie too starts forward. They go down together in a clattering tangle of limbs and cleaning equipment.

CUT TO:

9.3.1.2

Janette, pelting down the corridor. She runs into the solid figure of Mrs Lawrence, coming from the stairs out of shot.

MRS LAWRENCE
Here here here. Now, what's all this about?

JANETTE
(pointing back to where Hunter and Ronnie
are just rounding the corner behind her)
Get them oot ae here!

MRS LAWRENCE
Janette … That's your father … and
that's your little brother.

Ronnie and Hunter arrive.

JANETTE
(helpless now, anger spent, unprotected by its energy)
I know who they are … get them OOT …

MRS LAWRENCE
Janette! They're here for your birthday.

JANETTE
(hesitating slightly before saying)
It's not my …

HUNTER
(overlapping, interrupting her,
appealing to Mrs Lawrence)
Janette … I'm sorry …

Hearing that word, Janette is suddenly calm. Face red, tears
still in her eyes, but with a voice like an angry Goddess,
she echoes it.

JANETTE
"Sorry?"

As if he was hearing the word for the first time too, or as
if he were hearing it properly, Hunter acknowledges her
acknowledgement of his apology. He nods and hangs his
head. She considers him a moment, then speaks from the
depths of her experience, whatever that experience was,
but it wasn't good by the sound of it.

JANETTE
You've got nae idea.

Lawrence himself, still nervous, appears. The following
dialogue overlaps.

LAWRENCE
Mister Hunter … is it? I'm Bob Lawrence.

HUNTER
(to Janette, ignoring him, finding himself ambushed by
his own emotion, his own strength of feeling at what
he is coming to understand is the critical juncture

of his Quixotic enterprise of family reunion)
I want to make it up tae ye …

JANETTE
(to Mrs Lawrence)
I DON'T want to talk to these people …

LAWRENCE
(concurring entirely with the idea of
Janette and her bottom not communicating
with these interlopers in any way)
Mister Hunter …

HUNTER
(desperate, not even sure he can talk,
but knowing he must try)
Janette … just let me …

JANETTE
(to Hunter)
Please … Christ … can't ye hear me? Just leave.

LAWRENCE
Mister Hunter … if Janet doesn't want …

HUNTER
… fourteen years …

9.3.1.2.1

And he feels it. Suddenly. Cumulatively. All he lost. Every
dawn. Every endured day, every thankless, restless night.
He understands too, I think, dimly, that he has been
hiding all these years from the depth, from the reality, of
his own hurt. He has been wrapping himself in purpose as
a shield against the emptiness. He has been covering an

open wound. And now that the project of anticipation that had sustained him through those howling, vacuous years is actually at the point of fulfilment, it is also at the point of hazard. He had blinded himself to how bad his situation, their situation, really was. And now, in her eyes, he can see it. Right now, he sees too, it might all fall to pieces. The recognition of his danger, of just how much he now depends on this young woman who he scarcely knows ... strike that ... that he doesn't know at all ... is overwhelming. He had had a role for her all mapped out in his head, but now that he recognises her independence, he has also got to understand that at this moment he is entirely dependent on her, on whatever kindness or reason or sentiment she has in her for him, on whatever emotion she feels for him, on whatever love she can find or that he can earn from her. And that he has no way to know or influence anything about her. He is achingly projecting his love, of course, and his need, but he cannot anticipate her response. He does not know how to deserve her. He is entirely in her hands.

9.3.1.2.1.1

Would that all of us sometimes knew our helplessness in so clear a way. Would that all of us experienced our utter reliance on a love that we have no right to expect.

9.3.1.2.1.1.1

(Protestants — or the Elect Few, anyway — used to get that kind of love from God — Justified by Grace. I suppose some people still think they get it from their golden retrievers. Unconditional love appears to be one of those human needs that the world (which, as aforesaid, is only that which is the case) is not at all disposed to afford us. Which means we have to negotiate it from each other. Which causes all kinds of problems. But also affords us opportunities and the possibility of salvation, whether there's a God involved or not. In my opinion anyway.)

9.3.3

She looked at him then, Janette. And though I'd like to report that in that moment of her regard there was also understanding, or even forgiveness, there really wasn't to be honest. There wasn't even hatred or rejection. She was herself, I think, so wholly banjaxed as to be careless of her existential responsibilities, let alone the fact that she could with the slightest touch entirely change the direction of (at the very least!) three lives in this moment; that in this moment, the world was wet clay on her potter's wheel.

9.3.3.1

It is perhaps of significance that at this moment of her maximum agency, it was not Janette who by conscious choice selected her destiny, or Hunter who changed gear from his "find the kids" mode to the "make a family" mode of being and doing; it was actually what Mrs Lawrence then said (a figure of marginal importance to this narrative and one with, comparatively speaking, only a small stakeholding even in the moment I'm making such a fuss about), that proved to be decisive.

MRS LAWRENCE
Now, I've booked a table for the three
of you for lunch ... Our treat.

Everyone looks at her aghast.

JANETTE
What?

LAWRENCE
What?

RONNIE
What?

HUNTER
What?

MRS LAWRENCE
You can serve Janette today, Bob. I think a nice
family luncheon, round the table ... is just what
the doctor ordered. There's no better way to
celebrate a reunion. Or settle a family quarrel.

9.3.3.1.1

Of such banalities, despite the best efforts of philosophers,
does history consist.

9.3.1.2

JANETTE
I don't WANT to ...

LAWRENCE
(to his wife)
Dearest ...

MRS LAWRENCE
(definitively, to Lawrence, and to the warring Hunters)
Families are important.
(turning to Janette)
Now, Janette, if you still feel the same way
after lunch, I'm sure your father will be
reasonable. Won't you, Mister Hunter?

HUNTER
(understanding he's just been rescued from destruction)
Janette … just gie us a chance … I promise …
I'll leave … if ye want … if ye just …

MRS LAWRENCE
(to Janette)
Now, I think that's fair. Don't you?

She looks between them. Janette, trapped, dully certain of
further, future, unspecified unhappiness, lowers her eyes.

9.3.1.2.1

Satisfied, Mrs Lawrence, playing the matriarch she's never
been, speaks to Hunter and Ronnie.

MRS LAWRENCE
(looking at her watch)
Twenty minutes, then, in the dining room.
(to Janette)
You get changed love. Take the day off. Enjoy yourself.

Everything sorted, moved almost to tears at her own
wisdom, at *helping!* … Mrs Lawrence sails … nay, floats …
towards the stairs. Lawrence follows her.

LAWRENCE
Margaret?

MRS LAWRENCE
(turning on him, moved, her eyes damp)
What on EARTH'S the matter with you, Bob?

He is startled at her emotion, at her not having the first
clue what she thinks she's doing, at his not having the first

clue what she's crying about. Unencumbered therefore, she sweeps on. Mr Lawrence turns to see Janette running away upstairs to her room, and Hunter put his arm on Ronnie's shoulder to lead him back to theirs. Then he is alone.

LAWRENCE
(to the silence and emptiness)
Oh, bollocks.

He follows where his wife has gone.

CUT TO:

9.3.2

Hunter, Ronnie and Janette further up the corridor.

HUNTER
(to Janette)
We'll see ye doon the stair, then?

Janette, a hand covering her face, waves him away.

RONNIE
(to Janette)
Is the scran good? cos I'm fuckin starvin.

HUNTER
C'mon Ronnie.

RONNIE
I don' want nane ae yer garlic shite.

Hunter looks at Janette as he hustles Ronnie past her.

(to Hunter, as they go)
I'm tellin ye, she was fourteen, in a fuckin
kid's hame, and she goes VEDGIE!

They leave Janette, who, shaken, goes alone up the stairs.

CUT TO:

9.3.2.1

INT. JANETTE'S ROOM – SOME MOMENTS LATER

Janette reaches the little attic room that she repainted in
simple eggshell, with its lovely view of the loch. We see
a collection of framed photographs of her family, of her
father, of her mother, of Ronnie and herself. Like a shrine
on her dresser. She looks at her suitcase, already nearly
packed. She looks at a picture of herself on Hunter's
shoulders on the beach at Portrush a lifetime — a hundred
lifetimes — ago, and she dissolves in helpless tears.

9.4

Meanwhile, on the other side of the Ochils, another
multiply complex confrontation was taking place in the
police station in Callander, where Padraic Macreesh,
even having been coaxed off the roof and back into his
clothes, or at least into wrapping himself in a blanket,
was still steadfastly continuing to withhold his cooperation from the Black and Tans, and was no more inclined
to cooperate at the sight of Superintendent Bellamy
accompanied by Messrs Frank and Joseph Wheen
coming through the door of the cell to which he had
insisted on retreating.
    "No, no, no," he said, "you fuckers keep away from me!"
    Bellamy, bland leading the bland, was all emollience.

"Did he say where he was going, Patrick? You don't mind if I call you Patrick?"

"It's pronounced Poraig, ye ignorant, Scottish bastard … Keep away from me. I'm sick of the lot of ye."

Bellamy sat in the wooden chair opposite the little bunk bed where Mr Macreesh had huddled protectively, while Frank and Joe, floating like boxers, flanked him, saying nothing, promising much.

"You're identifying with your kidnapper, Poor Egg … that's the Stockholm syndrome, isn't it," Bellamy opined. "You're an educated man. You'd know about that kind of thing"

"Go and fuck yerself," yelped Padraic, with decreasing conviction and rising vehemence.

Bellamy, veteran of the soft terror of his trade, was in his element. He almost purred.

"You also know … as an officer of the court … that aiding and abetting an armed kidnapper … in this case, the kidnapper of a minor, is an extremely serious offence. Let alone a dereliction of your duty."

He said this with the forward-leaning, intimate generosity of giving the traumatised social worker a recipe for eggs Benedict.

A moment of frozen silence waxed a mask over Padraic's expression. He wanted to reply, "Get bent, filth," as might have been said by Ronnie Hunter or one of his other charges in similar circumstances, but Mr Macreesh was handicapped, in this instance of danger and immediacy, by his having an intelligent interest in the future that made him wary of giving into the total commitment to the present tense involved in the satisfaction of impulse.

It is this mediation of immediate desire by concern for consequences that is the mark of a civilised individual. It is also how the bastards get you. There are many positive aspects to decent inhibition. But it is, no matter what anyone says, one of the mightiest tools in the oppressor's box.

(If you have a mortgage and you want to have a pension, you don't kick a policeman in the face. Even though it's just THERE!)

"If and when we get him, Mr Macreesh, and we find out that you knew where he was going and that you didn't tell us, then whatever satisfaction you are deriving from your current irresponsible attitude will be short-lived. We are doing our best to look out for the child, Mr Macreesh, the child towards whom, till his sixteenth birthday next week, you owe a legal duty of care. We need to know what Tommy Hunter wants. We need to know what he's doing. Where he's going. You yourself can testify that he is an extremely dangerous man, so you would be doing no less than your duty as a human being, let alone as a social worker, to tell us everything he told you. Where is he going, Poor Egg? You need to tell us."

Macreesh looked at Bellamy, heard his tone of reasoned threat … and looked at the Wheen brothers, at Frank's desperate, miserable fear for his own security, and at Joe, with his plain relish for the sound of snapping bones and he felt his resistance dribble in shame between his thighs.

He knew these men. He knew them in his flesh, in his history and in his education. He knew the bullying nature of their nihilism, the terrible certainty of their narrowness. These men were the kind of men who ruled the world, ruled it from within the sociopathic limitations of having no imaginations. He knew their genetic lack of sympathy and ideological scorn of solidarity. He knew that they would kill Tommy Hunter if they could, and that they would kill him too without hesitation if they had to.

And they wore him down, of course. Such is the weariness of postmodern humanity that even the good-hearted, when faced with the apparent invincibility of evil, give way.

We know that death wins in the end. We know that for cosmologically certain now. So it is hardly surprising that death has its cheerleaders, and that those cheerleaders, those devotees of the common sense view of the inherent hopelessness of everything, seem so strong and persuasive to the rest of us a lot of the time. We think they might be right. So that even the best of us, and blameless Padraic Macreesh was surely one of the best, feel ourselves pre-defeated by the sullen drift of everything towards equilibrium without hope, towards the heat death of the bioverse, even as the worst of us feel emboldened by the same physics to get away with the most unpardonable shit imaginable. We are all signatories, after all, to the same murder-suicide pact with nature. And there are some among us, the worst and most fearful and most powerful of us, who ache to accelerate the worst possible outcomes in the meantime.

In resistance to them, we can only assert that while it is undeniably true that darkness and decay and the red death shall in the end hold illimitable dominion over all, there is no need to abandon all memory to death's share price in the meantime. The meaning and value of life lies precisely in its resistance to the inevitability of extinction. The uncertainty, unlikeliness and contingency of living richly here and now is life's beauty and its joy and its only defensible purpose.

But we must forgive each other too ... that's the hard thing. Forgive each other for sometimes betraying our weakness even while accepting that our weakness made us do it. We must forgive Mr Macreesh. It is a lot harder to be joyful and beautiful when you are staring at the wrong end of a senior policeman accompanied by his two confederate gangsters ... let alone a policeman that you confidently believe to be a big, bent, Presbyterian bastard who'd set fire to you as soon as look at you, you poor, liberal, bog-trotting Fenian twat.

9.4.1.1

Which is why, at exactly the time Mr Lawrence served the overcooked venison sausages to Ronnie, Janette and Tommy Hunter (see 9.5.2.3.2.1), Mr Macreesh told Mr Bellamy and Messrs Wheen exactly where they were, and felt his heart sinking in shame. They were on their way out of the room, the three of them, when Bellamy's phone rang.

9.4.1.2

DS Boyle, having stood for a moment in Jack Webster's vacated room, looked at the blood on the walls, the blood soaked into the bed and the carpet, and having taken in the room being empty of any further trace of habitation, though its walls fairly screamed the dreadfulness of what had happened there, having sent Maggie downstairs to use the car radio to get the Glasgow polis here to close off the crime scene, was on the phone. He called his boss to tell him that Jack Webster, who had done time with Joseph Wheen and who was suspected of taking part in the original robbery with the Wheens and Tommy Hunter four-teen years ago, was likely dead and definitely disappeared.

Bellamy, answering his phone when in the same room as Padraic and the Wheens, allowed no sign to appear in his voice or face that he was being told anything very inter-esting. But everything was changed by this news. It is my belief that Bellamy, as he looked at Joseph Wheen's angry, stupid mug and Frank's anxious, cunning one, already knew who he should be asking about Jack Webster, had he been inclined to ask anyone.

And just like that, he wrote them off, the Wheen broth-ers. He dismissed them from his future plans. They'd gone too far. He wasn't going to even try to protect them any more. They joined the ranks of ordinary mortals from whom a man in a position of responsibility keeps secrets.

It took all of his political skill for none of this to register in his face as he looked at the sweat on Frank's upper lip. And the baboon smirk on Joseph's puss.

"I'll get back to you, Danny," is all he said.

CUT TO:

9.5

Darkness. Exhausted, deep unconsciousness.
RONNIE (V.O.)

Dad!

CUT TO:

9.5.1

INT. BIDE A WEE HOTEL – BEDROOM – DAY

Hunter awakes, his eyes opening from his dream. He is lying on the bed. Ronnie is sitting beside him. They are handcuffed together.

RONNIE
I'm starvin.

Hunter sits up, knowing that his deep sleep the moment before and his anxiety now betoken that his quest has reached its pivot.

CUT TO:

9.5.2

To a thunder of pipes and drums, the Hunter family sat for lunch in the Rob Roy Room. Ronnie and Hunter arrived first, as inconspicuous in these chintzy surroundings, as Raymond Chandler once put it, as tarantulas on a piece of angel cake. More florid than ever, Mrs Lawrence bustled about them with talk of specials and the soup of the day. Hunter looked strangulated by the sitting still. Mrs Lawrence was all sympathy at his red face. She had clearly decided it was her duty as a Christian, and as a fan of daytime television, to bring together the dysfunctional in a controlled setting, unconsciously trusting that the fact they were in public, and together for something as comforting and familiar as a family meal, would moderate any extremities of behaviour. She wasn't to know that "a family meal" was as familiar to these people as the arachnid and the baked goods aforementioned.

Janette arrived soon after, looking, if anything, and despite her comparative familiarity with the environment, even more ill at ease than her father. The look that passed between them was so full of regret and guilt and fear as well, on his part, of yearning, that it would have taken a heart of stone not to be moved. Mrs Lawrence heaved a sob. Ronnie looked out of the window.

Outside, Ronnie could see a camper van pulling up painted with symbols of the Dakota and Lakota tribes. In it, at the wheel and in the passenger seat, appeared to be two old white men dressed as Red Indians in full buckskins, warpaint and feathers. He turned back to his father and sister to tell them … so that he didn't see Denise, the hitchhiker, get out of the back of the van. Wearing warpaint too, as it happens.

"There's fucking INDIANS out there," he said, but they ignored him. They were deep in silent negotiation with each other. Ronnie looked out of the window again.

What was it about the country, Ronnie wondered incoherently, that made the cunts in it go balmy?

9.5.2.1

Why people do the things they do has of course been the subject of every philosophical speculation from the analects of Confucius to the structuralism of Claude Lévi-Strauss and every treatise of every kind between. Since the beginning of recorded thought, the primary theme of culture has always been "Did you see that? That was batshit crazy! Why on earth did they do that?" The nature of human knowledge can be attested by the fact that although this question has been comprehensively answered again and again and again, still, every day, we are taken entirely by surprise by someone doing something new that's so batshit crazy that we say to ourselves and to each other: "Did you see that? Why in the world did she do a thing like that?"

9.5.2.1.1

Why, on such short reacquaintance with her rediscovered parent, did Janette agree to go on holiday with him and her frankly unappealing younger brother?

That she left the hotel where she worked immediately after the unlikely family meal arranged by her employers, Mr and Mrs Lawrence, is a matter of record. That she made this decision in the midst of a hail of tears, screaming and gunfire is, I contend, incidental. The immediate circumstances of her departure (see 9.6.4.1.3.1) do not constitute, in my view, sufficient explanation of her decision.

Indeed, the mysterious thought processes of Janette Hunter, who, of the whole family, was surely the one who came closest to what we call "happy", may well provide the essential test case for the relevance of this entire undertaking. If this narrative can accommodate both the extremity of a Tommy Hunter and the competence of a Janette, then it may have gone some way towards things unattempted yet in song or rhyme, and justify the ways of things to folk.

9.5.2.2

Hunter, still our main subject of enquiry despite the contrary fascinations of his daughter's motivations, was of course compromised in his erstwhile decisiveness precisely because he had now achieved almost all, or two-thirds anyway, of what he had set out to do. He was now unarguably on holiday with his children. That he had achieved this by means of kidnap and deception was incidental. A good percentage of his dream, long held, had now come true. That he was yet to translate his energy and focus from the instrumentalism of the search to the emotional register of what he was supposed to do now that he'd found sixty-six per cent of what he was looking for, is understandable, predictable and even forgivable.

His immediate problem now was that Ronnie, although a stranger to him in matters of personal detail, was of a type and genre of individual with which he was familiar from the slammer and from his own past. Janette, on the other hand, a capable and self-organising young woman at ease in social and work situations, was most decidedly a horse of a different colour.

When dealing with his daughter, Tommy was not in Kansas any more.

When Hunter looked at Janette as she sat down with him and Ronnie in the Rob Roy lounge, he saw her mother in her. You bet he did. He saw Janice's wit, her quick intelligence, her sharp temper, and felt her flashing blade of interrogation. But he also saw, I think, something else. That if Ronnie belonged to the world only in so far as even his uncontrolled behaviour was exactly what was expected of him, and if even Hunter, as a criminal lunatic, was only anomalous and disturbing until he could be locked up or otherwise violently disposed of, Janette seemed to belong to the world in the way that we are all theoretically supposed to, but in fact, that very few of us do. She was relatively at home in it. That is, she looked at the world not necessarily as a friendly environment, but one where she felt equipped and confident to make the best of it.

(That we regard sanity and competence of this order as in any way normal is more of a testament to our need of wish fulfilment than it is to our powers of observation.)

Hunter, meanwhile, didn't know what to say to her. He didn't know what to do. He felt tears of regret, of horror at himself, of relief and joy at once, stabbing at the back of his throat. He knew how desperately he needed to tell her things, but he couldn't speak. So he didn't say anything. Ronnie wasn't much for conversation anyway, and Janette was too tangled up in her own angry and guilty complexities to simplify matter with either small talk or profundity

9.5.2.3

MRS LAWRENCE
Leek and potato soup to start?

There was a heavy silence at the innocent question. And now, for reasons she didn't yet recognise or acknowledge, even to herself, Janette took over and managed the immediate crisis.

JANETTE
No thanks, Mrs Lawrence ... we'll just have two venison sausages and mash and one vegetarian. Thanks.

9.5.2.3.1

The preliminaries of ordering over with, they were now

left exposed to the silence, to the fourteen and a half years of silence between them.

9.5.2.3.1.1

Again it was Janette who, having spoken once, now found herself feeling obliged, unaccountably, to make this family occasion "work", "go smoothly" and such. She was frankly annoyed at putting this expectation on herself, and wondered whether it was her minimal social conditioning and/or her biological destiny and/or an unworthy access of nostalgia for a past that had never been, that prompted her to give a flying fuck as to how well her "men" behaved in public.

Somebody had to say something, was as far as she got at the minute. Would we could all get that far so fast!

9.5.2.3.1.1.1

She was sitting in her place of employment too, of course, that had to be a factor in her wanting to manage the situation, and she felt again a certain surprisingly conventional sense of duty of showing her family her workplace to advantage, or at least towards compensating for its flaws. Though only nineteen, Janette had been consistently employed in the catering industry since leaving school. So she knew what was good about the Bide a Wee Hotel … (its location) … and what wasn't … (everything else) … perfectly well. It had been a stop on her journey, that was all … a journey which one day, she hoped, would lead to her running places a damn sight more substantial than this … and glory be to God, without the medley of Victorian tartan tripe that assailed the eyes and ears still all too frequently in places of this kind.

"Did you come far this morning?" she heard herself ask, as if Ronnie and her father were customers she hadn't met before, which, of course, to all intents and purposes, they were and she hadn't, so it wasn't really such a stupid thing to say as it sounded in her ears as soon as she'd said it.

"We left early," said Hunter, equally incongruent, employing that understatement he had the habit of employing that I told you about (see 1.3.2.1.1.1).

"He fuckin kidnapped me!" repeated Ronnie. It was a tribute to how low was the regard his sister held him in, that, once again, she entirely ignored and discounted this both truthful and useful information.

It was at this point that Mr Lawrence appeared with the sausages.

9.5.2.3.2.1

LAWRENCE
Smoked venison sausages … from our
local smokery. World-famous.

HUNTER
Thanks, thank you.

9.5.2.3.2.2

Lawrence wobbles out, nervously. Occasionally through-out the following, we must imagine him sneaking a look at them from the kitchen. Hunter didn't see that. Hunter just looked at Janette, who, being a clever and to-the-point sort, then asked the apparently simple question to which there is never a simple or comprehensive or even reliable answer.

9.5.3

"What do you want, Dad?"

9.5.3.1

Hunter handed her the white envelope he'd been clutching since before they sat down.

> HUNTER
> Happy Birthday.

> JANETTE
> It's not my birthday.

"I'm making up," he said, which was true in so many ways.

9.5.3.1.1

She sighs. She opens the envelope. She sees the two thousand pounds inside, then drops it, horrified and insulted, on the table. Some of the money falls out where Ronnie can see it too.

> HUNTER
> It's a lot of birthdays.

Ronnie stares at the money

> JANETTE
> (she shoves it across the table at him)
> I don't want it.

> RONNIE
> It's nearly MA birthday. I've had a
> lot of fucking birthdays.

Janette glares at him. She hardens in her resistance at the sight of her father's hurt. Damn right this should hurt, she thinks. And doesn't touch her dinner.

9.5.3.2

Now, this refusal must have been, for Hunter, potentially catastrophic. The future on which he had entirely constructed a good deal of his past hinged upon the simple enough — you would have thought — contingency of his being of help and comfort to his children in the future. It had been going not badly with Ronnie, all things considered. But the firmness and apparent equanimity with which Janette had just rejected the money, and thus rejected him, might have been terminal to his hopes. Small wonder he changed the subject, or at least decided to approach the possibility of pursuing his project of familial rapprochement by an alternative sentimental avenue. Her eyes flashed, ready for him.

9.5.2.1

HUNTER
D'ye remember much about yer mother, Janette?

JANETTE
(deliberately, her eyes clear, her voice fighting for calm)
I remember the two of ye screamin aw the
time. I remember you gaun aff yer hied when
she left ye wance when I was about three and
you breakin everything in the house.
(she turns to Ronnie, who is snarfing down his potato)
I remember feedin him out the fridge till the food ran out.

HUNTER
Janette ...

RONNIE
(indicates the money, then to Janette,
through a mouthful of mash)
Seriously, can I get it?

9.5.2.1.1

Hunter and his daughter look at each other now, and look
inward at the same time, reflected one in the other. And
she finds herself the stronger of the two.

JANETTE
I remember you comin hame just after that. I can see it.

He knows what she means. But he has never, till this
moment, seen himself fully as he was that night through
another's eyes. The experience is shocking.

HUNTER
What?

JANETTE
Blood. Blood all over ye.

9.5.2.1.2

Hunter looks down. He can feel tidal floods inside him,
like he'd been injected with something radioactive before
going into a CAT scan. It feels like he's wetting himself,
it feels like her vision of him is going right inside of him,
washing him, cleaning his blood, maybe killing him.

RONNIE
(through a sausage)
Mum's blood. Right? Was it Mum's blood?

9.5.3

And Tommy Hunter, whose force of will had carried him through a Sahara of lonely pain and had over-come his emotional inarticulacy by the sheer force of his unquestioning energy, was then in a place he had never dreamed of being. He was at his moment of ful-filment of his lonely dreaming and at the nadir of his loneliness. His dream had come true, and he now found that exactly those qualities that had sustained him for so long in his solitary hell unfitted him entirely for his suc-cess as a reuniter of the scintillae of his family. He could see that, however estranged, Ronnie and Janette shared not only a history, a history of unguessed at and probably awful detail ... but a present. The two of them were of a kind and that kind did not include him. They thought he'd killed their mother.

He found himself feeling more helpless and less capable than he had felt since that afternoon when in the exter-minating van he had succumbed to the Wheen brothers' admonitions, and had brought himself to this solitude, a solitude that had served him, that had enabled his sur-vival, but that now seemed more of an affliction than at any time before. He had been living alone in hell till Ronnie and Janette had dropped in, passing through, and had reminded him of where he was by making him aware again of the heaven he had lost, that he had turned his back on. And he knew pain then, Tommy did, in a way he'd forgotten he could feel it.

9.5.3.1

The prickling at the back of his eyes pushed past them. Tears, hot and humiliating, fell. He gasped in shock at himself. He hadn't cried since childhood, the penalty, in the circumstances in which he had been raised, had been swift and punishing for such transgression. All too suddenly he knew now that the real reason that boys don't cry is not the offence of tears against masculinity, but rather that the tears of another remind us of our own pain. They fill us with the terrible fear that if one of us breaks down and admits the true horror of living, the true helplessness of it, then the rest of us will be forced to look at it too. To hate someone else crying comes from fear of our starting to cry too. I wish we found strength in weeping together for our shared weakness, but we don't. Not nearly enough, anyway.

9.5.3.2

Tommy Hunter wept in front of his children now, and predictably, as they had been raised to, they despised him for it.

CUT TO:

9.5.4

EXT. BIDE A WEE HOTEL – BACKYARD – DAY

Lawrence is sweating as he saws down the barrels on a shotgun. Mrs Lawrence comes out with a cup of tea.

> MRS LAWRENCE
> (handing him the tea)
> Now what do you say?

> LAWRENCE
> Thank you very much.

> MRS LAWRENCE
> It seems a terrible shame to do that t' that gun.

LAWRENCE
Better safe than sorry, Margaret, if
we're going to get proverbial.

He keeps working.

CUT TO:

9.5.5

INT. BIDE A WEE HOTEL – DINING ROOM – DAY

Hunter has now dissolved into great gulping sobs, his body heaving with the effort of releasing all that regret and self-pity from whatever chamber of the heart in which he'd been hiding it.

HUNTER
(howls)
I love her.

RONNIE
Gonnae shut up, Dad.

Ronnie looks to Janette for help.

Gonnae make him shut up?

HUNTER
I'd never hurt yer MA!

He still sobs.

RONNIE
Shut up, will ye!

JANETTE
(fiercely)
I don't care. Cry all ye want tae.

HUNTER
Believe me.

JANETTE
I don't CARE.

9.5.5.1

"I don't care if ye got raped in the showers," she might have
said to him; "I don't care if you were on drugs and fuckin
suicide watch," cos I was there TOO. "I was banged up fer
something YOU did … and noo yer oot? And yer greetin
at me? So fuckin whit? Am I supposed tae light a fuckin
firework? I've got a job, I've got a PLACE here. It's MINES,
it's got nothin tae do wi you or my MAW, wherever the hell
she is. I don't care if ye buried her or not. Ye buried me."

9.5.2

Hunter, recovering, sniffing, puts the envelope and the
money back in his jacket pocket. Ronnie's face falls.
Hunter takes out the postcard and puts it on the table.
Janette stares at it. Elsewhere, out of his vision, Mrs
Lawrence anxiously looks around the doorjamb. This is
not going according to the daytime television plan.

9.6

HUNTER
She sent me a postcard.

Janette stares at the card, she blinks.

Yer mother. She sent me this, while I was in prison.
(he takes her hand)
Janette, yer mum's alive and she's
waitin for us ... here. Look.

The blood drains from Janette's face. Time stops.

9.6.1

Suddenly Janette bats the card out of Hunter's hand. It falls to the floor.

HUNTER
(in supplication)
Come with me. Come with us ... We'll find her. Together.

JANETTE
(distraught for reasons we don't know yet)
Get up ... stand up ...

HUNTER
Come wi us.

We hear the lobby phone ringing. It continues throughout:

9.6.1.1

Lawrence approaches the table and picks up the card from the floor. He tries to pretend that what is going on in front of him doesn't really terrify him. He looks at the card.

LAWRENCE
Calgary Bay ... that's on the Isle of
Mull. Lovely spot, that is.

(he looks at them, Ronnie chewing and dribbling, Janette and Hunter looking down, hollow with pain, not eating)
Everything all right, is it?
Hunter stands, holding his napkin. He snatches the card from Lawrence.

HUNTER
(still shaken and tearful)
No. It's not all right. I was in Peterheid and the scran was better than this. Yer sausages taste like shite.

LAWRENCE
I beg your pardon.

HUNTER
Like turds fae a donkey's arse.

Phone bell continues.

CUT TO:

9.6.2

INT. BIDE A WEE HOTEL – LOBBY – DAY

Mrs Lawrence answers the phone in the lobby.

MRS LAWRENCE
Bide a Wee Hotel ...
(she listens)
Police? Tommy Hunter? Yes ... Mister Hunter's here ...

CUT TO:

9.6.2.1

INT. BIDE A WEE HOTEL – DINING ROOM – DAY

Hunter looks at his children.

> HUNTER
> (to the kids)
> 'Scuse me.

Janette watches him go, with Lawrence at his heels. Ronnie takes a bit of sausage from Hunter's plate and puts it in his mouth surreptitiously.

CUT TO:

9.6.2.2

> MRS LAWRENCE
> (on the phone)
> Yes, he is here, he arrived today …

Hunter walks past her into the lobby. Lawrence is following.

> LAWRENCE
> Where are you going, Mister Hunter?

He catches up and gets between Hunter and the door.

> HUNTER
> I just need a breath a air.

> MRS LAWRENCE
> (watching this, on the phone)
> I think you'd better speak to my husband.

> (to Lawrence)
> That's the phone, Bob.

LAWRENCE
I think it's quite clear that you're not
welcome here, Mister Hunter.

MRS LAWRENCE
Bob …

LAWRENCE
I think you should leave now. Before
we have any more fuss.

MRS LAWRENCE
BOB!
(mouthing silently)
It's important.

Lawrence turns to his wife, and Hunter walks through the
front door.

LAWRENCE
What is it?

MRS LAWRENCE
(mouthing silently)
It's the police …

She holds out the phone. He takes it gingerly.

LAWRENCE
Hello …

CUT TO:

9.6.2.2.1

EXT. BIDE A WEE HOTEL – DAY

Hunter emerges from the hotel, feeling faint, taking great gulps of air. He looks over at a group of hippy types and Indians climbing into a van. He recognises Denise between two middle-aged men in buckskins and full war regalia. Something like recognition penetrates his fog of upset for a moment before dissipating as the Sioux drive off to whatever destination. He watches them drive away, thinking what to do himself, touched by something, he doesn't know what it is yet.

(see 13.0)

CUT TO:

9.6.2.2.2

INT. BIDE A WEE HOTEL – LOBBY – DAY

Lawrence is on the phone.

> LAWRENCE
> What am I supposed to do about it?

CUT TO:

9.6.2.2.2.1

INT. CALLANDER POLICE
STATION – OFFICE – DAY

We see Macreesh, still wrapped in a blanket, on a bench, now in the front office. On the phone is Superintendent Bellamy.

BELLAMY
Mister Lawrence, if Tommy Hunter is
there, we'd like you to try and keep him
there until we can get a team to you.

CUT TO:

9.6.2.2.2.1.1

INT. BIDE A WEE HOTEL – LOBBY – DAY

Lawrence is on the phone.

LAWRENCE
Keep him here?

CUT TO:

9.6.2.2.2.1.2

INT. POLICE STATION – OFFICE – DAY

Bellamy is on the phone. Frank and Joe look on, tense,
waiting for the off. Macreesh sneezes.

BELLAMY
Yes. If you can. We should have somebody
with you in about twenty minutes.

CUT TO:

9.6.3

INT. BIDE A WEE HOTEL – LOBBY – DAY

Lawrence on the phone makes no reply to Bellamy. He

looks through the front door to see Hunter pacing. He puts the phone down.

CUT TO:

9.6.3.1

INT. POLICE STATION – OFFICE – DAY

FRANK
If they take him alive, we talk to him
first. Is that understood?

BELLAMY
Oh, there's nothing to be understood, Mr Wheen.
Frank's eyes narrow, suspicious. He doesn't trust this cunt any more than anyone in this room can trust anyone in this room. Joe laughs unaccountably. Macreesh farts quietly.

CUT TO:

9.6.4

INT. BIDE A WEE HOTEL – DINING ROOM – DAY

Ronnie and Janette argue at the table.

RONNIE
God, I am starvin … can't I just EAT?

JANETTE
No …

RONNIE
Just a ROLL …

JANETTE
Shut it, Ronnie.

CUT TO:

9.6.4.1

EXT. BIDE A WEE HOTEL – DAY

Hunter walks up and down, muttering to himself.

CUT TO:

9.6.4.1.1

INT. LOBBY – DAY

Mrs Lawrence has joined her husband. She is putting the newly sawed-off shotgun behind the counter like we were in Wyoming or somewhere.

MRS LAWRENCE
We could make the room complimentary.
Maybe he likes fishing, he could have the boat.
I think you should go and talk to him.

He stares at her. This day, which started as badly as he imagined a day could, is getting unbelievably worse by the minute.

CUT TO:

9.6.4.1.2

INT. BIDE A WEE HOTEL – DINING ROOM – DAY

                        RONNIE
He came efter us wi a GUN ... he stuck ma
social worker in the BOOT ae the MOTOR.
What was ah supposed tae do?

                        JANETTE
Ye mean ... he kidnapped ye?

                        RONNIE
                     (exasperated)
                        Aye!

                        JANETTE
Jesus CHRIST!

She stands up and heads straight for the exit.

                        RONNIE
Where ye gaun noo?

She storms off. Ronnie fills his napkin with sausages.

                        CUT TO:

                        9.6.4.1.3

              EXT. BIDE A WEE HOTEL – DAY

Hunter breathes the air. He looks at the car ... he could just
leave. He could just leave the kids. Get out of all this com-
plication and emotion. Maybe he should. Would they miss
him? Surely not. He could just leave them some money
and go. Maybe everyone would be better off? Maybe he'd
be better off. He certainly wouldn't feel as challenged as
he feels now. Maybe he'd even be better back in prison,
knowing what's going to happen every day.

In his own brown study, Mr Lawrence approaches him, no longer telling him to leave but all solicitous, working very hard for some reason to get him to stay.

Hunter stares at him, impatient to either get back to his kids or go. He wishes everyone would make up their minds so he didn't have to.

CUT TO:

9.6.4.1.3.1

INT. BIDE A WEE HOTEL – LOBBY – DAY
Janette storms through the lobby.

> JANETTE
> (to Mrs Lawrence)
> Is my Dad out here?

Mrs Lawrence doesn't answer, and Janette doesn't wait. She goes out of the front door.

> MRS LAWRENCE
> (calling after her)
> Janette …

As Janette exits, Ronnie comes into the lobby, with his napkin folded like a bag.

> RONNIE
> (to Mrs Lawrence)
> Hiya.

He heads to the exit. Mrs Lawrence picks up the shotgun.

CUT TO:

EXT. BIDE A WEE HOTEL – DAY

A moment earlier. Lawrence talks to Hunter.

> **LAWRENCE**
> I was just going to say I was very sorry about the sausages ... and if there's anything else you would like off the menu, please, take it with our compliments.

Janette comes out of the front of the hotel.

> **JANETTE**
> (furious)
> What's goin on?

> **LAWRENCE**
> We're very fond of Janet here, Mister Hunter.

> **HUNTER**
> (to Janette)
> What?

> **JANETTE**
> Mister Lawrence!

> **LAWRENCE**
> (panicking)
> I didn't do anything wrong.

> **HUNTER**
> What?

> **LAWRENCE**
> (turns to her as she arrives)
> Janette ...

Mr Lawrence looks between them.

I've done nothin I'm ashamed of. I'm not ashamed.

                    HUNTER
            (alarm slowly dawning in him)
                    What?

                    LAWRENCE
                 It was nothing.

                    HUNTER
              What was nothing?

                    JANETTE
            (realising, hands over eyes)
                 Aw Jesus ...
                (to Lawrence)
      You've never said anythin to him, have ye?

                    HUNTER
      (eyes narrowing dangerously, his past feckless
      wish to run away from his family responsibilities
      now subsumed by a growing apprehension of his
      daughter being of an age of sexual activity, and
      this weird wee bloke with his weird wee wife ...
                    Said whit?

There is the sudden blast of a shotgun from indoors.
Janette and Lawrence freeze. Hunter starts to run towards
the door but Lawrence hurls himself at him with a despair-
ing cry which ends up in a sort of rugby tackle. The two
of them crash to the gravel and scuffle ... Mrs Lawrence
appears in the doorway with the smoking gun in her hand.

MRS LAWRENCE
(to Hunter, less posh)
Stop it. Gerrawayfrumim!

Then Ronnie emerges from behind her and punches her in the back of the head. She goes down like a stalk of wet broccoli. Ronnie shakes his sore hand.

RONNIE
It was only a fuckin sausage. She
tried tae fuckin SHOOT me.

Hunter goes for the shotgun. But Lawrence is only interested in his wife. Bless him.

LAWRENCE
Margaret …

HUNTER
Get the money, Ronnie.

Ronnie scampers back indoors.

(to Janette)
Get yer stuff. Get in that motor.

JANETTE
Tae hell. No way.

HUNTER
I don't think you're workin here.

JANETTE
I fuckin LIVE here!

She looks over to where Mrs Lawrence is coming to.

Lawrence is with her. Hunter grabs Janette.

> HUNTER
> Were you SHAGGIN him?

> JANETTE
> (hesitant)
> No … no …

Hunter turns to stare at Lawrence. He starts to move towards him.

> (grabbing Hunter)
> No, Jesus, leave him alone … all right.

Hunter pulls away from her. She makes an extraordinary decision.

> I said all right. I'll be as quick as I can …

She runs inside. Hunter goes over to Lawrence who is desperate by now that his guests should be gone.

> LAWRENCE
> The police are coming!

> HUNTER
> The police?

> LAWRENCE
> They were just on the phone. They'll be here
> in twenty minutes. Take the old road …

Janette and Ronnie emerge together. She carries a suitcase, Ronnie has the carpet bag.

HUNTER
Give me that.

Hunter takes the bag from the reluctant Ronnie, and
draws his pistol from it.

JANETTE
Dad …

HUNTER
(his voice is clipped, as an outraged
proper parent suddenly)
Get in that car, my girl. I'll deal with you later.
(Hunter crosses to Lawrence.)
You been shagging my wee lassie, Mister Lawrence?

JANETTE
(having followed)
Christ … NO!

Lawrence sees the gun, howls and collapses to the ground
beside his wife.

He never touched me. Honest tae
CHRIST he never TOUCHED me.

HUNTER
Are you telling me the truth, young lady?

JANETTE
Yes … yes … I am …
(dragging Hunter away)
Will you get in the fuckin CAR?

HUNTER
(tutting like a hen)

In the name of the wee man!

He tosses an envelope onto the ground beside the Lawrences who, swear to God, are NEVER going to recover from this.

That's twenty quid for the sausages.
They were okay, actually.

He turns for the car, keeping the few onlookers who are gathering covered. He gets to the car and finds Ronnie, holding the gun and the carpet bag, in the driver's seat.

RONNIE
Can I drive?

HUNTER
Get tae fuck over there.

Janette gets in the back as Hunter gets in the front.

9.7

£24,587.04

FADE TO BLACK.

10.0

As indicated earlier, all the stories about Tommy Hunter turn out to be true: even when they can't all be accurate or verified as such, or even logically consistent.

10.0.1

By way of example, there are multiply attested sightings of the Hunter family that Thursday afternoon as they enjoyed their brief Highland vacation which simply cannot all be "true", for reasons of time and relative geography, but each of which may as well be, poetically and thematically speaking.

10.0.1.1

Mr Arnold McHugh of Birnam will swear blind to this day, if anyone should ask him, that he it was who accepted a reconditioned vintage racing green Jaguar off a suited, gravel-voiced man and his two sullen teenagers in exchange for the 1986 Hiace Camper van he'd advertised by means of a cardboard sign in his driveway on the afternoon in question. He has attested further that this had been a private transaction between consenting economic agents and was therefore, in and of itself, no concern of the authorities. (He had been delighted, of course, thinking he'd got a hell of a bargain!) The credibility of Mr McHugh's account of the change of vehicles in this informal manner lies in that by some means or another, Hunter did indeed "lose the motor" as he may have put it, and thereby threw the Wheens and the Busies off the trail for long enough for the events which we now know to have happened later on (which were publicly known to have involved a Hiace van) to have actually happened.

10.0.1.2

The car the authorities and their associated gangsters were still looking for hours later was described by Mr Lawrence in his statement to the Pitlochry constabulary at 1.45 p.m. when they arrived at Kinloch Rannoch. Mr Lawrence's memory was later exactly matched to the description of a car reported stolen in Bishopbriggs a week or so before-hand ... and the registration number that Mr Lawrence, even in extremis, had remembered so exactly, was in fact a dummy that had been originally assigned by the DVLA to a Ford Transit van written off four years before that. This was indeed the same car that turned up for sale through the next week's issue of *What Car?* as advertised by Mr McHugh, who was later unsuccessfully prosecuted as a receiver of stolen goods by the said Busies in an act of petty attempted vengeance at their renewed humiliation. Mr McHugh successfully defended the case but lost the car and was never compensated for the van, which he will tell you about at inescapable length no matter how soon you have to catch your train.

10.0.1.2.1

So it would seem that Mr McHugh was indeed the source of the almost parodically family-friendly transportation that evaded detection for a vital further twenty-four hours before the powers that be put two and two and two together and came up with the Ossian's Viewpoint Estate Incident as being the next properly verified sighting of Tommy Hunter and his offspring (see 12.4.2.2).

On the other hand, Lothar Wendt and Matthias Erzberger, a recently happily married couple of Scotophile Schweitzers who had purchased a holiday retreat in Fortingall, also testified quite compellingly the following Monday (once all this had been on the telly over the weekend), that they had been approached on foot by a man and his two teenaged children at 1.40 in the afternoon that Thursday, when they had just parked *their* right-hand-drive Hiace van in Glen Lyon (in the car park of the forestry commission hillside walk to Bridge of Balgie — which can be thoroughly recommended not only on the grounds of the scenery and historic interests of the Campbells' Eastern Glen, but also for the cardiovascular benefits of the short but steep excursion from that car park through the forest and on to the hillside, and for the cholesterol-laden cream tea awaiting the rewarding of sweat and virtue in the Bridge of Balgie cafe after).

Lothar and Matthias both spoke excellent English when they made their statement to DS Boyle, but confessed to having been baffled by the sub-Gaelic patois of the stone-faced man they had encountered, let alone whatever tongue was spoken by his unnervingly Goblin-like, skipping son and his apologetic daughter, who translated for them, being used to tourists, that what the gruff-voiced man wanted from them was to hire their van for a couple of days and here was five hundred pounds in a white envelope for their trouble.

10.0.1.3.1

However, despite circumstantial details of their account tending to corroborate their story, their being visibly both foreign and homosexual meant that their account was dismissed by the puritanical and parochial DS Boyle. Maggie

232

Singleton opined to him (in order to shore up his prejudice with something like a rationale) that maybe Lothar and Matthias had simply read about Tommy Hunter in the papers and wanted to join in with the Jacobite romance of his flight from the redcoats. To confirm her suspicion of their enthusiasm, they were found to have the translated, collected works of Sir Walter Scott in their possession (in a rather nice nineteenth-century German edition) and were later bound over to keep the peace in the same spirit of petty resentment that initiated the unsuccessful attempt to prosecute Mr McHugh.

10.0.1.4

Then there is also the later discovery of a burnt-out Hiace van (the same type of van that was testified to have broken through the security cordon at the Ossian View site very early the next morning). It was found abandoned in the similarly burnt-out remains of the Indian Encampment. This was felt to be a very satisfying result. Except that the scorched number plate in fact proved that THIS wee camper had been reported lifted from the Landmark Forest Adventure Park near Aviemore that Thursday afternoon.

10.0.1.4.1

There were, of course, several dozen vehicles belonging to the Ossian View encampment found abandoned that weekend after the battle that ended the occupation, so there was nothing more than circumstantial evidence to tie this burnt-out van specifically to the Hunters.

10.0.1.4.2

Further potential circumstantial corroboration that this *may* however have been their vehicle temporarily, is that

Ronnie may well have remembered and remarked that "Landmark" was actually a place he had been to before on one of Mr Macreesh's Away Days ... an "away weekend", in fact ... where Ronnie, then nine years old, had been one of a group of waifs taken up north for some free air and self-expression back in those prerecession days of social liberalism, when it was believed that preventative redemption of underclass juveniles might be effected by introducing them to the outdoor pursuits of their distant social superiors, on the theory that giving the unwanted offspring of the lumpenproletariat a bit of the skiing and snowboarding and tobogganing on Cairngorm enjoyed by lads from public schools might result in a bit of that rugged, tweedy character-building rubbing off on their ill-clad personalities.

Included in this trip, there had been a morning of diving on and off the treeline platforms and water slides of the park. "We fucking wrecked the joint," Ronnie could have happily recalled. This may have prompted his father to sanction a return visit in the spirit of holiday-making where novelty and nostalgia can sometimes so happily congeal. One can also picture Hunter himself, in his suit, making a giddy goat of himself, whooping and laughing and turning the air blue as he enjoyed, for once, physical thrills that were of no harm or threat of harm to himself or anyone else. One can see Janette, in a newly adult, vaguely uneasy posture as she stood and watched this strange man and her young brother, seeing how Ronnie had actually become young for maybe the first time she could remember, finding the boy in himself in the presence of the older man.

10.0.1.4.3

And what did Janette find herself feeling (if this touching family scene ever, in fact, took place) is the intriguing question? This young woman who had endured abuse and boredom, neglect and very occasional disinterested encouragement from one sadly short-lived substitute teacher; this girl, almost a child herself still, who had essentially schooled herself in the box making skills of dividing her experience into discreet, watertight compartments, with the tiniest allowance of space for hope that one day she would be someone, that she would run things, that she'd be looked up to as a strong and capable employer of a small but hard-working team of professional, imaginative, attractive young people like herself, a team who by skill and dedication to the art of catering would take a rundown caricature of their country like the tartan nightmare of the Bide a Wee Hotel, and turn it into a hip and groovy rest stop for the hip and groovy traveller, a place where for a modest outgoing, the best of local produce sourced with global consciousness would afford repast and accommodation to the kind of people who make the world a better place one square mile of lifestyle at a time, what did she make of her new and unlooked-for situation?

10.0.1.4.3.1

Janette had already come a long way, at least in her own mind, from the unheated room she'd shared with her parents in Agnes's house. She had already transcended the hunger and violence and, worst of all, indifference she'd endured from her unwell, underqualified, exhausted, bitter great-grandparent, and from her later disposition to the intermittent competencies of the care and fostering system. She'd done better than survive. She had her self-worth intact. And yet here she was (if in fact she was) standing in this ecological theme park watching a pair of overgrown testosterone cases make loud and obnoxious arses of themselves ... standing there caring for them and disapproving of them like the caricature of a model of family life, that she, like them, had never really known, but into which she, like them, now found herself falling, the wish for stability seeming to transfer itself without pain to the "family" and temporarily away from the ambitions of grooviness that had held the threads and episodes of her life together this far.

10.0.2

It was happening to all of them that day, wherever they really were, this seemingly preordained, species-defining, evolved need of binding and cleaving. Almost as if it were meant, almost as if this were some tendentious story about human nature that someone was making up, just to prove a point. That we are meant to be together. That we need each other. That the atomising criminals who keep us apart to keep us weak and hungry are not simply morally wrong; they are up a gum tree. That there is that in us which makes us one. And that this thing in itself about us is as much in and of the way things really are as are gravity, cancer and quantum uncertainty.

10.0.2.1

Whatever the circumstances philosophically or circumstantially, it is, of course, the fact of the change of vehicle that is significant in terms of plot. Their evading detection and capture for twenty-four more hours was what was significant within the genre of flight and pursuit. It might be said that, no longer a throwback to seventies gangster aesthetic, the Hunters were now a family on holiday together in a mobile home in a road movie. And by osmosis or otherwise they were in fact becoming, however eccentrically, a gestalt, a social entity, a family.

10.1

Albeit in a mobile one, for the first time in any of their lives, they were at home.

10.2

As a matter of purely personal preference, for one reason and another, the scenario in which I choose to invest my belief similarly has Janette standing looking on in contemplation of her life as Hunter and his son behaved badly, but not in any modern eco-aware leisure facility, rather in far more sublime and terrible surroundings, evocative of history, stuffed full of geology, in a glacier-cut channel leading down to the Western Ocean and America beyond, a slow ice sculpture of water, stone and sky, echoing with the shrills of raptors. However unlikely in mundane terms of driving times and distance, I choose to believe the early evening testimony of a party of Harry Potter fans who were photographing the second most spectacular monument from the heroic age of railway engineering anywhere in these islands, the highlight of any visit to the West Highland Railway. The Glenfinnan Viaduct at the head of Loch Shiel is, of course, featured on bank cards and postcards as well as appearing in all the Harry Potter films as the essential landmark en route to the Public School Fairyland of that singularly inexplicable subset of teenage wish fulfilment, so you can see why comparatively normal people like the Hunters might want to visit it.

10.2.1

The fans' testimony was that they'd been terrorised by the sudden appearance of a gunslinger and his vile apprentice loosing off some practice rounds at the nearby Glenfinnan Monument, a Victorian folly built in Gothic imitation of a watchtower at the spot where Bonnie Prince Charlie was said to have raised the Royal Standard in 1745, gathering the clans, inaugurating his last-ditch desperate attempt to reimpose papist absolutism on a land already irredeemably lost to Justification by Protestant Ascendancy. Two magical symbols of lost dreams of childhood and tyranny then, in a single photoshoot on the same sea loch, truly one of the most breathtaking and dramatic meetings of history and culture and sea and landscape anywhere on our magnificent and midge-infested coastline, all framed by swooping crags reflected in the glassy rippling of Loch Shiel and thoroughly spoiled for the schoolgirl party from Hampshire, by the wild swearing and shooting of a madman and his pasty-faced and hellish brood whanging their high-calibre gunfire off that Sentimental Tribute to purposeless Jacobite yearning at the apex of sea and sky and shore. The kind of vehicle they were driving was not described but that absent detail is hardly necessary to the credibility of the sighting which, if solely judged on grounds of mythological resonance, must be judged definitive.

10.3

The most cursory of glances at a map makes it unavoidably evident that their itinerary cannot possibly have physically placed the Hunters at all of these places on the same afternoon. To pursue the physical analogy, their confirmed observation at one place precludes the possibility of their being observed by their effect, like protons, at another location. Best, then, I think, not to try pin them down. Best that the Hunters, for that one afternoon of freedom they enjoyed together as a family grouping, however tenuously, however contingently, remain in the realm of probability and uncertainty. On grounds of realism, perhaps, and for the sake of consistency, we should probably assume

£40 spent on petrol at some stage, we should estimate the remaining contents of the carpet bag at £24,587.04.

10.3.1

If we do not find truth but only make it, as has been variously alleged by all the sages of our disappointed epoch, then can we not allow ourselves not to know? Can we not forgive ourselves a little, and leave to the Wheens and Bellamies and Boyles of this world their false consolations of certainty, their unreflective acceptance of appearance, their spurious purposefulness. Freedom, if it means anything, bears the price of flux, of being unsettled, of not expecting "truth". There is slavery in what passes for common sense. Given that procedural confidence was largely placed in the description of a vehicle that Hunter, in whatever circumstances, had abandoned, and given that the needs of escape did not, I think, enter into his mind ... that rather he was thinking that his children needed a place to sleep where he could watch over them under the very special conditions of their being fugitive together ... can we not find a little generosity in our hearts, give a little benefit to doubt?

10.3.2

This Scotland where he found himself (wherever exactly he was) was new territory for Tommy in more than the merely topographical sense. However much he might have welcomed some insight into the exterior landscape of his old and weary country, its bleak and surprising beauties, the real landscape of novelty was inside himself and his children. These strangers to him were not strangers to each other, he found to his amazement, and once he had got himself over that barrier, he found himself enjoying their company, the intimacy and ease with which they traded abuse. He was jogged back towards sociability by the habitual nature of the interactions they displayed, by their unconscious ease with each other. Unlike him, they just talked and shoved and mocked each other quite naturally, with a spontaneity entirely alien to him. For him, after so many years of solitude, every movement of conversation had to be thought through, every utterance weighed and its consequences anticipated. He felt his otherness from them then, I think, he witnessed himself as they saw him and he was probably quite sad about that, even as he knew joy at being able to witness his own, lost children. He could only have felt then, probably, when he was near them, how far he had fallen away from them.

10.3.2.1

So as he drove he let them talk, their liquid babble washing through him, mainly without his understanding it, but cleansing him nonetheless. It hardly mattered what they said to each other. What astounded him with its novelty, and that he noticed that they didn't notice, was that they changed each other. Ronnie became animated and actually quite witty in his sister's company. Janette he knew less about, but she too seemed to relax and enjoy her younger brother in a teasing, sarcastic sort of way. He wondered if they were changing him too. He wondered what it meant to change. Whether being changed might be a good thing for one's identity and not a threat to it, as had been the case in all of his prior experience.

10.3.2.2

Hunter was beginning to understand, I think, that he had no way to know the journey he and his children had been on apart and together. He had no insight, for example, into the value each of them, undescribed but constant, had always placed on the mere fact of their relatedness. Everything in their world of social care, like in his world of rather more astringent regulation, had been designed upon the Cartesian principle of the isolated soul, the atomised individual, whose relationship with "society" was regulated solely through their measured conformity to the systemic demands and eccentricities of total institutions. The guiding belief underpinning all such institutions being that it is only submission to the practices of these institutions that offers happiness, normality, morality ... humanity even, to those humans damned to dependence on them, and to the irreducible loneliness of mere being. Sod that, as it were, had said the brother and sister, who had in their prior relation to each other an alternate standard by which to judge and find wanting the good intentions of the state in its taking the place of their absent parents. And now, in the restored but aberrant return of the father, in the sudden substitution of the parent for the state, they likewise had a standard to which they could hold him to account. Hunter, like Her Majesty (or at least the District Council) before him, found himself in nominal charge of their destinies, true enough. But that didn't mean that Ronnie and Janette would put up with any snash from him, thanks very much.

10.3.2.2.1

And their defiance, their mockery of him delighted him, I'm happy to say. He found in their cautious mockery a loosening of the sclerotic plaque of his protective rigidity, and, exposing his nerves though it did, he recognised that his only hope lay in their carelessness. His only acceptance was in their forgetting of who he was in their simple celebration of each other, who they were. His achievement, he was staggered to learn, was not that he had reunited them with him, but that he had reunited them for the moment with each other.

10.4

Talking away to Janette, Ronnie would never have admitted, not even to himself, how glad he was to see her, how much he had missed her, how grateful he was he had her back, or, how angry he was at the deepest depth of his soul that she had abandoned him to the professional care of others who could not, with the best will in the world, love him. She annoyed him, she amused him, she patronised him and she flattered him all at once, and he felt in himself the dangerous revival of feeling, of that flexibility of the soul we allow ourselves when we feel safe. And with that happiness there came to Ronnie the terrible fear that it could be taken away again. And to the defensive hardening of his heart the vulnerability of that feeling ate at him unconsciously all day, which probably explains both his poisonous mood in the evening and the catastrophe he was to precipitate that night. How Ronnie's resentment at an imagined slight led him so astray, and in turn incited the climactic incidents of this Scottish Western, we'll be exploring later on. For now, in any case, by comparison with Janette, his father had arrived in his world like a visitation. Janette, by contrast, he knew now he had found her again, was his whole world.

10.4.1

As for Janette herself, she could not help being a little flattered by her father's clear regard for her. He respected her navigating and accepted her advice as to where to go next utterly without question or without ever allowing his rank as an adult to manifest itself in adult defensiveness. Once they were embarked, once she had accepted their expedition, she was acknowledged as the expert, she took charge, and he let her take charge, enjoying her authoritative advice as to routes, eateries and destinations. It was Janette who had insisted, for example, on their being self-sufficient in terms of accommodation, hence the change from the austere and manly vibe of the vintage Jag to the two-wheel-drive domesticity of their new home. It was Janette who knew about places like Glenfinnan Viaduct and Landmark, the Commando Memorial at Spean Bridge, the Roads of Glen Roy and so on … and her wisdom in matters of tourist attractions also seemed to evidence itself as exceptional emotional intelligence.

She carefully enquired about what her father remembered of the night they'd lost her mother, for example, and he willingly told her about their dropping Janice off at a service station at a roundabout on the outskirts of Perth. He had done this at her insistence, he told his daughter. He had appreciated that she perhaps needed to assimilate the then new reality for her of being on the lam, as it were, like Bonnie and Clyde, and with a pair of toddlers in the car, she had felt understandably uncomfortable about it. Hunter had, as always, acceded without demur to what Janice had asked of him, satisfying himself with telling her he would get in touch with her via Agnes and then tell her where to come if and when she decided to join them later. He had confidently expected that she would, he told Janette, and showed her the postcard again as evidence of his absent wife's continued interest in maintaining their relationship.

He looked at her then with a child's eagerness, a frightened need for her assurance, desperate that Janette, who he had come to respect as an emotional authority, should confirm him in his hope.

Janette understood then, from his anxious, naive plea for her blessing on his lunatic expectations, that for her father, the fourteen years that had passed between that journey and this were merely an interruption, a small detour, a momentary distraction from a holiday itinerary that he had kept in his shattered mind for all this time as the only consistency available to him. That this journey they were on right now was not only the fulfilment of his prisoner's pipe dream; it was the only thing holding him together at all. His surface calm, his clarity of purpose, his reality itself, all these were as fragile as the wings of butterflies. He depended utterly on the little things she was doing to make their day together fun and interesting. He was as utterly and vulnerably reliant on her goodwill as he'd been on radio contact with their base in Crossmaglen when he and the Wheens had been khaki boys together in the wilds of South Armagh.

10.4.1.1

Is it possible this responsibility moved her? Is it possible she felt pity for her father? Or is it possible she felt something else as she took, at his urging, another closer look at the postcard of Calgary Beach with the Tobermory postmark from two years ago? What was the meaning of her wordless response, her inexpressive accession to his request to look at it again? Is it possible that Janette knew more than she had told him so far? Was there something in the look she gave him as he handed her again the postcard that she had swatted to the floor in the Rob Roy Room back in Kinloch Rannoch that indicated guilty knowledge? In any case she was lost, for a moment, in interior contemplation, not listening to his story till her father's barked confession that having dropped Janice off all those years ago, he had, like an idiot, forgotten, in the turmoil of parting, to fill the car up with petrol and that this was why they had stopped at the gates of Drumochter Pass and the polis man from Coupar Angus had come across them there, and Hunter had been arrested and he and his children had been flung into the wilderness ...

"So that's the last time you saw her?" asked Janette.

"Sure," said her dad, "do you not remember?"

10.4.2

She was sorry she did not, and had to bite her tongue to stop herself from telling him (yet) what else she knew.

10.5

They drove along in silence for a few moments, or rather, drove along to what was to the children the thoroughly incomprehensible country boogie of Lowell George and Little Feat. Ronnie asked then where they were going, which though it seems an entirely reasonable question leads us into a sticky point of narrative procedure which was that where they were going was not at all where they ended up, and how they ended up where they did and not where they were going is the proper subject of the next chapter.

10.6

What remains in this chapter is a description of the scene of the last chapter some ninety minutes after the Hunters had left it.

10.6.1

Here, in the car park of the Bide a Wee Hotel, surrounded by perhaps thirty policemen of various ranks and functions, including an armed response unit, Joseph Wheen, sitting in the passenger seat of Frank's Beamer, was snickering mirthlessly, inanely and annoyingly at some private joke he was enjoying while Frank looked through the windscreen towards where Superintendent Bellamy was sitting on a reclaimed park bench with the Lawrences outside the windows of the Rob Roy Room, staring as if he could lip-read what they were saying, irritated beyond measure at both his dependence on Bellamy for useful information and at the clear evidence (in the form of sniggering) that brother Joe was enjoying this ridiculous game of real-life Grand Theft Auto into which that maniac Tommy Hunter had tipped them.

10.6.2

Mrs Lawrence, who was now bandaged and saddened at human nature, and Mr Lawrence, with his arm consolingly around her, were doing their joint best to recall details of what the Hunters might have said to each other about where they might be heading off to, before they'd headed off — leaving so much upset in their backwash. They'd just told Bellamy about the postcard, and Mr Lawrence had just recalled the detail of where it had come from … Calgary Beach … and Bellamy had dredged from his own memory that that annoying wee prick "Danny" Boyle had been up that way somewhere a year or two back the last time this ghost had revived, risen, gibbered and begged for reburying. And even worse, that Danny was heading there right now.

10.6.2.1

"Bollocks," he said out loud. Mr Lawrence looked at him anxiously.

"Was that not helpful, Superintendent?" he asked.

Oh yes. Oh yes it was, thought Bellamy to himself and very much gave no indication of the thrill of power in knowledge that he had over that nasty, arrogant man in the car with his nasty idiot brother over there. Bellamy was making plans even as he straightened and looked around the car park to the fields and hills beyond. And none of those plans were intended to be of any benefit to Frank Wheen.

10.6.3

Bellamy now looked over at Frank and shook his head sadly, as if Lawrence had told him nothing that could help them.

10.7

"Fuck," said Frank, and Joe chuntered his unhappy wee laugh again.

"What the fuck are you laughing at?" asked Frank.

"Nothin," said Joe. "Wouldn't you like tae know?" he added. Maddeningly.

Bellamy was walking over to the car. Frank prepared himself for him.

"Think he's gonnae look in the boot?" asked Joe. Not paying any mind, Frank was already opening his window so Bellamy could update him.

"Sorry, gentlemen," Bellamy was saying. "There's no new information. I'd suggest there really isn't anything useful to be done here. You'd be better heading back."

"So what are you gonnae do?" asked Frank.

"Procedure, Mr Wheen. We have a good description of the car. It's bound to get spotted. For the moment, I think we should use our local resources to identify known contacts. We know he spoke to someone at a Glasgow payphone before he left the Wallace Arms. Carntyne. A little cross-checking around that location using your sources and ours might well turn up something."

Joe burped one of his wee laughs out.

"But in the meantime," Bellamy went on, "leave it in our hands. Be sure we'll be in touch if we turn up anything."

Bellamy smiled tightly at Frank, and glanced briefly at Joe with ill-guarded contempt, then put his hat on and went back to his own car to alert certain trusted cohorts by CB radio to the lead he'd now withheld from the Wheens. He hoped he'd done enough to send them home to be dependent on what he chose to tell them. But Bellamy had not reckoned with the information that Joe was about to enjoy sharing with his smarter, younger brother.

For now, Joe, in response to Bellamy's patronage, let a single obscenity escape him.

"Cunt," he said. "If he thinks he's gonna turn up Jack Webster in fuckin Carntyne, he's got another think coming."

10.7.1

Frank looked at his brother, awful suspicion tingling in his toes, and working its way upwards towards his medulla oblongata.

"What do you mean?"

Joe shrugged.

"What happened with Jack?" Frank insisted.

"Well you know how it is, Frank," Joe said, wise in the ways of the world. "He didnae want to talk to me."

Joe grinned.

"Where is he?" asked Frank, his stomach turning to an icy lump on top of his intestines.

"He's in the boot," said Joe, with studied, simple brutality. He then added, innocently employing the heavy mockery so ingrained in his nature, "D'ye want me tae show him to yer mates?"

Shockingly, he opened the passenger door suddenly, and thirty highly trained firearms officers turned their heads automatically towards the sudden sound.

10.7.2

Joe enjoyed watching Frank's colour changing from red to white to red and back to white again as he slowly closed the door and Frank wordlessly started the engine, not knowing what else he was supposed to do, not knowing where he might be going, especially as he knew that the unholy thing he wanted to get away from was in the car with him. But Frank didn't know yet how else the last act of his tragedy was supposed to start.

10.7.2

"Course, he talked tae me eventually," said Joe before Frank could get the car moving. "Told me a lot of things."

Joe smiled like the masterful bad guy in the substandard movie he had always dreamed he was.

"He told me Tommy had money. Tommy paid him in cash for a motor and a gun."

Good taste and a proper regard for dramatic tension would have stopped Joe right there, leaving the next question unasked and hanging there between them like a bad smell. But taste and dramaturgy were not in Joe's range of aptitudes. So he probably said something obvious like, "Where'd Tommy get fucking money, Frank? It couldn't have been from you. You're fucking skint all the time. At least that's what you always tell me!"

Frank must have stared at him then. The unattended engine flooded and cut out.

10.7.2.1

Of course, there are those who think that Frank must have known about poor Jack all along – DS "Danny" Boyle later certainly proceeded on that assumption. But I think that something like the above conversation probably took place and precipitated the Wheens' otherwise unexplained departure from the entourage of Superintendent Bellamy. Of course, I wasn't with them in the car, but given that it was from the car park of the hotel that Frank and Joe disappeared off the public radar for the next twelve hours or so until their dramatic reappearance at the gates of the Ossian's View Estate, I am confident that my account is reliable (see op. cit. 12.4.2.2 *passim*).

10.7.2.2

You fuck, thought Frank to himself, feeling sick. What have you done to me?

He turned the ignition key again and let out the clutch too fast. The car jumped like there was a learner driver at the wheel.

"Drive slowly, Frank …" Joe cautioned. "You wouldn't want tae crash in front of these cunts."

Frank gagged, he nearly threw up … and Joe's soul knew the highest, deepest pleasure of its unlamented time on earth.

11.0

Still as one, for the first and possibly last time, the Hunter family stood that night in the doorway of normality. Hesitating on the threshold of a family diner, they breathed it in, the kaleidoscopic smells of it – chip fat and piri-piri chicken, lager and Irn-Bru.

11.0.1

The family restaurant that served the campsite they had chosen as well as the B&Bs of the locality, The Jaco-Bite, doubled as a cabaret venue for local and touring talent. The band onstage tonight, the Ted McPherson Experience, was already playing a disconcerting series of medleys of eighties cover versions on guitar, keyboards and drums, all of which climaxed with an eight-minute "Don't You Want Me?" by The Human League. To which question the answer was "Almost certainly not".

11.0.1.1

On the cliff edge of this mirrorball-and-spotlit all-you-can-eat dining experience, Ronnie and his father balked at the sight of all those other people, and Janette smoothly took over the practicalities, having already made the decision that she was going to put her father straight about a couple of things while she had the protection of being in a public place. She inwardly prepared herself for revelations and admonitions as she chatted easily with the waitress, who was called Elaine, who had spotted a table about to open.

11.0.1.1.1

Janette may well have known Elaine at least by sight. Though it's crowded, the Scottish catering community is nonetheless tight-knit, and itinerant though its members tend to be, they do form a bit of a clique. They recognise each other by the behaviours they have learned, the specialised social reflexes they have assimilated, the shared culture they inhabit. They are a fellowship, like sailors and chemists. They exchange practical information, too, about good employers and bad, and the story about Mr Lawrence and Janette's knickers may well have been like an Icelandic Saga to them for all I know.

11.0.1.1.1.1

Prisoners are clannish like that. Prostitutes and professional mercenary soldiers and dentists are hugger-mugger in like fashion. Parents of young children and pensioners are fraternities and sororities. Even dog owners and joggers that meet only in the park of a morning are like that. Everyone, the possible singularity of Tommy Hunter being excepted, is like that. We are social animals, like everyone says, but not in the way that everyone means it (as if it were a surprise that we are not purely auto-directed windowless monads), but in the very genetic and epigenetic bone.

11.0.1.1.1.2

We are not, we are never, alone. It is at least arguable that we can only legitimately consider ourselves to be "individuals" in as much that none of us share exactly the same nest of composite collective identities with anyone else. We all of us inhabit multiple communities, culturally and occupationally. Our uniqueness, far from being essential to us, or based on any intrinsic difference from anyone we happen to bump into, is purely a Venn diagram function of social happenstance. What makes you "you" and not "me", is that our composites of samenesses, our mixtures of relatedness to others are accidentally and invariably slightly different from each other's. Our accidents are individual, but our essences are identical, I think. We are only marginally and circumstantially ourselves. The only existential uniqueness to which any of us can legitimately lay claim with any weight of evidence (through our ancestors' and cousins' looping chains of bases) is that we all, like daffodils and Labradors, belong to the "class of things that are not dead," itself a vanishingly small subset of actually existing stuff.

11.0.1.1.1.2.1

The primal, protozoan bacterial soup from which we emerged and to which we will return is where we still live, mostly, materially considered. We still belong to the bacterial world, to most intents and purposes. It is only our temporary consciousness, our having self-contained bodies and minds to wander about and do stuff in, for an eye-blink of time, that deceives us into thinking it is only when we have lives that we are alive. In fact, from the point of view of life as such, we are effectively immortal, the stuff we're made of having been alive since life began, and likewise remaining so, long after a small and inessential bit of us is dead or is not playing temporary host to consciousness, whatever that may mean, any more. In common with all living things with more than one cell, we animals and plants are a rampantly florid eukaryote disease of limited duration, and as such, have perversely yet compellingly been evolving for the half a billion years as superficially autonomous organisms who are actually as close to each other as are bananas in a bunch.

11.0.1.1.1.2.1.1

Bananas included.

11.0.1.2

Most of us recognise each other, we living things, in our degrees of separation and in our ultimate unity, and that we have meanwhile evolved in emotional as well as physical landscapes we are shaped by, whatever else is our inheritance. We are temporarily and only contingently "ourselves" very much in the short term and in the meantime, as it were. Our knowing this about ourselves, as we all do, as we always have, and our not being very happy about the idea of death, is just one example of evolution teasing us with the theory of forever while confining us to a limited tenancy in ourselves as ourselves. Bananas don't, so far as we know, have this problem.

Our being doomed to inhabit "reality" as two entirely distinct locations all the time has had both happy and unhappy sequels, among which we might count inventing religion and culture and right and wrong as being the very least of the compensations that we felt we owed ourselves. Being capable both of conceiving of the infinite and the eternal, while all too aware that we ourselves are neither of those things, we occupy the universe with the deepest imaginable insight, yes … but aware at the same time that this insight is entirely inappropriate to our mortality. This paradox is just another bloody thing we have to put up with, it seems, several thousand years' worth of pen scratching by the cleverest people we've got making next to no headway in squaring the circle, let alone in adapting our behaviour to the realities of both our human and our extra-human natures. No philosophy or religion has altered the base reality that we all live in two worlds at once but that we are evolved to cope in only one place at a time, and even then are only really happy with living when we can do so without thinking about it, with the concomitant outcome being that we are as habitually and roundly defeated by the slightest change of air as might be a pit pony on a Ferris wheel. Some of us are like landed fish when we have to buy a pair of shoes.

11.0.2

Hence, Ronnie's vague unease at how well his sister and his father were getting on had become a prickly brittleness in him even before they started eating. This kind of jealous vulnerability was hardly new territory for him. Every good thing that had ever happened to him had been so unreliable that none of it had ever really made him happy. But, complex of deprivations and improvisations though he was, he lacked real experience of familial complexity.

11.0.2.1

Lonely boys are very simple in some ways, like happy boys are simple in others. We are all distinguished very early on in our learned responses to things like knowledge, insult and fear. According to nurture, we each become wise in some ways, and remain infants in others.

11.0.2.2

Ronnie, who was well capable of handling himself in situations (of confrontation with authority, for example) that would render most adults into blubbering wreckages, was well out of his depth with the kind of negotiations with loved ones that are already second nature to comfortable children by the time they reach double digits. For Ronnie, emotional vulnerability of any sort had always been a crime that was to be immediately punished in others, and for which one expected immediate punishment. Consequently, since he was bright (though God forbid he'd ever let you see that) policemen and educators and social workers had found in Ronnie a kung fu master of defensive evasion, angry irony and cheek.

But even in this short time today of his being, once again, somebody's child, there had flowered within him all unheralded — as well as unwanted and confusing — a need and capacity for love that was crippling him with awareness of his own infantilism in this specialised regard. Unguarded because of his inexperience, at this moment Ronnie was openness itself to hurt as well as joy, and he hated feeling like that without having the geographical knowledge of his own hinterland that would tell him what it was he hated and what he might do about it. Consequently, the only therapeutic remedy that occurred to him for feeling bad was to make somebody else feel worse.

11.0.2.3

His father had already turned down a game of pool with him while they were waiting to order and now Hunter and Janette were back going on about something to do with what she wanted to do with her life. Hunter was leaning in to hear her over the noise of the PA system. The noise of the band meant that Ronnie couldn't really hear what Hunter and Janette were saying to each other, and even the fistfuls of coated crispy fries he was eating didn't do much to reconcile him to their isolating him like this. Isolation, his haunting core reality, ate at him faster than he ate the chips. It was testament to Hunter's inexperience as a parent and to Janette's preoccupation with what she was about to tell her father and how she was going to do it, that meant that neither of them noticed the slow build-up of Ronnie's misery.

11.0.2.3.1

They did nothing but talk, these two, about nothing. And it was me he kidnapped first!!

11.0.2.3.2

Ronnie took his ego in his hands and decided to intervene and tugged at Hunter's sleeve, and was enraged by the wee patient smile Hunter gave him as he asked him "What?"

"Do ye want tae play that game of pool now?"

"No," said Tommy pressing a coin into his hand. "On you go and fuck up the locals."

Ronnie looked down in contempt at the 50p his father had just handed him.

"They take pounds!"

Hunter dug for the change, and ended up handing Ronnie a fiver.

"Don't spend that all at once," he cautioned and turned back to his daughter.

Ronnie felt tears he didn't want to explain to himself pricking at the back of his eyes. Like a man dying of thirst in the desert who has been given a sip of water, only to have the cup removed almost before he's registered the taste, Ronnie found that his jealousy was as disproportionate as his need for love, once awakened, had proved to be. He was voracious now in his hunger for the food he had never tasted, that he had never trusted the world enough to admit that he even wanted from it. He had opened himself unconsciously to his father, and now his father, all unwary, was closing him down.

11.0.2.2.4

On his way to the bar, Ronnie saw that the pool table was being used by two snotty children in bright T-shirts decorated with anthropomorphic animals, laughing at their own incompetence in a way that completely wasn't as fucked up as he was. As he took the change and turned to watch them as they rushed back to the loving arms of their loving parents, Ronnie's mood had sunk from sullen to murderous.

11.1

All unaware of the churning turbulence inside his son, Hunter was indulging himself in the calm surface, and for all he knew, depths, of his daughter. She knocked him out. He was stunned and delighted by her wit, her poise, her obvious intelligence. He wanted to know her secret. How was it possible to live in this terrible world that well?

11.1.2

Janette, appearances suggesting she was making the best of her ambiguous situation, was now about to tell her father as much of the truth as she thought he could deal with for the moment, or as much of the truth as she felt she needed to tell him, yes, for reasons of conscience as well as immediate utility. Old-fashioned in this way, she felt she owed him something. Why did she feel this? Was she simply being controlling? Had Ronnie known that word, he would certainly have said so.

11.1.2.1

She had accompanied them, yes, on an impulse, but having acted impulsively she was now thinking systematically, balancing contingencies ... if this then this ... This capacity for forethought, for the future being, for her, a region of thinkable alternatives, distinguished her from her male relatives, one of whom, her father, acted on impulse but always returned to the tramlines he had set himself, and the other of whom, Ronnie, alike acted on his own testosterone-complected version of impulse, but had not, unlike his father, a governing objective to which to return after whatever disaster he'd just brought about. Janette had possible futures to Hunter's one possible future. Both were rich compared to Ronnie, whose best version of the future was a present tense that was pretty much dreadful going on forever.

11.2.1.1.1

In fact, the chain of events that Janette's ensuing conversation was about to precipitate was going to radically challenge all of their desires and calculations as to what was going to happen next.

11.2.1.2

As a unit then, with Janette at the centre, the family had by now achieved, however precariously, a combined emotional intelligence that was considerably more than the sum of its parts. And while both Hunter and Ronnie were wary of acknowledging the change, Janette, as the focus of the new paradigm, as the head of the family, in the literal and figurative sense of that word, was comfortable with improvising in a systematic way, with weighing contingencies and fallback positions.

11.2.1.2.1

After all, she had not committed any crime when she had left the Lawrence's employ. She had had no formal contract she was breaking. Her stuff was mostly still in her room, of course, but she was used to travelling light. She had packed her favourite clothes. She had thrown her small collection of family photos in her bag, and Mr Lawrence was welcome to her remaining knickers.

11.2.1.2.1.1

And Janette, we should now reveal, was already committed not to an ideology or career path as such, but to a way of life. She liked the countryside, nature. All that stuff. She even wanted to save it from people. She felt the existential threat it faced from hardhearted and soft-headed men. She'd actually thought about joining the Green Party.

11.2.1.2.1.2

Can you imagine, could Tommy imagine, a child of his inhabiting the world so securely as to actually think about changing it, to actually consider involvement in civic activity? She never told him that. I'm not sure he'd have known how to cope if she had! Anyway, they weren't going to have anything like that kind of time together.

11.2.1.2.2

When she had decided to come with Hunter, aside from the fact that she had already been more than ready to move on, we shouldn't forget that for all of her apparent equanimity, Janette retained the rootlessness of a childhood passed without roots, but I think perhaps, I hope, with a positive intuition that the freedom and resilience this early education in fragility afforded her could be parlayed into a way of living in the world in the twenty-first century that had general application and correctness.

11.2.1.3

The world would be a saner place if we all acted according

to how tenuous our hold on it is. She was sure of that. One can only hope that one day Janette will write it down for our philosophical consolation, even for our pragmatic adoption.

11.3

She looked at her father's face. It was open. It loved her. He was eager to take whatever she wanted to share with him. That was how far he had come. If she had understood, really understood, just how far that was, she might have acted differently and spoken more softly. We'll never know.

11.3.1

And besides, she was there. On the spot and in that moment, and she did what she felt was right. What more can you ask of anyone, really?

11.3.2

Her time here with Hunter, she thought, looking into his face, about to break his heart, afforded her most of all the opportunity she had needed to complete her renegotiation of her past, to put it behind her, to move on, not simply from the Lawrences, but from her childhood itself. She had had to do that. We all have to do that. It wasn't just that she was forced to talk to her father by her being here with him as she was. She actively wanted to.

11.3.2.1

And this wasn't a sudden thing. She had actively wanted to get through to him for some time, as she was about to explain. She had dreamed of him when she was a girl. She had memories of him from a very young age. She had imagined him at night and practised telling him things when she'd been alone. She had had many, many conversations with him when he wasn't there. She'd used to tell him everything. Of course, he had been in prison and she had just been a little girl, and till a couple of years ago she had never even thought to write to him.

11.3.2.2

Even when she did send him that postcard from Calgary Beach, it had been from a moment of impulsive intention to communicate, rather than a real attempt at communication per se. That was why she had sent the card without her name on it. Sending the card, writing his name and address on it, she had been making him real to her, unaware that at that moment she, or rather "the sender of the card", would become real to him. It had been a rather daft, rather self-involved thing to do. She hadn't really imagined that him getting that postcard from her would give him ideas, let alone that he would have wrongly concluded that the card came from Janice and that those ideas he had were going to have been about her mother and not about her. Such unintended consequences might have been amusing in another context, rather than cataclysmic. But she was very young when she sent it, after all.

11.3.3

The fact that her handwriting looked very like her mother's wasn't something that Janette was even aware of. But it was. Such are the vicissitudes of inheritance.

11.4

It was, of course, her decision that now was the moment to reveal the authorship of the postcard as being hers that was to prove so devastating to their hard-won and sadly temporary functionality as a family unit.

11.5

JANETTE
Da?

HUNTER
What?

JANETTE
What if I told you yer never gonnae find her?

HUNTER
I never hurt her. I got a postcard.

JANETTE
(pause)
Mum never sent you that postcard, Dad.

She pauses for a moment. He tries to smile. Does she relish, just a little, her power over him at this moment? In memory of those fourteen years?

It was me.

And now she's said it, and almost immediately, despite her having done the right thing by any moral standards, she finds herself rather regretting it. She stumbles a little now.

I know you never hurt her. I've saw her. I've
talked to her. It was just the once.

Hunter is staring at her now, his face bloodless, his eyes wide, unreadable.

It was when we were in care, still. Ronnie was too wee to remember. She turned up at a hostel we were in. Kiddin oan she was wer auntie ur somethin.

His mouth moves. She speaks before he can.

She was a wreck, Da. She was high oan somethin. She was a junkie.

Saying this, hearing herself, her own emotion unexpectedly fills her throat, constricting her breath. Janette looks down at the remains of her vegetarian chilli burger. There is a line between the pragmatic disposal of information and dredging up pain from your own oesophagus that Janette has just crossed without meaning to. She finds there are tears in her eyes and that she can't speak. Hunter's mixed and private feelings for his lost lady-love are at this moment, very much to his credit, trumped by his concern for his daughter, however much he is attempting to distract himself from the terrible shock his system is yet to really absorb. He cups her chin in his big hand and says, gently:

HUNTER
Hey ... Hey ...

Janette, strategically or not, takes this solicitude to be questioning her veracity. In fact, she is speaking from a combination of defensive, retrospective doubt at the reliability of her witness as a ten-year-old, of her memory, and a fresh fear that she won't be able to get through this without making a fool of herself.

JANETTE
I grew up in care, Da. I know a fucking junkie when I see one.

The brutality and undoubted truth of this statement silences and reconciles him to hearing from her now what she has to say. He will make no further attempt to shut her up by sentimental solicitude. She has made herself a platform now. She has set herself a stage.

When I was sixteen, I went to find her. Just like you.
I went to the address of this squat she'd gien me. In
London. She wasnae there. Nobody knew anything
aboot her. I sent ye that postcard ... when I was up
workin there ... on Mull. I was working in a hotel
there. I don't know why I did it. I suppose I just wanted
to tell ye ... I suppose I wanted ... I don't know ...

She hesitates. He doesn't know why, but it's because she's considering lying to him again in order to keep her options open. While she is thinking about that, he makes the beginnings of his new understanding of things verbally manifest for the first time. A little obviously, he is asking her a question that is begging her for a comforting answer.

HUNTER
So you sent it because you wanted tae see yer Da?

He smiles, sadly, but in appreciation of her simple, childish wish, to which she reacts with some fury.

JANETTE
She's fuckin dead, Da! She got a mass burnin at some
place where they burn junkies. Probably ... Okay? She's
fuckin dead. Yer never gonnae see her again. All right?

Hunter, still in shock, still nowhere near processing this, looks across at his son angrily banging the stripes about the table. She drags his attention back to her.

Ronnie knows fuck all.

"Right," he says. And sinks into himself, feeling once again open beneath his feet the yawning abyss into which he fell all those years ago, and from which, like Dante, he had only recently been climbing. First, ascending from hell, with Ronnie as his Virgil, he had glimpsed the sky and the mountains. And now with Janette as his Beatrice, he had come further into the light than he could ever have anticipated. He had had a really good day, his first really good day on earth. He had touched the earthly paradise and glimpsed up into heaven. And now it was gone. All gone. Inferno's darkness fell on him again like a hammer, obliterating him. His vision actually failed him, like he was having a seizure. He could not speak, he felt utterly incompetent, utterly alone, utterly helpless and afraid. The story he had told himself since the arrival of the postcard was that he would find her, find Janice. His dream, his lunatic dream that hat he would bring his family together and make them the gift he'd owed them all these years, the gift of togetherness underwritten by a cash injection, was wet ashes all round him and over him and inside his mouth and eyes. He felt dirty. He could smell himself. A blizzard of dark covered him. He could not see or hear.

HUNTER
(after some moments)
Efter the morra, I'll let ye go.

JANETTE
(stunned that new information she's given him has
not made him pragmatically reconsider his plans yet
— which was expecting a bit much to be honest)
What about tomorra? What are we doing the morra?

Hunter, clinging, she thinks, to unreality, takes the post-card from his pocket to look at it.

Did ye not hear me? Did ye not hear what I just told ye?

He looks at her. She can't read him. He can't understand anything himself yet.

HUNTER
Efter the morra, I'll let ye go.

She stares at him nonplussed and a huge cheer goes up from the assembled revellers. The band on stage has started playing "The Birdie Song" and there is a surge of relief at the crowd's being spared any more New Romantic rubbish as the floor fills with grannies and grandpas and children, with the generation in the middle proudly looking on at the organised cuteness of it all.

Hunter looks away from his daughter as the tears start, silently this time, just flowing without effort of his lungs over his stone face. Janette — seeing that he's crying again! Jesus! — turns to watch her brother scoop enough pound coins from the pool table to get himself a drink, then she looks back at her silently weeping father to whom she has just confessed her awkward gesture of sorrow and love. He's taken it all wrong.

She wishes she'd never sent the bloody postcard now, as her comparative competence in matters of the heart is found wanting. Janette watches her father mourn his wife, her mother ... watches as for the first time, maybe, he gets past denial and passes into grief, and she wonders if she's done the right thing.

The bill for dinner was £44.58. Hunter left the change from the fifty as a tip. I don't know if he did that because Janette told him that's what you do.

11.5.1

£24,492. 04

12.0

By coincidence or serendipity, depending on your preference, at that very moment and in the very pub where Janette had been working when she'd sent the postcard of Calgary Beach by moonlight, namely the Mishnish in Tobermory, Detective Sergeant "Danny" Boyle and Maggie "Single" Singleton had already fallen in love, had a shower together and come down for a drink before dinner.

12.0.1

It had started in the car, innocently enough. They had just turned left at Scotland's crossroads, Crianlarich, as you do (the drive by Loch Lomond having exhausted his theories about Hunter and poor Jack and Agnes and the Wheens, which had come very close to the nub of things as I see them — an employment of the heuristic method of analysis of a very high order — Boyle being quite the Thomist), when Maggie asked him if he'd got any brothers and sisters.

12.0.2

Now, she'd never asked him this kind of thing before, it ranking, as a question, just above "what's your favourite colour," but there was something about the landscape and the sunshine and the moon being out in the daytime that rendered all things more simply themselves, and just eased the question out of her without forethought ... and maybe it was the glow of the green and brown masses of the rising hills, the open sky, that encouraged Danny into talking with genuine warmth about his hitherto unmentioned brother — Michael, the priest, and how they'd always done everything together, and how he'd been out to visit his brother in Rome and then on a mission station in the Ivory Coast, and what a transformative experience Africa had been for him, not out of political sentiment, but simply in changing his perspective on life's expectations — and Maggie told him what she'd been doing when she'd watched the Live Aid Concert and about her relationship with her own sister who suffered from bipolar depression and how time spent in a psycho ward with your sister drained of life, lost in sheer pain in the minimum act of merely existing also told you a thing or two about what's what and whether it matters or not, and then they were on to the fact that Danny too had been in a seminary but that he'd fallen in love and abandoned his plans for the priesthood but then it turned out that she was no good, Helen, she'd been cheating on him the whole time, and maybe that sense of betrayal was why he had this fear of emotional commitment ... and they steered away from that one, thank you very much, though both had deftly taken note of it, she as information that explained so much about him, poor lamb, and he in surprise at having heard himself say anything so personal to anyone at all let alone to another woman after all these years alone, even though he'd known and liked and admired Maggie for years and looked at her now, wow, in the reflected light from the waters ... how it lit through the ends of her hair ... and Maggie, flushing at his scrutiny, talked about her own fascination with religion and how she'd never really understood about transubstantiation and that led Danny into a fairly lengthy disquisition on the ins and outs of the Monophysite and Arian heresies he'd studied at the seminary and how when he really got down to it, it was history as a mental discipline rather than spirituality that he loved — the retention of fact and its dialectical relationship to mastering narrative, and by that time they were on the CalMac car ferry from Oban to Mull and he'd made her laugh over a coffee in the bar with some scurrilous tales of the early mediaeval papacy and the famous reluctance of anyone to take the job as the odds were they'd end up strangled, and the conversation hit a sticky patch at the mention of the word "murder" and her stomach almost fell out of her with disappointment as he went for a walk on deack and sank deeper into bitter gloom in the whipping wind as they crossed the sound at how the bastards on top always seemed to get away with it but she countered brilliantly by getting him on to international finance which was a little more abstract and as the ferry hove to at Craignure they found they both had hidden free radicals inside them who were longing for a way out of the cultural depression and politics of pessimism we all share, and they found themselves sharing anecdotes of the little kindly things that people sometimes do to redeem themselves, the little things that charm and surprise you and give you hope and by now they were driving along the road from Craignure to Tobermory and it was a glorious day and they passed through Salen and both said aloud at the same moment that it would be really nice to live in a place like this and they'd joked together about the wee hand-knitted police station there and imagined what their duties would be on an island where nobody could get away with anything except on the ferry and then they both avoided wondering any further about what Tommy Hunter, a fucking thug like that might want in a beautiful place like this, no they both suppressed that thought, that reminder of why they were here as they drove down the steep hill flanked by the waterfall and the distillery, down into the picture-book Northern Naples vista of Tobermory harbour with its self-coloured houses and sailing boats and famous cat and its chocolate shop and that really nice bakery where you can get a first-class sandwich, no, they avoided, purposefully all thought but each other and when he booked just the one room for the two of them at the

Mishnish without even asking her, my God, just knowing, she felt herself open up inside and the blood pounded in his pelvis and they both knew exactly what was happening and they could hardly breathe and they climbed the narrow stairs of the hotel tripping over each other, and barely made it into the room before they had torn each other's clothes off.

12.1

The moon was still pale in the late sunlight when the Hunters got back to the campsite and Tommy wordlessly went for a walk around the perimeter, his scheme of things in shards. Ronnie asked Janette what were they gonnae do? What was up with Dad? She lied and said she didn't know and looked at her father in the distance as the last light left the sky and the lamps of the campsite flickered into life.

It was time to consider, Ronnie thought, that seeing as he had been removed by force at gunpoint from the Dryry Street hostel, they might be expecting a little attention from the powers that be and that quite shortly given that the manner in which she'd departed from HER work had been a bit unorthodox as well. Janette looked then at the face of a passing fellow camper who she thought was looking at her curiously and, a bit thrilled at the thought, Janette decided she'd better check online on her phone to see if there was anything about them on the Internet. Having googled around a little, she told Ronnie with a gasp about the hostel burning down and held her phone out and showed him the pictures and it has to be said neither of them got too sentimental about the old homestead. But it did make them think, even though there was nothing on the news yet that named any of them, that their situation did need some consideration between the pair of them especially as their Dad, immersed in his own crisis, had left them alone to talk, though Janette did remark to Ronnie that he was keeping an eye on them ... that his peregrination of the campsite perimeter never went as far as him actually losing his direct line of sight.

"There he is there. He's still watching us."

"What does he really want?" Janette asked her brother. "I mean, he was going on about Mum and going on holiday and stuff; do you suppose he's just mental? I mean, do you think he might hurt us."

They both thought about that for a minute. Ronnie asked her if Hunter'd told her about the money: "He's got thousands of pounds ... and a gun ... I mean what is he gonnae do with it and what are we supposed to do?"

"I told him Mum might be dead," said Janette.

"Everyone knows that," said Ronnie

"Except she isn't," Janette told him, not looking at him. Rather ashamed of herself. "She's not dead."

Ronnie stared at her. Rather than let him ask her anything, she went on as if this information she was sharing was of less than paradigm-shattering significance.

"But if I tell him that, if I tell him I think I know where she is he'll just want to go there and he'll keep us with him. What do you think we should do? Should we tell him we want away from him or what?"

And he looks at her still, and understands that she's out of her depth. She's not asking him this question like she usually asks him questions: like she already knows the answer and she's waiting for him to say something stupid so she can tell him he's said something stupid. No. She genuinely doesn't know what to do.

Had she now gone even further, and told him that not only had she a pretty good idea as to where to find their absent mother, but that her choice of tourist destinations and itinerary had in fact been points on a journey towards where she had reason to suppose her mother might be, and that right now her mother was quite possibly less than ten miles away as the crow flew … there would potentially have been a series of consequences that she hesitated to confront, which explains why she didn't tell Ronnie those things yet. Had she told him everything she knew or thought she knew, everything might have turned out differently. But she didn't, so it didn't, the world being only everything that is the case.

"What do you think," she asked him. "Should you and me not try to get out of here? Should we say to him, 'Come on now, you've got to let us go' … I mean, I thought when I told him she was dead that he'd let us go anyway. That's why I told him that."

"My mum's not dead?" said Ronnie.

"I was gonnae tell you," she said.

He looked away, not sure how he should feel, not sure if he really felt anything.

"Ronnie …?"

He turned on her angrily.

"You never fuckin change do you?" he said. "You've always got to know everything and …" he struggled for words and breath … "be fucking smart …"

"Ronnie …" she said again. Really sorry, and really not telling him that she only did what she did because she didn't know what else to do.

(She wasn't going to tell him that. She was his big sister, after all.)

And Ronnie was looking at her now in bewilderment and hurt, and thinking again, maybe, about how she'd left him, she'd abandoned him the moment she could, when she was sixteen she'd just upped and left him to fend for himself, and now it seems that that's exactly what his mother had done to him as well, that she had escaped from whatever shit he and his sister and his father were in that night on this same narrow road into the deep north, so maybe it was him, it was something irredeemable in Ronnie himself that was simply so disgusting that no one could bear to be near him and look after him and love him. And who needed any of them anyway? He'd be fine, he didn't need his father, who, now he thought of it, had come to get him from Dryry Street but as soon as Janette came into the picture had only been interested in her, the bitch, who'd betrayed him like everyone betrayed him and how he didn't care because he knew better now, he knew now that the only people you can trust are the people who you know in advance you can't trust, and having thought all this through in the time it took to look down at the grass and look back up at her, Ronnie was smiling strangely, crookedly, duplicitously now and thinking as he looked at his sister's anxious face in the fading light, well see how you and him and everybody think you know so much ... maybe there's some things that I know that you don't.

Only he didn't say any of that. Especially that last bit. He just asked her if he could look at her phone ... Janette's own guilt stopped her thinking anything of this request other than that he was pining for YouTube so Janette said okay and she was going to talk to Dad and ask him what the hell was going on and she walked away; that's when Ronnie unrolled the wee tube he had made of Frank Wheen's card with his phone number on and while she was walking over to talk to Hunter, Ronnie went behind the van out of their sight. And he called Frank Wheen.

I told you he was going to do something stupid.

12.2

Now the Wheens weren't the Sopranos. They didn't own a *salumiere* where they could chop dead bodies up. They didn't even own pigs they could feed them to. In fact, for all of their fearsome reputations, this was only the third unlawful corpse they'd ever had to deal with. Fourth, if you count Agnes, which niether of them did.

Frank was a wee bit squeamish as you've heard earlier,

and though the sight of Jack's mashed-up face and concave skull weren't quite as disturbing as Agnes's puddle of putridness had been, the soft grittiness of shattered bone inside the burst bag of Jack's cranium and the leak of grey matter on to Frank's shoes and trousers had made Frank even more miserable than he'd expected as they lugged the clumsy, heavy thing that had been poor Jack Webster on to the path and then carried him into the woods and the peat bog they'd located.

Frank and Joe didn't do any of that professional mafia stuff like wash the body or bury the head and hands separately. They didn't have the gear, or, frankly, the stomach for that kind of thing. While the light lasted, they did search Jack's clothes for identifying papers, and Joe smashed up his teeth with his heel and Frank's snow shovel. But that was more because he thought that might be a good idea than it actually was a good idea. Jack's DNA was all over the car boot and their clothes and they were stuck changing either of these for a while. But for the Wheen brothers, I suppose, Perthshire was the back end of beyond where no bugger ever came anyway, so to their way of thinking, just off the A9 was the far edge of the universe and they probably hoped that they'd be safe enough.

They took turns digging one at a time in the bog with the wee snow shovel, ruining their shoes and suits in the sucking black peat, while the other one held the tiny map-reading torch. They didn't do very well. They worked for an hour nearly, and it seemed like the hole never got any deeper. Frank got more and more depressed, and Joe was still humming and chortling to himself like he didn't care at all what a nightmare this was. Thing is, that though they were making a bit of a cunt of this whole badass number they were running here, Joe was still finding his brother's discomfiture more amusing than he was embarrassed by his own lack of skill and judgement. They were both, as their aunty might have put it, on a shoogly peg.

But Joe, holding the torch at the moment, didn't seem to mind a bit.

"Ah doano whit you're makin the fuckin face fer," he was saying. "I'd nae choice."

"Ye just had tae put him in my fucking CAR, did ye?" said Frank, slipping and going down in one knee in the freezing stinky swamp.

"Fuck!" he said, and the phone in the breast pocket of his jacket that was hanging on a branch started singing "Nessun Dorma". Joe didn't move.

"Ye gonnae fucking get that?" yelled Frank, who was expecting, or rather hoping for a call from Eleanor enquiring after him, a call conspicuously, he had not received all day.

Joe took the torch beam off him just as Frank was lifting one leg out of the suction pump that passed for ground around here and Frank went face first into the hole he was digging that kept filling up with water. Joe laughed and pointed the torch back at him and Pavarotti stopped singing.

After a few more grim capers getting out of the swamp, and not recognising the number when he finally looked at his phone, his shirt and underpants now full of slimy grit, Frank called the number back and Ronnie answered instantly, telling Frank the name of the caravan site, and no he didn't know where it WAS he wasn't David fucking Attenborough but they were in for the night and driving a shitey wee blue van honest to God it looks like a toy or something. Hi Ace van or something … and at that point he rang off as he saw Janette and his father approaching.

In Laggan Wood, his face dripping, Frank looked up at his brother. Joe had picked up Jack's body by the armpits.

"Mebbe it'll just fucking sink?" he suggested. And Frank went through a variety of things he'd like to do and the order in which he'd like to do them.

INT. CAMPER VAN – LATER THAT NIGHT

Ronnie lies awake looking up. He listens to the silence. He sits up and looks over to where Hunter is asleep. The gun is beside Hunter's hand. Gingerly Ronnie swings out of bed, and, as silently as he can, tiptoes in stocking feet towards Hunter and picks up the carpet bag from where Hunter sleeps, still with shirt and tie on. He reaches over for the gun, watching his father's sleeping face. His hand closes round cold metal. He puts the gun into the bag.

CUT TO:

Janette. Asleep. Ronnie, a jumper on now, comes over to her. He looks into her face. Is there something like regret in his silent farewell?

12.3.1

EXT. VAN – NIGHT

The rain is teeming down. The door opens gently, and Ronnie emerges, his shoes in his hands, as well as the gun and carpet bag. The caravan park is still dimly lit by floodlights down to half power so you can see your way to the toilet bloc. But there's no one else out. Happy families in caravans and tents and campers are either asleep by now or up late whispering over games of German Whist. Ronnie can see warm light from their windows and through tent walls. He shrugs inwardly. He has made his choice. He is going to be a free man, free of all that, free of family life, free of any demands on him but those made by his own being. He is wearing the bright-orange pacamac his dad got him in the outdoor-wear shop. He sits on a stone to tie his new shoes. He looks around him wondering which way it is to the main road. His shoes tied, he takes the gun from the bag, picks a direction and sets off. But he neglects to shut the camper van door properly.

12.3.2

INT. VAN – NIGHT

Some moments after Ronnie's departure, stirred by the breeze, by the change in temperature and sound picture, Janette's eyes flicker open. She sits up. She sees the open door. She finds herself yelling.

> JANETTE
> Ronnie!

Hunter awakes with a start.

12.3.2.1

EXT. VAN – NIGHT

Ronnie is already running, panicked by the shout he's heard from Janette, bag in one hand, gun in the other.

CUT TO:

INT. VAN – NIGHT

Hunter is up, pulling on his trousers, looking for the gun, the bag.

> HUNTER
> (to Janette)
> Where's he gaun? He's got the gun!

CUT TO:

EXT. WOODS – NIGHT

Ronnie, not seeing the road, running hard, is heading for a path out of the campsite that leads into the woods.

CUT TO:

EXT. VAN – NIGHT

Hunter, yelling back at Janette as he leaves the van.

> HUNTER
> (finishing tying his own shoes)
> Stay there!

But Janette is already putting her boots on as Hunter sets out after Ronnie.

CUT TO:

EXT. WOODS – NIGHT

Ronnie, looking back from the dark path, sees Hunter in the lights in the campsite heading straight for him. He thought he'd seen the entrance to the campsite. He'd thought it was this way!

> HUNTER
> (in the distance)
> Ronnie!

Ronnie turns and plunges off the path into the dark woods to his left. Ronnie, of course, is a city boy, so he's never been in dark like this before. He didn't even know that it could get this dark! He sounds like an elephant to himself. Everything is louder and smellier suddenly. Soon, he's stumbling blindly. He trips over something and recovers, pulling a muscle slightly. He limps on.

CUT TO:

Hunter reaching the path, plunging straight down it ... then stopping, hearing noise to his left. He walks steadily into the trees and looks into the darkest darkness, waiting for his eyes to adjust, his training serving him.

CUT TO:

EXT. CAMPSITE – NIGHT

Janette, moving more cautiously through the last of the campsite light, heading for the path.

JANETTE
Ronnie!

CUT TO:

EXT. WOODS – NIGHT

Ronnie. He's only yards off the path. He might as well be on the moon. He's already entirely lost. He stops, breathing hard, staying still, and listening. He hears the sound of a stream somewhere to his left, he heads for it, more slowly now.

CUT TO:

Hunter, also in the dark, also moving slowly. But implacable. In his primitive element. Lord of the Jungle.

CUT TO:

Ronnie, stumbling noisily into the stream. The rain is clearing. The moon is peeking from behind a cloud affording some silver glimmers on the water. Ronnie splashes through the stream.

CUT TO:

Close on Hunter, his face dripping, listening to the splashing sounds. Then he's on the move, swift, silent.

CUT TO:

Janette, staring into the dark forest.

JANETTE
DAD!

CUT TO:

Ronnie, on the riverbank, taking shelter in the roots of a fallen tree. He crouches, waiting.

CUT TO:

Janette. Blue light bathes her face. She looks up. In the sky, the moon is breaking strongly, full, through the clouds.

CUT TO:

Hunter, in the coming moonlight, by the river. He sees a flash of orange twenty yards or so away.

CUT TO:

Ronnie, watching his father being lit up. Seeing Hunter turn, seeing him … and moving towards him.

The light goes out again.

CUT TO:

Janette, her face going into darkness.

CUT TO:

Ronnie, getting up, running, tripping, falling, going headlong into the shallow water. He scrambles to his feet. He's dropped the carpet bag. He's terrified. He can hear the splashing of his father's feet. He sees nothing.

RONNIE
(terrified)
Get AWAY fae me!

He falls again, stumbles up. His foot goes into something soft. The moon breaks through again, and Ronnie finds he is standing in a sheep. Sodden, rotten, a week dead in the river. At that moment, Hunter speaks, close to him.

HUNTER
Ronnie.

And Ronnie spins and fires the gun wildly and repeatedly.

CUT TO:

Hunter, standing in the river, as a bullet hits his hand and spins him, dropping him to his knees in the water. Janette is near now, she runs towards Hunter and Ronnie.

JANETTE
Ronnie!

Ronnie stares, gun in hand, at Janette trying to lift Hunter.
He yells at Janette, extremity finding the little lost boy in
him.

RONNIE
Ah found him first.

Hunter raises his injured hand to look at it. He's lost a
finger on his left hand. Blood is pumping steadily from the
stump. He's going into abstracted shock. Janette grabs the
gun from Ronnie and flings it away into the darkness.

Hey!

HUNTER
Sorry. It's aw my fault.

JANETTE
Aw, Jesus …

HUNTER
Ah shouldnae have showed ye the money.

Ronnie looks around him, suddenly struck by something.

RONNIE
The money? Where's the fucking money?
I've lost the fuckin MONEY.

Ronnie scrabbles about looking, ignoring Hunter.

HUNTER
I wanted ye tae COME wi us, I couldnae …

Hunter raises the carpet bag in his good hand.

Ye dropped this.

Ronnie grabs the bag from his father, clinging to the course he chose. Janette screeches her frustrated rage and goes for him, struggling with him. He shoves her away. Hunter watches, swaying on his knees in the stream as Ronnie scrabbles through the bag, strewing out empty white envelopes. Ronnie throws the bag down and grabs his swaying father.

> RONNIE
> (with strangled fury)
> You CUNT! It's not in there.

> HUNTER
> (smiling, his speech slurring like he's drunk or having
> a stroke, repeating Ronnie's intonation exactly)
> It's not in there.

Ronnie stares at him.

> RONNIE
> What?

> JANETTE
> What?

Hunter smiles still, his eyes closing. Ronnie throws the bag at Hunter. Hunter CHUCKLES and sways, and picks up the bag.

> HUNTER
> (fondly)
> Ya wee shite. That's a good bag.

RONNIE
Where IS it? Ya BASTARD.

Hunter holds up his injured hand. He passes out, his head lolling backwards as he sits back on his heels in the water. The moon bathes the tableau of the three of them in the stream.

CUT TO:

EXT. CAMPSITE – NIGHT

Some minutes later, Ronnie and Janette emerge from the woods, supporting Hunter between them. Hunter's injured hand is tied grotesquely to his neck with his tie. All three of them are soaking wet and covered in his blood. They walk through the campsite. Other holidaymakers, woken and alarmed by the gunfire, stare at them as they approach. Janette has the carpet bag in her hand.

JANETTE
Were ye gonnae LEAVE me, ya wee bastard. Fuck off and leave me wi NOTHIN, was that yer fuckin plan.

RONNIE
I'd have fuckin made it if it wasnae fer you, ya bitch. You and him coulda just kept fuckin TALKIN about shite.
(to an onlooker)
What are you lookin at?

They reach the van and dump Hunter through the still open door on to the floor. Ronnie gets in to pull him.

JANETTE
Tie his arm up tae something ...

Ronnie glares at her. She slides the door shut, and walks round the van to get into the driver's seat.

CUT TO:

INT. VAN – NIGHT

Janette sees that Hunter is still on the floor.

JANETTE
Tie his arm up tae somethin, or he'll DIE!

RONNIE
He's your fuckin pal, YOU tie him up!

JANETTE
I've got tae DRIVE.

RONNIE
I don't CARE.

JANETTE
HE knows where the money is, right? If he dies, he'll no be able tae tell ye where he planked it. Right?

Petulantly, Ronnie does what he's told, tying Hunter's injured hand up to the door handle. Janette looks out at the rain. She needs to decide where they're going now. But she has always known, maybe, that one way or another, she'd be asking the Indians for help. Her decision is made. She starts the van.

12.4

A good thing too. Because just as Janette started the van's engine, Frank and Joe, with Joe at the wheel of Frank's

Beamer, were pulling up to the entrance of the caravan park. They, like the Hunters, were not enamoured of nature's delights at this moment. They'd ended up just putting Jack back in the boot, vaguely planning some way where they could maybe put the blame on Tommy for his murder (and Frank was running through desperate scenarios by now, I imagine, where he could blame Tommy for Joe's death too, and kill Tommy in "self-defence" so Tommy couldn't tell anyone what had really happened), but in truth they were pretty much helpless, hopeless, wet, cold and clueless by this point. So that when the Hiace van drove past them heading east towards the A86, it took them both a moment to register Ronnie's face in the windscreen lit for second in the full beam of their fog lamps.

12.4.1

The chase wasn't long. As Janette told Ronnie even before she'd understood that they were being followed, the land occupation that she'd thought her mother might be part of was taking place only minutes up the road. The situation there, which we'll explore in more detail later, was fairly stable. There had been a brief flurry of activity when it had begun the month before, and catching the powers that be unaware, being organised on Facebook with no mention of Islam under the flash mob code name of Wovoka, and what with taking place on a massive private estate to which there was no access by public road, it had been a few days before law and order had recovered its poise and it had already been too late to just send the heavies in before anybody noticed. The place was regularly featured on TV before you knew it. Indeed, had any of our little cast of characters been at all attuned to the right kind of social networking activity, it would have been clearly obvious right from the beginning of this story that this was where it was all going to end.

12.4.1.1

It must be explained that, although there was only one narrow private road into the estate, infiltration had been very easy for the protestors to achieve on foot, and by way of the railway station anomalously nearby this haven for the rich in the wilderness, and as no one was trying to leave, this being an occupation, and no one had tried to get in for a couple of weeks, the entranceway to the estate was relatively lightly guarded, especially at this time of night.

12.4.2

In any case, Frank and Joe argued between them as to whether or not this was indeed the Hunters' van they were following, and concluding that it probably was (who else would be LEAVING a campsite at midnight other than fugitives), they then fought about tactics, as to whether they should content themselves with following the Hunters ... knowing nothing about how heavily armed they might be, for example ... and call in police reinforcements, or whether, for fuck's sake, Frank, we're already so far past legality that we can't even see it if we look behind us. Let's drive the cunts off the road and fucking finish this.

12.4.2.1

Whatever the strategy was, Janette, having seen that they were being followed, was now flooring the van while Ronnie shouted at her to go faster ... which brought the wretched junk heap up to nearly sixty. Hunter, in the back, tied up and tourniqueted, but still bleeding profusely, seemed to be singing something about a Dixie Chicken. It was also roughly at this point that Ronnie found the money stuffed into the glove compartment and began putting it all back in the bag.

12.4.2.2

Frank and Joe were still tailgating the van and loudly debating as to whether they should come alongside the thing and open fire, when Janette saw in the light of her fog lamps, a few hundred yards ahead of her (guarded by a few sleepy representatives of the shadowy security firm hired by the Estate's equally shadowy owners), what she thought she might be looking for, that is, a row of Indian tepees established along the roadside by supporters of the main protest which was taking place in the Estate itself, and she had turned hard left into the lightly patrolled entrance way to the Ossian Viewpoint Estate and past the security men before Frank and Joe knew what was happening. As a consequence of which, though he hit the brakes pretty hard, Joe was a long way past the unmarked turn-off into the private road before he managed to bring the Beamer to a screaming, smoking halt that left the car nose first in a ditch with the transmission entirely wrecked and Frank suffering from whiplash. Joe got out of the car as the security men ran towards them having noticed that the impact of the crash had sprung the boot open revealing the shattered muddy remains of their old chum. Dazed, he ran round to the back of the car and tried in vain to shut the trunk as Frank turned his sore neck to see that however badly he'd thought his day had been going up till now, it was about to get catastrophically worse. He scrambled out of the car and yelled to his brother, "Run, you stupid cunt!"

12.4.2.2

He and Joe, all traces of civilised living now shed from them, plunged off the public road into the private darkness of the Ossian's Viewpoint Estate, running, stumbling, weeping, laughing.

12.4.2.3

"Where the fuck are we going?" Ronnie asked his sister as Hunter, his tied arm dislocated by the sharp turn, bless-edly lapsed into an unconsciousness he'd not wake from for fourteen hours. While Janette, for her part, weeping herself in fear, but being pumped with adrenalin, just about kept the van on the unlit private road, keeping her eyes on the distant but now approaching council fires of the Lakota.

12.5

And the clouds were gone. And the full moon sailed in the sky.

13.0

You're just going to have to take my word for most of this.

13.1

To Tommy Hunter, on his back in his sleep, a voice comes. It's male, American, a little nasal. Midwestern but hard to pin down to any place special. Intoning, yes, but studied in its not wishing to make a big deal of what it tells; bashful to intrude, even. Flat and uninflected, it's a young voice from when the world was young, impossibly young, it's impossible that anyone ever was that young.

Tommy swims upwards through black cotton towards consciousness. His eyes flicker open, and he misses the next few words, staring as he does, firstly, at a timbered, low ceiling of some antiquity (white, paper peeling, in need of paint, with a patch of damp in the corner) and then, coming into focus in the foreground, at two craggy, friendly looking, late-middle-aged, early old-aged faces that now hove into view from the left and right sides of his perspective, peering down at him into the well of his sight. He notes sleepily their weathered skin and brown eyes, and he reliably intuits, even through his fog of fever, their amused, ironic benevolence — surely our best hope from the company of strangers. He notices almost incidentally that they are both wearing the full facial paint and feathered head-dresses of medicine men of the Hunkpapa Sioux in time of war.

"Is he awake?" asks the slightly taller one, the more authoritative in his bearing as a head man of the Lakota.

"His eyes are open, ya dick!" says the other, his disrespect for his chieftain clearly tolerated between the two, perhaps even acting as a signifier of this cultural element of the tribal ethic as a whole.

"But can he hear us?" insists the first among equals. "Cunts can't hear ye sometimes." The smaller man shrugs, not caring much, enjoying the poem. His leader leans down closer to Tommy, looming, till Tommy feels his tobacco breath, the red and white stripes on his face catching some light source Tommy can't see. "Can ye hear us, big man?" he asks Tommy slowly, old pipe smoke in a stale haze around his words. Reminded suddenly of the grandfather he hasn't thought about in years, whose loss at an early age precipitated his own plummet into delinquency, Tommy tries to reply in the affirmative, but his tongue is heavy in the mud of his mouth, and he is already slipping back into sleep, comforted at clearly being in the care of experts.

He starts up out of the darkness again, as he feels himself being shaken back awake.

"Ho!" says his secondary attendant, demanding his attention and respect for the other man, who now introduces himself with the appropriate ceremonial form.

"I am known as Short Bull," he says, "cos ah'm no big and ah talk shite."

Short Bull's eyes keek owre tae Tommy's right at the smaller but no less smiley face of his sidekick, who introduces himself thusly also.

"I'm called Kicking Bear, eh? Cos I like tae get naked when I'm huving a boogie," says the other, smaller man, with an upward inflection at the end of the sentence that even to Tommy's uneducated ear is clearly an Edinburgh accent. Strangely enough it is the incongruity between the Scottish accents of these Indians rather than that these apparent redskins have Scottish accents at all that makes him wonder fleetingly, "Who are these guys?" before returning to his simple, laudable acceptance that the present, however weird it gets, is real. He is reassured. Soothed, even.

Tommy's eyes start shutting again.

"Wir gonnae hivtae call you 'Stuck Pig'," says Short Bull, fading out at last, "cos you were bleeding like a fucker last night."

Tommy sees no more for the moment, but he is aware once again, as he falls back into the comforting swell of blackness, of the recorded, ancient voice of a young Bob Dylan reciting his "Last Thoughts on Woody Guthrie" at Carnegie Hall way back in 1964, at the other end of space and time.

13.1.1

Short Bull straightened his back and punched Kicking Bear on the shoulder.

"Ho!" said Kicking Bear again, rubbing at his doeskin tunic.

"It might be fucking your fault," Short Bull told him. "Not everyone likes Bob Dylan."

Kicking Bear tchached contemptuously at the very idea — to his way of thinking, there was no sound on earth more congenial with which to return to consciousness than a bootleg recording of the individual approach to key changes of that small Jewish genius of the Northern Plains.

13.2

Kicking Bear's monomania on the subject of singer-songwriting was only an aspect of the kinetic certainty that had brought him and his friend so far since their enforced redundancy at the shared age of fifty some twelve years back from the then downsizing (and now entirely shut) engineering works where they had both turned their tools ever since their Bonanza and High Chaparral-soaked boyhood. They had jointly brought the focus and energy and love of doing things well that had distinguished and sustained them as craftsmen to bear on their Scottish yearning for all things American and for the Wild West in particular: a yearning that had begun as a merely vicarious participation in what had always seemed a more abundant life but that had now vivified into something far more transformative and full-time with the advent of the Internet. These two redundant pipefitters had become amateurs in the best sense, in that they were now well-informed self-educated enthusiasts for the history, culture and contemporary resonances of the alliance of Plains tribes known as the Sioux. The friends had always, sentimentally speaking, been on the winning side at the Battle of the Little Bighorn (as the White Eyes called it) or the Fight at the Greasy Grass (as the blood brothers had now learned to say), delighted at the alliterative immediacy and pragmatic concrete poetry of the appellation of that last gasp of elegiac victory in the long sad story of aboriginal defeat to which they felt drawn with an irresistible historical sympathy. The twain had become proper experts now in the culture whose deep complexities and ethical structures had only become capable of acknowledgment by the Palefaces in the literal moment of their destruction some years later just down the road from the Black Hills at the little creek called Wounded Knee.

They had progressed from some fairly serious collecting of artefacts to latching onto the craze for historical reconstruction that has crossed the Atlantic of late. The highlight of their mere pageantry had been a nearly full-scale re-enactment of a Santee raid on Fort Ridgely which they'd held on the banks of Loch Lomond that had even been filmed for the telly! And why would they have wanted to just go home after something like that? Now Short Bull and Kicking Bear, completists that they were, had eschewed the obvious options of merely doing Red Indian versions of re-enacted Bannockburns over and over again on consecutive weekends, and had instead jumped in at the deep end, improbably and fully identifying, as Scots, with that other lost nation, the Indian nation. So instead of going back to their families and their disappointments, they, like Sitting Bull before them, had headed north to another country, one where they hoped that the banal blandishments of the White Man's consumerism couldn't reach them. And every day they had separated themselves from the consensual numbness that had exploited and robbed and lied to them all of their lives, the more certain they had become in their chosenness. These genial and determined eccentrics, first in their reconstructions, and then in a series of land occupations of disputed territories of Scotland, had been progressively joined and confirmed in their reinvention of themselves by a growing multitude drawn from other generations of the discarded, the bored and the optimistic. Just as the two of them (once their identity as working men had been stripped away from them like skin being flayed from a captive) had longed for another way to be themselves, so had those others who were likewise insulted by the crass bullshit of these last, stupefied days of the enlightenment project and had now joined them, feathered Quixotes all, in search of El Dorado.

They had reinvented themselves as the future of the human race, as noble savages, rebels, internal exiles, self-defining, the last free people of the world. They might be, to outside eyes, a loose collective of anarchists, environmentalists, dropouts, lunatics and ne'er-do-wells. To themselves they were freedom and hope itself. They lived in light. They had acquired clarity and all they had sacrificed in exchange was "security", that most profound and seductive snare of death's dark kingdom. Now there were nearly two hundred of them who had escaped from the allures of equilibrium, a wandering band of nostalgists for the future — a future that had seemed cancelled by the sheer unimaginative moral idiocy of the present's propertarians, but that they had now recovered with a naivety at which others might scoff, but without which, we'd all be living in caves or concentration camps. They, like the Covenanters or the Amish of old, had set themselves free from the preterite sphere of Old Corruption, and it was merely a matter of timing that the coming moment of their sacrificial apotheosis at the hands of that rude and rejected power should coincide with the arrival among them of Stuck Pig, as they would call Tommy Hunter for the short remainder of the space and time that his Great Spirit coincided temporarily with theirs.

They were used to vilification in the public prints, of course, but were, that morning, on the BBC and Sky, unhappily concerned at now being referred to with the same mixture of awe and contempt that the telly usually reserves for suicide bombers. They, like the Salafists, were now seen to be placing their faith in themselves above the laws of property and clearly could not be allowed to persist in such perversity. Tommy's arrival with his family in a now crashed and useless camper van (and the coincident discovery of Jack Webster's multiply shot and muddy corpse in the boot of Frank Wheen's car, even though it plainly had nothing to do with the Indians) had brought public concern to a head, it seemed. The call to "do something" was being heard throughout the land.

Having been watching the telly earlier on, Short Bull and Kicking Bear (who barely even answered to Douglas and Alec any more) both knew that catastrophe was upon them and left Tommy to go and prepare their people for the consummation of the Ghost Dance. It was time to get the bulletproof shirts on.

13.2.1

In like contrast with Tommy's wounded stupor, for the

other characters in our little passion play, things were moving towards crisis point at a likewise rapid clip.

The looming apocalypse, for Danny Boyle and Maggie Singleton, had begun with renewed joy as the erotic possibilities of uncomplicated happiness had further unfolded themselves to them twice that morning in ways that quite frankly startled both of them. They were in such a state of stunned ecstasy even after they'd enjoyed a shower together that they only slowly became aware of the appalled news broadcast from the mainland of the hideous discovery made at the gates of the Ossian's Viewpoint Occupation and didn't understand the direct import of that news until the repetition of looped images inherent in the twenty-four-hour news cycle finally broke through to Maggie, as they drank their fruit juice and dragged their eyes from each other's elated, stupefied faces towards the world, or at least towards the television.

Maggie it was who first caught sight (or thought she did) of Superintendent Bellamy in the background of a piece-to-camera. The officer was walking behind a breathless reporter in company with another man she thought she sort of knew the face of. Another shot revealed her boss again in the background in urgent conference at the edge of a high and treeless moor with this chap who she now recognised as Donald McCormick, sole proprietor and manager of the licensed Scottish franchise of the reputable security firm that had (once upon a time) been transporting used notes for disposal all those years ago, and had been, as aforesaid, among the pioneers of the private-sector provision of prison services, including running one institution that had played lucrative host, in times past, to Tommy Hunter, Joseph Wheen and Jack Webster at various junctures (see 1.0.1.2.2). The camera then showed the silver BMW in the ditch by the road where it had ended up, axle snapped and boot sprung open, and the reporter then gestured towards the partially wooded uplands where the car's living occupants had apparently fled.

"Is that …?" Maggie managed to say before "Danny", his face purple and his throat strangled, asked the surly waitress to turn the volume up. Jumping into the broadcast halfway as they did, they learned first that the discovery of a murder victim in the boot of a wrecked car now seemed about to precipitate some action of some kind against the land occupation that had been going on for some time much in the same way, that whatever the merits of the case, the attack on the Twin Towers had precipitated the invasion of Iraq.

"Jack Webster …" said "Danny". "That has to be Jack Webster!"

"They used to be here, you know?" said the waitress, delivering them their "two full Scottish with Fried Egg and Black Pudding," bewildering them.

Swift questioning of the waitress and continued attention to the News quickly revealed that the "they" the waitress was referring to was "those bloody hippies" who were now in illegal occupation of the huge Central Highland estate outside of which the forces of law were finally gathering, it appeared, to some purpose. "When were they here?" asked "Danny", light dawning on his investigatory intelligence.

It transpired through the waitress that two years before the Indians had taken over Ossian's Viewpoint on the mainland, the Lakota Nation, so called, had occupied the tiny island of Ulva (yards off the coast of Mull but accessible only by swimming, rowing and an occasional ferry roughly the size of a bathtub) for nearly a year, upon the occasion of its ownership changing hands. That the timing of this earlier action had so neatly coincided with the sending of the moonlit postcard of nearby Calgary Beach (!) that had lightened the interior darkness of Tommy Hunter so decisively with regard to his sense of purpose upon his release, immediately lit a fire in the guts of Detective Inspector "Danny" Boyle that had him up and out of his seat and paying the bill almost before Maggie could take a breath. Indeed it was while Boyle was precipitately packing that Maggie ascertained from the waitress that a certain Janette Hunter had been employed in this very hostelry at that time, and had been rumoured to have occasionally rowed or swam over the sound of Ulva to pay the dangerous lunatics there a visit.

The joy of all this revelation was leavened by DS Boyle's equally sudden understanding that he was currently about a hundred miles to the west and south of where the action was and that he had made something of a vainglorious fool of himself. Maggie's heart lurched in fear that this operational error on "Danny's" part would acquire a dimension of moral failure for him, and would now be associated in his mind with his recent abdication of duty in favour of passion. And indeed, Maggie saw, as they clambered into the car, that "Danny", to her unexpressed horror, his purpose now renewed, seemed to have shed his happiness like a skin. He was all raw and humiliated again. He wasn't talking to her any more, he wasn't even looking at her, as if he were mortified at their dalliance, as if he had been caught and was now being punished for the moment of happiness they'd shared, and was now ashamed that their freedom and his recklessness had distracted him from his rivalry with the hated Bellamy, that now he hated her for having been the occasion of his lapse. Maggie felt her soul plunge into her comfortable walking boots as they started back on their way off the island, away from that isolated joy they had shared at that special time and place, that was already becoming a despised memory now they were on their way back towards the guilt and compulsion that they had abandoned with their clothing last night while they sank their teeth and tongues into each other. For that liberation had been yesterday's child. Once again, the lovers were the slaves and not the masters of the present.

Maggie didn't dare say anything as they drove, for fear that her reminding him of the snuggle-bunny he had briefly been to her would cruciate him further and take him from her for ever. He felt a fool, she knew he did. "It's not my FAULT," she felt like saying to him, but dared say nothing at all as they drove in silence for about thirty minutes to catch the ferry at Craignure.

She looked at the map and charted a route for them from Oban to the high road past Spean Bridge and she tried to keep her voice level and her bearing professional even as she longed to appeal to him, to be as naked and open in her need for his spoken love as she had been to his body the magical and fading night before.

Ironically, unknown to her, "Danny" was admitting to himself that he *was* feeling a little more nuanced about life than his usual straightforward anger at the world for refusing to lie back and cooperate usually allowed. "Danny" too was wondering how to fold his new contentment into his old routine of flagellation, and was even wondering how to find the words to say to Maggie that would express how much he still wanted her, that he wanted nothing more than to find a way to accommodate both what he had to do as a policeman and what he had to do as a man. But "Danny" was handicapped in his interior search for articulation because he had never actually stopped to consider what it was that Maggie might have seen in him, so now that things had changed again he didn't know whether what had just happened was just one of those things he'd heard about happening to other people or something else entirely that was meant exclusively (and lastingly) for him. He was even wondering, a bit desperately, if she'd be disappointed in him now if he were less than immediately and miserably focussed on the solving and fixing of everything like he had been yesterday. Doggedness was the quality he most admired in himself, and we are prone, we humans, to imagine that it is that which we approve of in ourselves that others will also find attractive — many, many years of the reverse, if anything, almost always proving to be true, teaching us nothing.

13.2.1.1

Teaching us nothing seems to be one of the things that experience is good at.

13.2.2

He and Maggie did get married on completion of the enquiry and report he undertook for our Procurator Fiscal eighteen months later, just to save you wondering. And he was promoted to Detective Inspector when Bellamy took early retirement six months after that, so you might say that things worked out very well for him, though, of course, he never lost that sense of grievance which fuels the fire beneath many a Scotsman's career.

13.3

Meanwhile Elspeth Dewar (whose evidence to that enquiry was to be of great importance) had clearly watched the same news that morning as had "Danny" and Maggie, a bag of frozen peas still over the bruises that Frank had inflicted on her in uncontrolled frustration early the previous morning. What she saw on the telly suggested to her that now might well be the time for her to reconsider the strategy of silence she had pursued since Colin's (or Eric's) complicity and tragedy in the founding event of Frank Wheen's fortune. Elspeth got in touch with the authorities the following Monday having thought about it as the news of what had happened up north continued to come in over the weekend, and her sworn statement, most of which was true, along with Danny's completed report, led to the unsuccessful attempt recently by the Crown to seize the assets of Frank Wheen as being in a heritable sense the proceeds of crime. These official attempts on the sanctity of her property are to this day being fiercely resisted by the ferocious legal team employed by Eleanor Wheen, co-owner of that fortune, who, I imagine, daily thanks her lucky stars that she had been so wise as to insist long ago that all that was Frank's was hers, and that all that was hers was hers as well. In contrast to Elspeth's dithering, Eleanor, watching the same broadcast that Thursday morning and recognising her husband's car, hesitated only till a minute past nine to contact that fearsome collection of legal minds at her solicitor's firm in Edinburgh, days before Elspeth, in her own little underprivileged way, made her first contact with the constabulary to charge Frank Wheen with assault.

13.3.1

Frank's physical isolation that morning in the frozen, dew-wet company of his hated brother was all of the world that he really had left. Had Frank had even a signal on his phone in this ungodly location in the Wild West of Scotland, perhaps he would have been able to do something by rapid transfers of ownership via his Internet banking facilities and their handy app he had on his Samsung to protect himself from what was coming to him. But to his disbelief, his network had no coverage in this land that time and all the gods forgot, and he damn well wasn't going to make his way back to the road in search of Wi-Fi, or to the Indian encampment that he and Joe were now spying from the ruined Pictish broch on the high ground misnamed as "Ossian's Viewpoint" by a previous owner whose tastes were rather more romantic than the Dubai-based holding company which currently held the paper ownership of this sixty thousand acres of Scotland.

Having been walking most of the night in the wind, the brothers were now in the comparative shelter of the ruins. They had even made a rudimentary windbreak from some plastic sheeting they had found, but you still couldn't call them exactly cosy, both having left their coats in the car. But Joe's old field glasses were being pressed into service as he scoured the area for signs of Tommy Hunter. Frank was leaving him to it, eying the piece of inflamed skin at the nape of Joe's neck where it met his skull and wondering how it would look with a bullet hole in it. All the narrowly focussed Joseph Wheen could see right now were the tents and lodges and caravans and campers of those inexplicable savages in the glen below them, those and the old Youth Hostel, of course — the eighteenth-century dower house that had been converted back in the thirties for the use of the then nascent Ramblers Movement and whose closure by the new owners of the Ossian's Viewpoint Estate, despite their solemn promises that they wouldn't when they got planning permission, had been the inciting incident of outrage that had sparked the land occupation by the environmentalist would-be aboriginals in the first place — and from which Short Bull and Kicking Bear now emerged in an unheard but animated conversation as to what the hell they were to do with their uninvited guests.

13.3.1

Like Tommy, Frank and Joe had had some survival training in the army years ago, of course, but now, helpless and cold in the Pictish broch whose nineteenth-century misnaming as Ossian's Viewpoint, despite being ab-anthropologically inept, still gave the whole estate its name, Frank lay back and watched the clouds scud over the azure sky as the wind freshened from the west and sunny morning turned to overcast afternoon. He talked to himself about even he knew not what.

Although I'm aware that I'm reconstructing these events from the scattered indications in the public record about the disposal of dead bodies and such, and that the mental state of Frank Wheen that Friday is still a matter of legal dispute, I'm willing to assert within the necessary limitations of narrative the common-sense opinion that Frank was already perfectly well aware how tired and sick and hungry and scared he was, and how his judgement was already being distorted by the multifarious extremity of his plight. It stood to reason in the circumstances. And besides, if he hadn't been scared, sick, tired and hungry like he was he wouldn't have been remembering now that when they had put Jack's body back in the car after their abortive attempt at burying the reproachful cadaver, that Jack had definitely winked at him. He remembered it distinctly that Jack's open eye had closed and opened again.

Now Frank knew very well that this hadn't really happened. Of course he did. Other than in his occasional moments of fear, anger and ecstasy, Frank was nothing if not a rational sort. He also knew very clearly that he hadn't started remembering the way that Dead Jack had looked at him until well after the fact — that it wasn't a memory so much as a retrospective hallucination that was gradually overcoming him, and that this obsessional ideation was symptomatic of his imminent mental collapse. He even remembered quite distinctly the first time he had remembered contact with Jack's departed, vengeful animus — he knew that it was only during the last cold and sleepless and nightmare-haunted night that the vision or dream or whatever it was had come to him with all the force and conviction of recollection. He was only thinking now that poor Jack, who he'd always liked, even when they were boys, who he'd always secretly rather admired for his positive attitude to life, and had even wished he was more like somehow, had winked at him with the malicious garrulousness of the recently dead as they had stuffed his stinking, ruined body back into the boot of the BMW. Even as he had had the memory, he remembered, he had known it wasn't really a memory of an event that had objectively occurred, rather that it was an exhausted projection on to history of a subjective and subconscious wish that Jack was still alive, that Joe hadn't killed him and that his own life wasn't consequently and comprehensively fucked up beyond all possible repair, that such things don't happen, but what with the cold and the hunger and his hateful, hateful brother occasionally sneaking ugly and vindictive looks at him, what with his fear of ruin, his certainty, really, that all he was doing now was twitching in his coffin on the way to the graveyard, that memory that was not a memory had started to reach the point of vividness now that he'd only to shut his eyes and sleep for just a second and yes, here he was, warm-hearted, lovely, laughing Jack, winking and smiling so understandingly and forgivingly and warmly at him that he couldn't help but feel his hard heart melt into sentimental acceptance along with the dark waves of sleepiness that kept washing over him and pressing down on his eyelids. Every time he fell into the arms of Morpheus, there was Jack now waiting for him, a beckoning, friendly spectre, summoning him to sleep, to death, to peace, like Fedallah on the whale, so that he had to keep catching at himself to save himself from that cold and muddy embrace, the spectre of which, he knew, was being manifested to him by physical exposure to the elements as much as by his own tortured and self-contradicting mind. Frank, all unknown to Joe, had spent the night dreaming he was trying to keep himself awake and thanking the heavens for it being dark for such a short time in Scotland after the spring equinox, and thanking heaven for the grey light that stole across the moor without a hint of warmth or cheer, for the thin smoor of moistness that filled the air as mist and that sometimes even fell as rain.

13.3.3

Crouched behind the binoculars that he'd stolen from a Land Rover on a joint exercise with the Yanks outside Hamelin years before, Joe had already thought he'd recognised Ronnie at one point, walking and talking in an animated way between three women, none of whom he recognised. Thinking he might be wrong, he didn't say anything to Frank, who seemed to be in a hell of a bad mood for some reason, having passed the hours of daylight so far, at least since they'd found some shelter in the ruins of a Pictish broch to the south of the Indian campsite, just staring at his phone and saying something to himself, his lips moving but no sentient sound emerging. Joe, who was rather enjoying the night-exercise nostalgia of all this, and who was feeling invigorated rather than enervated by the loss of creature comforts, had looked back for the boy and the three women, and found that he'd lost them and gave up thinking about them, rather preferring to continue imagining himself as John Wayne coming across the band of the Comanche that had kidnapped his niece at the end of *The Searchers*. Joe had made very plain his feelings on Frank's lack of manliness in actually paying Tommy Hunter his share of the proceeds of the robbery, and was sure, for his part, that Frank's silence now was the silence of shame, and that soon, somehow, they'd sort everything out and he, Joe, would have as much future access to Frank's money as he deserved and could wish for. Yes, Joe was as as happy now as he had ever been. Which makes what was about to happen to him a mercy of sorts. At least that's what I like to think.

13.3.3.1

Joe was of course, deluded in almost every word of this, and had he but known it, he had indeed spied their quarry among the women, and had he been paying proper attention to who those women might have been, then he might have died an iota less stupidly than he had lived.

13.3.3.1.1

As for the three women, his not recognising them was not wholly surprising. He'd never seen Janette as an adult. He'd never seen Denise (the hitcher from chapter 8.0) before, and he'd never seen Janice dressed in buckskins with long purple dreadlocks, hadn't seen Janice for fourteen years in fact, and anyway he, like almost everyone else in this story, had always thought that she was dead.

13.3.3.2

Janice, having been spoken to by Short Bull as well as by Janette, reluctantly made her way into the old Youth Hostel in reluctant search of her husband. Joe wasn't watching her while she did this, as he was concentrating, bemused and strangely intimidated, on what the Indians were doing.

13.4

Below the brothers, in the clearing by the old house, the hippies, or whatever the fuck they thought they were, all seemed to pulling on some kind of ceremonial overshirt of uniform shape, but individually decorated with paintings and embroidery. These white shirts seemed to be gathering in a circle, the people in them chattering like monkeys. Then, as Frank muttered to himself and looked up at the sky and Joe continued to search among them for their target, the dancers slowly, slowly began to move, to circle. As they did so, they fell potently silent. All around the encampment, suddenly, the birds stopped singing. Ions seemed to form in the damp, cold air, warming it eerily. The wind slackened and the quality of the light seemed to change. Everything tingled. And in the silence the brothers heard only the rhythmic shuffle and thump of feet as on every fourth step the collected boots and moccasins of the faithful beat on the ground. Everything got downright fucking spooky for a moment. You could understand how the Yellowstripes felt back in Custer's day in the face of this kind of collective and nature-based wisdom that made nonsense of their carbines and their actuarial tables. Joe felt the tension in the air and turned to look back at his brother. His skin crawled unaccountably at the sound of a different kind of history.

13.4.1

The brothers nearly jumped out of their skin when Short Bull's voice cut the air in an invocation of the sun and moon that he had learned off a CD and his precentor's voice was echoed and enhanced by the raised answering chord of his followers. They opened up their diaphragms and bellowed the wordless response in three long, deep notes. John Wayne and his companion were now seriously unnerved at the calm rightness of the sound that echoed off the hills like the noise the winged monkeys make in *The Wizard of Oz*. The mere materialism of their purpose was no match for the voices that were carved from the same landscape as the horizon. There were no words to the outpouring of the multitude — they hadn't done the studying that Short Bull and Kicking Bear put into their whoops and imprecations — but there was a simple full-throated authority to their unified voices to which the universe itself seemed to respond as the clouds thinned and parted and a shaft of sunlight fell upon the circle, warming it, lifting up its collective heart for one last, joyous defiance of the material world that was even now organising itself into raiding parties less than a mile away.

13.5

Tommy smelled the soup she brought him first. Then he woke and saw her. She didn't look at him. She started talking the moment she saw he was awake, afraid, maybe, to hear his voice, afraid to be interrupted before she'd said what needed to be said, saying the things she needed to say, saying the things he needed to hear, saying who knows what because for the longest time, he couldn't hear anything she actually said. He just hunched up on his elbows and watched her face moving, heard in the subtly changed music of her voice, saw in the now stiff and twitchy way she moved, how she had aged and suffered. He saw the light that fell on her, but he heard nothing she was trying to tell him. He just heard her voice. And felt what? After all this time what could he feel? What was it possible for him to feel other than vaguely let down?

He was stunned that he was hearing her talk at all, I imagine, that he remembered her voice at all, even. He probably thought he recognised the timbre and rhythm of her speech, and that her choice of words, her phrasing, was unchanged. Not hearing anything she was saying still, he looked at her talking and not looking at him. He looked at her pale face, and noted, like she was some specimen served up to him, that she was wearing funny, tribal clothes. He saw how thin she was, how the skin on her cheeks was drawn tight, how big and dark her eye sockets were. The thought came to him, as she was saying something now about regret and heroin, that she seemed to have acquired, somewhere in the interim, a nervousness either that he'd never seen or never noticed in the only five or so years they'd actually spent together (and that only intermittently for one reason and another), since she'd left Gerry Docherty for him when he and Gerry and Frank and Joe and Jack had all been in Hohne together in those innocent days just after the Wall came down and before Bosnia blew up, when the world had conned us into thinking that it was about to become, albeit briefly, a safer, happier place. He looked at her. He looked at himself as he looked at her. He couldn't have told you what he wanted to feel, what he ought to have been feeling. He couldn't even have told you definitively that he didn't feel it. But he didn't. There was nothing there. After all that time and longing, he felt nothing. Not even very disappointed.

Was he surprised? He couldn't even say he felt surprised. Strangely, though he was happy to see her, and though he was glad she was alive and okay and everything, now, as he looked at her, he felt free of her. He felt a bit sad and wise and he felt free. He'd not been expecting that. He hadn't ever anticipated anything even resembling that and he'd had plenty of time to anticipate most things. So while she went on about something to do with London and this really great guy she'd lived with for a while in Stockwell before he'd got lifted for trafficking, he thought about why he might be feeling slightly bored by what she was telling him.

He'd never really thought about her, he now realised. He'd thought about "her" all the time, but he'd never really thought properly about *her*, about how (for instance) time was passing for her too. That he'd been away, locked away, he knew, but that she had been somewhere too, and that that *away*, away from him, was an inadequate description of her location. That she too had been locked up in who knows what prison of her own and her circumstance's making, he had known in the abstract, but here she was now, in front of him, and he didn't know her. He didn't know her any more, and maybe he had never really known her when he was as young and stupid as he remembered now he'd been.

And so he barely knew himself either. He had, since their rupture, defined himself entirely as the man who was looking for her, and now that he had found her he had no idea who either of them might be. He may even have concluded that he wasn't hearing her words now precisely because he was realising, in that instantly accepting way that he had when dealing with reality, that the past and the present and the future were all unwritten. All in flux again, uncertain. That it hardly mattered what she was saying or what he was feeling because once again, as he had when he had pulled that trigger all those years ago, he was changing suddenly, but peacefully this time, into someone else, something unprecedented — that he was going to inhabit the rest of his life in yet another guise, another shape entirely, and that he had no idea yet what that might be — let alone who *she* was now he saw her again.

And that he was okay about that.

13.5.1

What we know of the events that followed suggest to me not that he was seized by a suicidal raptus as has been suggested elsewhere, but that at that moment of all moments, Tommy Hunter was happy.

I find that I need to believe that. I find that to be able tell the rest of this story I absolutely need to believe that Tommy really did find Janice and let her go and that this made him happy. That him letting her go was as important as finding her had been, that his insane quest had not been for nothing, even though it, like every other human enterprise, had ultimately been futile. For if the pursuit of the unattainable is *not* for nothing, then there is hope and there is redemption for us in this world providing only we are willing to let what we want go at the instant that we find it. I don't know how anyone can live and not believe that.

Don't we need to know while our lives may well be meaningless resistances to the irresistible dissolution of the universe into a flattened soup of particles dead and expanding forever, that those same lives, that same resistance is what salvation looks like, that the only salvation we can wish for lies in both the acceptance of and resistance to the way the world is? Don't we need to act as if we believed that there is that in us which is worth the saving and fighting for, even if it is only, inevitably, for the sake of a vanishing moment? Is it not as necessary as breath that believing in the promise of peace and justice at some point in the future, while not a practical ambition, is a categorical imperative in the here and now; that we can live decently in the present only when we act as if there could be a better world? That the truth that every life ends in death and that every dream dies in failure doesn't mean we shouldn't live or dream but rather tells us that life and dreams are exactly the business we have being here? Doesn't everything we know about our history illustrate beyond dispute that no one ever made a better world without living as if they were already there? That no one ever gets their freedom or equality except by behaving as if they were already free and just as good as anyone else?

That's why Tommy's story means so much to me. It's not just that he is an exemplar of the failings of our social and judicial arrangements, though he is those things. It is that Tommy Hunter embodies the hope that we can become more than ourselves. That we can change. That we can be saved. That's why I want to believe that she was there, that he found her, that they spoke, that they touched, even if it was only for a moment that, like all other moments, was immediately lost in time. Even though I am perfectly well aware that there is nothing in the public record to confirm Janice's presence at Ossian's Viewpoint or even her continuing existence per se, there is nothing to disprove it either, and that is going to be good enough for me.

I insist that, at the moment she was talking to him and he wasn't hearing her, Tommy was as content at the utter extinction of self as any man has ever been in the presence of God. It doesn't matter whether this meeting, like meeting God, was imaginary. After all, what else could it be? What else is anything that ever happens to us but something that happens in our minds, whether or not it happens anywhere else? I would find it unbearable if that were not the world which is the case.

13.5.1.1

For, like the Wicked Witch of the West when Dorothy threw cold water on her, Tommy was melting, the icy purpose that had been the superstructure of his sense of self all these years was dissolving and in his transitional state between solid and liquid, between fixity of intended outcome and the uncertain joy of mere being, in that slide from being a knife that cut through the world and becoming the embodied acquiescence that flowed through it, he hardly had the mental space to listen to what she was saying. The mere fact of her, and the fact of himself being with her at this evanescent moment, were everything. He had frozen her along with him in his cell, he now realised, he'd made of her something as fixed and unchanging as the monster of focus he'd made of himself, a doll, an artefact. And now that he saw her in the fluidity of time passed and still passing, even before he heard anything she said, he was paralysed at the poverty of his own understanding, at how banal and foolish had been his imaginings of this moment, this moment whose anticipation had kept him alive, and whose realisation was now neutering, cancelling, killing him. The anticipation had been its own present tense, its own frozen continuum. Now that he was actually with her again the past anticipation that had led him here was embarrassing, risible and behind him. In this new version of time, of the eternal present, he was changed utterly again, newly born, understanding nothing once more. He was breathless, spineless, and out of ideas. He was annihilated with relief at his liberation from himself. He smiled at her and without pausing for breath in her monologue she glanced at him a moment, uncomprehending. And he forgave and pitied her like Jesus forgives and pities all of us.

Tommy Hunter was lost now, lost forever to all that had held him to the earth, and it was good.

13.5.2

He relaxed. She kept talking. He lifted his hand. He stared at the sore white bulb at the end of his arm. He was bandaged. He remembered now being shot. He remembered Ronnie. He remembered the river in the dark. And now here he was in the light. With her. And she was speaking. Was she speaking? What was she saying?

"You've lost a finger off of that," she was telling him.

He numbly believed her. But he was still feeling like a man who had gained an unexpected limb rather than one who had lost a digit.

He sat up and swung his legs off the cot and on to the old stone floor of the dower house. She still didn't meet his gaze but she did stop talking. He realised with a jolt that he had no idea what she was feeling, seeing him again. Let alone what he wanted to say to her, whether in fact, he had anything at all he could tell her. Had he thought of nothing to say to her in fourteen years? It would seem not.

We can forgive him, I think. Just moments before he saw her he'd been someone else. And when he spoke to her now, at last, easily and authoritatively asking after her, it was with a strange and selfless assurance, an oddly benevolent warmth. He didn't say anything about anything much. Or have much idea what he was saying. He had no idea where this peaceful, new mood came from any more than he had any other idea of any kind in his head. The past was gone and the future was a territory which, for either of them, he held no prior claim. He spoke entirely in the present tense. He had no prescriptions or predictions or preferences. He had no expectations any more. He held his empty hands, hand, one mutilated, towards the present only. He was suffused with contentment and holiness.

What did he end up asking her, then? What words am I insisting that they finally exchanged?

I think probably he just asked her how she was and she told him she was fine. He longed to know, perhaps, much more. Maybe, in a moment of need and weakness, he wanted her to tell him that she needed him. But he immediately accepted that she didn't. It was probably harder to accept that she had never really needed him, or she'd not have left so easily, that even back then he'd been kidding himself about her, that his longing for her all those years had been so intense precisely because he'd been missing something he'd never really had, that the intensity of that longing had been inversely proportional to the feeling she had ever had for him.

But I think he probably managed that as well, however painful it must have been. I think he must have looked at her, and that maybe she looked at him with something like pleading in her eyes; pleading for him to leave her alone, to disappear from her life again, whatever life that was. And I think he must have taken a moment to feel that loss, quietly. That he drew in a breath, and that in that single breath of his time, of his life, he mourned for her and for himself, just till he breathed out again and smiled again for her, to show her he was fine, that he was at peace with knowing he'd never get her back, and that he'd never see her again.

"How are you?" he must have asked her again, obvious and warm, and if she had burst into tears or struck him repeatedly it wouldn't have mattered. He wished, surely, that she'd ask him how he'd been all this time, but I'm not sure she ever did. But I'm sure he accepted that, just as he now accepted that just as he had carried an idea of her about with him that had sustained him all these years, so she'd been carrying around an idea of him, pictures of him and the children, actual photographs, in fact. But in that brief moment of their reunion in the occupied Youth Hostel at Ossian's Viewpoint, even as he was renegotiating her presence, she was still speaking to his absence, to a picture of him that she did not want to flesh out in three dimensions. She still would not look at him. She must have been aware of his face and of things she could be asking him, but remained (as he had done all these years, perhaps, in his own way) more comfortable with the idea of him than attempting to deal with the reality. So she kept him at a distance, in the corner of her eye, as if he were a therapist and she were lying facing away from him on a couch.

I think he must have asked her though how had she been all these years, where had she gone that night? Had she gone back to Gerry, as he'd thought? And she probably answered him truthfully. But I don't think that even he can have had the courage to ask her then what he knew now that he had always known, that she had always been going to leave him. That leaving him had been in her mind and heart well before he'd brought on the crisis in their relationship by coming home covered with the organic remains of Colin (or Eric). Had she gone back to Gerry, though, he must have asked? She must have looked at him warily, thinking that he was seeking a way in, a way to make some declaration of continuing love to which she would be forced to respond, and respond in the negative, hurting him in order to protect herself. But I don't think it was like that. I don't think he had any such thought in his head. I don't think he was trying to get anything from her that she didn't want to give him.

He'd always known, he now suddenly remembered, I think, that Janice had never really committed herself to him. That Janette's parentage had been "doubtful" as the church and the law used to say. This had not mattered to him then, and mattered less than nothing to him now. Janette, like Ronnie, was a miracle in half her genes anyway. What did it matter who her father was?

It is evidence, perhaps, of his growth beyond his need of her perfection, that Tommy now, I think, felt an ache of pity for Janice, probably for the first time, at how insecure she must have been to have been so in need of assurance that no one could assure her, that she had never really trusted in him the way he had believed, absurdly it now seemed in retrospect, in her. It no longer hurt, even, that she had only ever accepted his love for want of something better. The pity of it was, he could tell from her now, that there *was* nothing better. It had turned out that nothing had been better for her. That there was no cure for the kind of pain that Janice had internalised long before he even met her. And that now, as then, there was nothing he could do about that. There was nothing either of them could really do for each other.

He had always known it had been complicated, whatever was between them. He remembered that now. He was startled that he'd forgotten all the time he'd been away from her how difficult and stormy and unhappy they'd been together most of the time they had spent in the same room. He understood now that back then, as a young man, and one who had never known security and love and acceptance, that his epic longing for her had been a retreat from reality, a rudimentary and rather sad poeticising of who she was and what she might do for him. Now her restoration to him had made it possible to rediscover that she had never really been there for him, never really loved him, and, saddest of all, that her hurt was even deeper and more incurable than his. Now that he was free Tommy found himself entirely without hope of love and justice or anything else, and was surprised at how liberating it was, to have nothing, to hope for nothing, to be nothing. How strong it made him to accept that quietly staggered him.

Those who interpret what was about to happen to him as mere suicide in the face of disappointment are insulting all of humanity, I think, by insulting him with so diminishing and dismissive an ending. Of those who go so far as to deny that she was ever there to have spoken to him, I cannot bring myself to speak.

13.6

Perhaps she told him:

They call me Wounded Dove. I can hardly remember you. I can hardly remember anything. Yes. I left you that night, I went to Gerry at his aunt's flat in Cardonald. I thought of coming to your trial. I thought about the children. But I couldn't. I stayed in Glasgow for a year with him. I wasn't using the drugs yet, nothing serious anyway. That got out of control later. I couldn't face Agnes. I couldn't face the kids. I was guilty at leaving them so I couldn't go back to them because I didn't deserve them. I thought I must be nothing so I tried to be nothing. I tried to die. Gerry got rid of me. I thought he was right. I thought everybody wanted rid of me. I wanted rid of me. I went to London. I lived in a squat in Haringey for a couple of years. I met a nice guy and he pulled me back to myself a little. He heard me talk, talk for the first time about the children, about having the kids and how they'd never forgive me and I hated them and I hated myself for hating them and he helped me find them. I was off the junk for a couple of years by then and I went to find Janette.

That's when I saw her in the hostel she was in then. Ronnie was with foster parents. I had another name. Agnes took me to her, said I was their auntie or something. No one gave a fuck what we said anyway. And it broke my heart because I could see Janette try when I told her I was her Mum, I could see her try to look as if that meant something to her but it didn't I could see it didn't and I ate my heart and I went back on the junk and didn't go back to the guy and the guy chucked me and I thought I deserved it and I overdosed and I was in a hospital down south under a different name and I wanted to die I was depressed the air cut me the world hated me and I looked out the ward window at the flowers in the park outside and they were made of mud the world was made of mud and knives and they cut me and I was all mouth inside myself eating myself and my teeth fell out and my hair fell out and I was nearer death than I've ever been and that's when he came to me.

Wovoka. He came to me and he saved me, he taught me that I had become nothing for a reason. I had become dead I had become a ghost and if I wanted I could make myself one with the other ghosts. The ones who will come again like in the Bible but not like in the Bible not like out of the grave but all together in white buckskins the ghosts of all the people who will come back with the buffalo and save us from the drink and the drugs and all we've done to ourselves since we lost the earth to the pigs who make all the money and have all the guns and bombs and if we dance if we can only dance the ghosts will come back and nobody will hurt us we can save ourselves and get the world back before it drowns in sin.

She looked into his face now for the first time needing him really to hear and believe her, needing his forgiveness as she hoped to forgive herself. And he smiled and put his hand upon her, blessing her, giving her up, saying goodbye.

Outside, the ghost dancers shuffled and chanted, men, women and children, all humanity dancing together, shiny eyed and loving, for a salvation that they surely knew would never come, wearing the ghost shirts they'd been making all this time (as Janice explained to Tommy), which would no more really protect them from the axe handles and pepper spray of hired security officers than had the shirts of their Indian forebears kept the Cavalry's bullets from the dead of Wounded Knee.

What had happened there at Wounded Knee was, to them, coda to a last, ludicrous, desperate yet beautiful hope that was being danced again here and now on Ossian's Viewpoint. Some of them may well have also been aware that Ossian, in Gaelic Lore, was yet another imaginary definer of culture and a hoped-for, wished-for ghost of something past and fictional, and that they evoked both him and Wovoka now in a spirit of ironic sympathetic magic. They knew, perhaps that one incarnation of Ossian had been in the shape of the eighteenth-century literary fraud that had culturally defined Scotland itself. It may be that such an ironic gesture of postmodern solidarity may have been a minority perspective, but I like to think that the reincarnated Kicking Bear and Short Bull, heroes of faith that they were, had made the Kierkegaardian discovery, through their living and breathing of the Ghost Dance, that it is better to act as if you believed something absurd that you know not to be true (in this case, that human beings have inherent value), than to behave in solidarity with the ruthless rationality of the killing, indifferent universe.

13.7.1

It had been the retelling of the Ghost Dance story at

Glasgow's Kelvingrove Museum some years before that had confirmed Short Bull and Kicking Bear, those two genial, grim old buffers, in their sentimental attachment to the aboriginal beauty of their sadness. That's where they got their names, too. They had learned at the display of the Ghost Shirt at that very popular Glasgow Museum that survivors of both Little Bighorn and Wounded Knee, among them the "real" Short Bull and Kicking Bear, had come to Glasgow in 1894 as performers in the world tour of Buffalo Bill's Wild West Show, that showbiz ancestor of the very Wild West film and TV genre that had so captured their boyish imaginations. They had learned that Short Bull had given, or sold, or had had stolen from him, a "ghost shirt" ... this being the ritual garb of the short-lived and almost unbearably whimsical Ghost Dance Religion that had been woven from the Christian myth of the returning Jesus by the Paiute shaman Wovoka and had briefly and tragically offered a last hope to those who had been cheated, forced, drugged and deceived out of their sacred (and treaty guaranteed) land in the Black Hills from which the discovery of gold had now barred them.

Wovoka had concocted a potent twist on the myth of the return of Christ in judgement, the twist being that Christ would come back as an Indian (possibly himself) and would bring with him all the dead ancestors — the ghosts — along with the vanished buffalo, to magically sweep the White Man into the sea. An unstoppable army of angels and of the returned dead would sweep through the cities of corruption, through the sinners of property, and return the land to the people and nature to which it belonged, restoring a lost ecological communism of humanity and nature. Catching on to the deferred hope and ritual longing for justice and the restoration of the lost that has made Christianity such a success story, Wovoka taught that anyone who wore a ghost shirt and danced the ritual dance would not only help to summon those glorious and avenging dead from their slumber, but would themselves become ghostly, would become, specifically, invulnerable to the white man's rifle fire.

13.7.2

We know that the Ghost Shirt was "returned" to the Lakota people after that display in Kelvingrove. We also know that there were various public trials and enquiries into the many events that culminated together on that strange and powerful day in the Grampian Mountains. The deaths of both one of the Wheen brothers and Short Bull and the injuries inflicted on many of the dancers by the security personnel are a matter of record now. But Tommy and Janice, Janette and Ronnie were peripheral figures to the various legal processes in which they were coincident elements, so there is a good deal less certainty about exactly what happened to them after the dancers formed their circle and the Hunters, *en famille*, hurriedly gathered by the ruined Hiace van to discuss the future.

13.7.2.1

I think I have already dealt with those who dispute that Janice was there at all to take her leave of Tommy and the children and go to join the Ghost Dance, and thus refuse the offer I am sure that Tommy made her to take her away with them. We do know that she was not with them when they made their escape from the encampment just as it was being attacked by the bomber-jacketed ranks. But to take it from that negative circumstance that she was never there in the camp at all, and thus to imply that Tommy had killed and disposed of her all those years ago is unconscionable. It is a logical possibility perhaps, but it is a moral nonsense to even suggest such a thing. Just because death always wins in the end, that's no reason to be on death's side, as Short Bull once put it.

13.7.2.2

The fact that Short Bull himself died of a heart attack some hours after the attack on the camp, despite the efforts of the medical teams, and indeed of the outraged DS "Danny" Boyle who went so far as to arrest the two bastards who'd set about the daft old fool, is a melancholy confirmation of the heroism of acting as if one had faith, perhaps. Besides, as is evidenced by the elephantine and still unfinished public enquiry, the joint private and public security action that afternoon disintegrated into a complex chaos whose details are still being argued about by very expensive lawyers. However, what we know must be true is that from early in the afternoon, a minority of the occupiers, possibly those without vehicular transport, or those who simply couldn't face or didn't fancy the martyrdom that the hired thugs of the holding corporation were gleefully about to inflict on those who remained, were already making their way in unorganised dribs and drabs towards the train station on the Moor well before the attack on the camp took place. The refugees could hear the hourly trains coming, actually, for nearly ten minutes before they could see them … the silent air carrying the sound of the engine and the clatter of wheels for mile after echoing mile between the peaks and across the moor and peat bogs.

(For those who wonder what on earth a train station was doing way up on Rannoch Moor where no one lived when so many much busier stations had been shut by Dr Beeching fifty years ago, I refer you to the earlier mention of the ritual slaughter of birds by rich people. There was no road into the wilderness, and the only form of transport to that particular corner of sublimity in the nineteenth century and up until the present day was indeed afforded by the railway line that had been and remains a single-track miracle of Irish sweat.)

13.7.2.3

Meanwhile, before any of this happened, here, beside their own ruined transportation, sat Ronnie and Janette and Denise. The two girls were getting on like a house on fire. It turned out that they knew some of the same people and shared an ironic view of the world and of young men in particular that they were both finding very diverting. Ronnie, still feeling a mixture of shame and stupidity for his actions of the previous night and in relation to being alive, Scottish and sixteen all at the same time, was considering going for a walk and getting away from the pair of them, when Hunter and Janice emerged from the hostel together and came and sat beside them.

13.7.2.3.1

It was at this point, of course, that the family were all reunited as Tommy had hoped and planned, but even for Tommy this must have been dreadfully anticlimactic as he had already almost forgotten that he had been wishing for this moment for all of those years, given the fact that Janice and himself, against his expectations, were other people now than those they had been and also that they were having this conversation in noisy proximity to a hundred rotating, chanting hippies, who were now spinning like Sufis as they sang and danced, driving fear from their hearts by way of dizziness, losing their fear in the noisy embrace of vertigo. Things had moved on so far for all of them that the climax of what had seemed to be their story up till now passed by all of them without comment. So there's no real reason for me to go into it in any detail either.

Despite the growing racket, Hunter probably produced the carpet bag full of money at this point, apologising to Janice about the contents having gone down from his original take at the robbery and how that had happened. It remained the case that £24,492.04 was quite a considerable sum, but nothing seemed to have quite coalesced as he'd anticipated. The direct vectors of his dreamed-of denouement to his journey, that he would bring his son and his daughter and his wife and this money to a single point in space-time, had seemed graphically clear and self-evidently pragmatic to him when he'd been in prison, or rather, since Frank had contacted him there shortly before his release to promise him payment of his share of the robbery in exchange for being left alone, for Hunter never coming back. Hunter, as he saw it, was merely fulfilling his agreement with Frank with the added and strategically unspoken rider that he was going to attempt to reconcile his family first and use this windfall as social cement, serving both the interests of family cohesion in the material world, and his own spiritual need to have nothing more to do with the blood money other than the getting rid of it to the benefit of Elspeth Dewar, Agnes, and Jack Webster along with incurred expenses and incidentals. It was not, he might have argued, his fault that Frank had deemed his reappearance in Oor Wee Toon for just long enough to make some financial reparations and kidnap Ronnie to be a breach of contract. Hunter had, in essence, done exactly what he had set out to do. The fact that a cash inducement and their mere proximity didn't turn his ex-wife and children into the Partridge family was hardly his fault either. Nor can the revelation of pre-existing psychic damage in the Wheen brothers legitimately be added to the tally of his faults as written in the Book of Life.

13.7.3

The only negative causation, of which one can be sure, I think, was that the maximum volume to which the dancers were now attaining meant that no one heard the shot.

13.8

Why did Frank shoot his brother? Well, I think we know the general answer to that question. But why did he choose that exact moment? We're again reduced to guesswork, but I think it probably happened when it did partly because from where they were perched in the ruins of the Pictish structure (the eponymous but misnamed "Ossian's Viewpoint"), they could see the stealthy approach from several directions of the forces of Law and Order. Among these were DS "Danny" Boyle and Maggie Singleton, who had made it with minutes to spare, to the chagrin of Superintendent Bellamy, though I doubt if the Frank spotted any of them individually.

Frank may also have calculated that all the noise the dancers were making would cover the gunshot. But it is my suspicion that Frank was already well beyond calculation by the time he killed his brother. That he was already weeping, in the throes of a nervous breakdown.

13.8.1

Joe was found to have been shot at point-blank range in the back of the head, forensics confirmed, while in a prone position. I imagine Frank had been looking at his brother for some minutes before the murder, and had prepared the nine-millimetre automatic, putting a round in the chamber and easing off the safety, waiting to do it. I think the noise and the electricity in the air worked on him below the level of consciousness. Add to this that it was entirely within Joe's character to have promised his brother retribution for the payment he'd made to Tommy as a sequel to finishing off Tommy Hunter himself, or that Frank had inferred such a danger from his brother's generally and specifically unpleasant demeanour, and I don't think motivation for the crime is any more difficult to discern than are the means and opportunity. We have already understood the level of aggression and unselfconscious mayhem of which Joe was more than capable, and that the prior killing of Jack Webster had already pushed Joe well over the edge from where Frank, with the best will in the world, could have recovered him. Frank may also have gleaned that it may well have been in Joe's mind that there was going to be some exciting but messy Mexican stand-off that would leave both Frank and Hunter dead and Joe standing, triumphant and no longer cash-poor. Joe may even have told his brother in so many words that he, Joe, was going to kill Tommy, and that he, Frank, was next. But whatever scenario Joe had in mind was cancelled by Frank, who picked up Joe's gun once he had killed him and numbly, barely sentient, started down the slope towards the dancers.

13.8.1.1

As the late, lamented Short Bull once observed to his friend Kicking Bear: "Some cunts are born cunts. Some cunts achieve cuntness. Yet other cunts have cuntitude thrust upon them."

13.8.1.2

Now, had Frank been capable of paying more attention, he'd probably have seen what Joe had seen, I think, immediately before Frank shot him. Joe had seen Hunter sitting and talking with his family. Joe had recognised him even after all this time. I think Frank probably had been sitting behind Joe ready to shoot him, when Joe had shifted his weight preparatory to telling his brother that he'd spotted their quarry and that it was at that instant that Frank had shot him more in panic than premeditation. Having set himself up to *maybe* kill his brother, it had been Joe's moving and breaking the spell of contemplation (or dwam as we say in Scotland) that had precipitated the actual execution.

13.8.2

Maybe Frank saw Jack's ghost again. Who can say?

13.9

After an exchange of their details on Facebook, Denise and Janette had already agreed to part as Denise went to join the circle of dancers as she must have done (her name appears later in the list of those arrested at the site that afternoon). However, I have to admit that it is only my opinion that Janice too left her family and went back to the dance, back to the security of the new family she had made for herself and rejected Hunter's offer of a renewal of their vows. Maybe he gave her an envelope full of money for her trouble. It seems likely, but I'm afraid I don't know that either. Let's say he gave five grand.

13.9.1

Leaving £19,492.04 approx.

13.9.2

The train they were trying to catch stopped at the station at 4.35. So I'm saying that at some time before 4 p.m. that

Thursday afternoon, Hunter and his children, money in the carpet bag in Hunter's hand, having been given directions by Denise, began to make their way from Ossian's Viewpoint across the moor three miles to the station. We know from the police report into the whole episode that it was on the way to the station where Joe's gun and the cat-atonic Frank were later found, so that we can only deduce that it was in the course of that journey on foot that they were intercepted by the panting spectre of Frank Wheen who called upon them to halt.

13.10

Picture them. Meeting again after all this time. Old friends. Frank and Tommy. Picture Tommy with his bandaged hand and Frank in his ruined suit. Picture the moon that rose through a hole in the clouds. Picture Ronnie and Janette, suddenly understanding that there were worse and more unpredictable things in the world than to be their father.

No birds sang. They could all see the sound of their own breathing. Janette hugged her brother to her as Tommy greeted the ragged, distraught figure who was pointing one gun at him while holding another limply in his other hand.

"Hello, Frank," said Tommy, genuinely surprised. "Didn't expect to see you."

It is again tribute to the variety of human perception that while Frank had spent the last few days obsessing about Tommy Hunter, that it had never so much as crossed Tommy's mind to think about seeing Frank again and that he was genuinely surprised and not unhappy to do so.

"Why couldn't you just stay away?" Frank must have asked him, pained and bitter.

"These are my kids," Tommy said as if they were two old chums bumping into each other on Byres Road. "This is Janette. You know Ronnie."

Frank threw his extra gun, the one that he'd used to kill his brother, at Tommy's feet.

"Pick up the gun," he told him.

"How's Joe?" Tommy asked him. "Haven't seen Joe in ages."

"Pick up the gun," said Frank.

Tommy shook his head.

"I'll kill you," said Frank. "I'll kill them."

"No you won't," said Tommy, and held his hand out and started to walk towards his old friend.

"I'm dead," Frank said. "You killed me," he added.

"I know," said Tommy, not knowing anything of the kind, and took the gun away from him. Frank fell on his knees, awaiting the end.

13.10.1

"Kill the cunt," Ronnie advised his father.

"Ronnie!" Tommy admonished his son.

He threw the gun away and turned his back on Frank without a backward glance. He and his family set off again up the moor.

13.11

There is little that remains to tell. Frank was found kneeling silently at the same spot where Tommy'd left him. He has not yet been found psychiatrically fit to stand trial for his various crimes against the tax authorities and for the original robbery or the murders of Jack Webster and his own brother with which he has been charged and to which his wife and children have abandoned him. There are those who think this mental disability fraudulent, now DI "Danny" Boyle (predictably) among them. But Frank met Tommy Hunter at the strangest and darkest moment of his life. And I think that is sufficient explanation of any amount of trauma. Any depth of silence.

13.12

Hunter and his children were among the last handful of refugees who stood in the exposed peatland of the moor listening to the train coming for five minutes before it could be seen. They didn't speak. They didn't ask each other questions about what had happened to them or about what might happen to them next. I don't imagine that Tommy, at this stage, thought that he was in any position to give any fatherly advice. It had only ever been possible for this family to have been a family for the briefest moment in time. He must have accepted that.

13.12.1

The train when it came up the single track laid by those heroic navigators in that bygone time itself proved to be something of an antique. It still had doors you had to open manually with the window rolled down. The doors still had those lovely brass door handles in the shape of a supine, stretched out number 8. The guard and the catering manager were probably surprised at the number of passengers getting on at so isolated a station.

13.12.2

It must have been before the train had picked up too much speed that Hunter gave the carpet bag with £19,492.04 therein to Janette, knowing that she'd probably do something sensible like pay the deposit on a flat for the two of them somewhere and put the rest in a savings account. Maybe they'd get somewhere nice like the West End or Helensburgh.

13.12.2.1

I like to think that Ronnie maybe apologised to his father then, maybe saying he was sorry he'd shot him. Maybe he even called him Dad again. Maybe Tommy tousled Ronnie's hair with his good hand. He probably advised them both before he left his seat that they should get off at a station before Queen Street. There were bound to be police waiting when the train got into Glasgow so they should get off before that. Singer or Partick or somewhere.

13.12.2.2

In any case, at some point when they were still on Rannoch Moor, Tommy opened the door of the moving train and stepped out into space. The kids didn't even see him land wherever he landed. They didn't see if he rolled and recovered, didn't see if he smiled and waved goodbye or if, the last free man on earth, he started walking into the infinite west, on his way to somewhere else beneath the moon.

13.12.2.3

Did Tommy let go of them the way he did – of his children, of Janice – because he finally understood? That he was not one of us? That he had no business being among us? That no matter what his intentions, his effect on everyone he encountered, from Elspeth to Agnes to Mr McIvor to poor Jack Webster to the Wheens, was destructive? Did he leave us for fear of hurting us more than we're already hurt? Is that why he's gone?

13.13

Of what we cannot know, we had best be silent.